Player
Haters

Player Haters

Carl Weber

KENSINGTON PUBLISHING CORP.
http://www.kensingtonbooks.com

DAFINA BOOKS are published by

Kensington Publishing Corp.
850 Third Avenue
New York, NY 10022

All Kensington titles, imprints and distributed lines are available at special quantity discounts for bulk purchases for sales promotion, premiums, fund-raising, educational or institutional use.

Special book excerpts or customized printings can also be created to fit specific needs. For details, write or phone the office of the Kensington Special Sales Manager: Kensington Publishing Corp., 850 Third Avenue, New York, NY 10022. Attn. Special Sales Department. Phone: 1-800-221-2647.

Dafina Books and the Dafina logo Reg. U.S. Pat. & TM Off.

ISBN 0-7582-0014-5

First Hardcover Printing: February 2004
First Trade Paperback Printing: December 2004
10 9 8 7 6 5 4 3 2 1

Printed in the United States of America

This book is dedicated to my fans—
those of you who have stuck by me
from the beginning.
Thanks.

Acknowledgments

First off, I have to thank God. Without Him none of this would be possible.

Thanks to all the book clubs and fans who have read my books. It's you who make this whole thing worthwhile and get me up at three in the morning to write. I think you're really gonna like this book. It's one of my best.

To Karen Thomas, my editor and my friend. You've taught me so much about the industry, more than you probably realize. Thanks. I'll always be grateful.

To Walter Zacharius, Steven Zacharius, and Laurie Parkin. Thanks for believing in me and my dream for Urban Books.

Thanks to Paul Chin, my attorney. Thanks for watching my back as I crawl through the maze of the publishing world.

Thanks to the brothers over at Aggressive Records. You boys are about to blow up!

Thanks to Linda Williams, Linda Gurrant, Valerie Skinner—my three readers. You also have been a help I can't even explain.

Big ups to my man Harold.

Thanks to Marie Brown, my agent and second mother. You've done a great job, and I may not say it enough, but thanks. Your hard work and support are highly appreciated.

Last but not least, I'd like to thank all the black bookstores that helped to make *Baby Momma Drama* the number one *Essence* bestseller for five straight months. I may not have gotten a chance to visit each of the stores this past winter, but I'm going to try to visit every one of them in the near future.

Well, until *The Preacher's Son* hits the stores next year, thanks for the ride. It's been great.

Oh, and if you get a chance, holler at your boy: *UrbanBooks@ hotmail.com.*

1

Wil

I pulled in front of my house and cursed under my breath when I saw my brother Trent's black Mercedes parked in the driveway. Trent didn't show up very often, but when he did, he always found some way to piss me off. Today was no exception. I'd told that fool a thousand times to leave space for my car when he parked in my driveway. But no, his arrogant ass always had to park in the middle of the driveway so no one would scratch up his precious Mercedes-Benz. I felt like taking my keys and carving my name in the black paint. Don't get me wrong. I'm not trying to hate on my brother for having a Mercedes, but his inconsiderate behavior was just one of the countless reasons Trent and I didn't get along.

When I walked into the house I got this eerie feeling that something was seriously wrong. I'd been having this uneasy feeling all day. I know it sounds crazy, but I had the same feeling right before I found out my pops had passed away. And again, right before 9/11. That's why I'd decided to leave work early today and come home to my family.

Now that I was home, there was no sign of them. The only sound I heard came from a radio playing upstairs. In my house, that just wasn't normal, 'cause I had a five-year-old son and a three-year-old daughter. You just don't keep kids that age quiet unless they're taking a nap. And it was way past nap time.

"Teddy! Katie! Di!" I shouted their names, but got no reply. I wondered where Trent was, too. That's when I heard this creaking sound coming from upstairs. I couldn't be positive, but it sounded like it was coming from the direction of my bedroom.

By the time I got to top of the stairs, the creaking and the banging had gotten louder and steadier, and it was definitely coming from behind my bedroom door. There was no doubt in my mind that someone in there was gettin' his groove on. I was just praying that it wasn't with my wife. I tried to give her the benefit of the doubt. Maybe she'd gone out with the kids and my brother was taking advantage of the empty house with one of his hootchies. Why he would do it in my bedroom instead of the guest room beats the hell outta me. Except for the fact that he's nasty. He's the type who'd do it and then leave without cleaning up, letting Di and me sleep on those nasty ass sheets.

I stood outside the door for a few seconds, listening for voices. I still wasn't sure if it was Trent in there or not. Whoever was in there sure wasn't the vocal type, 'cause except for the creaking and some heavy breathing, it was pretty silent for a while. When I finally heard a few words, I almost lost my lunch. There was no mistaking that it was my wife's voice I was hearing. Weak-kneed, I forced myself to listen to her as she coached her partner.

"Come on, you can do it."

Creak! Bang!

"You can do it! Just don't stop!"

Creak! Bang!

"That's it. Just a little bit more."

Creak! Bang!

"You're almost there!"

Creak! Bang!

"One more time!"

Creak! Bang!

"That's it," she shouted.

And she was right, that was it. I couldn't take it anymore. The creaking and banging had come to a halt, and all I could hear was Diane's unmistakable heavy breathing. Things were finally starting to make sense. Now I knew why she'd been refusing to make love to me the last few weeks. She'd been sleeping with my brother. Without thinking, I walked into my son's room and snatched his Little League baseball bat out of the toy chest. Then I busted into my bedroom like I was on an episode of *Cops*.

"Aha!"

Diane jumped back so fast she tripped over her StairMaster and landed right on her ass. "Oh, my God, Wil! What are you doing home?"

"What do you think I'm doing home, goddamnit! I live here. Or did you forget?" I raised the bat.

It took everything I had not to use her head for batting practice. But my brother Trent, he was a different story. I was gonna kill him. The only problem was that he was nowhere to be found. And for that matter neither was any other man. And now that I took a good look at Diane, she sure didn't look like I'd expected her to either. She wasn't anywhere close to being naked. She was dressed in her workout clothes, which meant she hadn't been having sex with Trent at all. She'd been working out on her StairMaster. I felt like a moron.

"Wil, what the hell is going on? And why are you carrying that bat?"

I didn't answer her. I was too embarrassed.

"Goddamnit, Wil Duncan! I asked you a question. Are you gonna tell me what the hell is going on?" She placed a hand on her hip.

I lowered my head and examined the bat in my hands. I didn't wanna tell her the truth, so I said something stupid to lighten the mood.

"Um, would you believe I'm thinking about trying out for the New York Yankees?"

Unfortunately, my little attempt at humor only succeeded in pissing her off.

"Hell, no, I don't believe that shit. What kinda fool do I look like?" She stepped away from the StairMaster and pointed a finger at me defiantly. "Now I wanna know what's going on, Wil. And I wanna know now."

"All right," I told her. I knew the truth was probably gonna get me in more trouble than I was already in, but it wasn't worth lying. My wife could smell a lie from a mile away. So I sucked up my pride and admitted what an idiot I'd been.

"Well, when I got home I saw Trent's car parked outside. Then I heard all the noise the StairMaster was making. And, well, to be honest, Di, it sounded like someone was having sex in—" She cut me off before I could finish.

"And you thought . . . you thought I would do something like that in your bed, with your brother?" I could tell by her tone that she wasn't just insulted. Now she was hurt. "What kind of woman do you think I am, Wil? You know I wouldn't cheat on you. And you know I can't stand Trent."

"I know that, Di, and I'm sorry." I tried to reach out to her but she pulled away.

"Sorry ain't good enough, Wil. Not after what we've been through." Her eyes got misty. I felt like I was shrinking in front of her. "How could you, Wil? How could you think I would mess with your brother?"

"I don't know, Di. You know how Trent is, and it really sounded like you were having sex in here."

"Sounded like?" She snapped as tears began to run down her face. "You couldn't open up the door and find out before you went and got a baseball bat? After everything that's happened in the past, I can't believe you're still jumping to conclusions."

I had to bite my tongue to stop from saying what I really wanted. See, Di knew a little herself about jumping to conclusions. In the past, it was she who'd nearly ended our marriage over some shit I didn't even do. She found some pictures of me in compromising positions with a few strippers, and the next thing I knew, all my shit was on the front lawn and the police were ordering me to leave my own property. But it's not what it sounds like. I was passed out in every one of the pictures, and I didn't even know the pictures had been taken. My boys, Kyle and Allen, thought it would be a harmless joke at Allen's bachelor party to get a few shots of me and the girls with my own camera. They figured I'd get the film developed and get a kick out of their little joke. What they didn't count on was that my wife would be the one to take the film to the pharmacy and find what she thought was enough evidence to put me out on the street and threaten to move my kids down South.

The time that I was living away from my wife and kids was the worst time of my life, and it took some creative payback from my boy Jay to convince Diane that things are not always what they appear to be on film. So obviously, we'd gotten back together since that crazy misunderstanding and for the most part we were a happy little family again. But whenever something threatened to dredge up memories of the incident, things could revert to shaky ground in a heartbeat. That's why Di was standing at the doorway, arms crossed and lip poked out, obviously still very hurt and angry.

"Oh, and for your information, Trent borrowed the van so that he could take the kids to Chuck E. Cheese. He called himself giving me a break from the kids," she said with a smirk as she left me standing there, still clutching the bat like an idiot.

I waited about half an hour before I came downstairs and looked for Diane. I found her watching TV in the den. I was hoping that she'd cooled off a bit by now. As I explained before, Diane's been known to hold grudges. Long, drawn-out grudges. I really didn't want this to be one of those times. Especially since I was still having that eerie feeling that something bad was about to happen.

"Di," I called from the doorway.

"What?" She never looked up from the television. It was obvious she still had an attitude, but her voice was a lot more civil than it had been upstairs.

"You still mad?"

"What do you think, Wil?" She finally looked up from the TV.

"I think we should go get something to eat and put this behind us. I saw the crab man set up over on Farmers Boulevard. I was thinking about going over there and getting some crab legs. You want me to get some for you?" There was no question that Diane was upset, but if there was one thing that could help me get back in her good graces, it was crab legs. She loved them.

"You really think you're slick, don't you?" She stood up and stepped in my direction.

"Look, Di. I don't wanna fight. I made a mistake, all right? I jumped to conclusions. It's not something I'm proud of, but it's not like you never jumped to conclusions." There, I'd said it. And to my surprise, she didn't go on the defensive. She just pursed her lips together and looked away. I would've expected at least a little fight out of her.

"Look, Di," I pleaded, "I just wanna get past this."

"You think buying me crab legs is gonna get your ass past this?"

"No." I sighed. "I just . . ."

She picked up her purse and spoke to me without any trace of emotion.

"Let's go, Wil." She stood and looked at me. Her face didn't give any clue about her emotional state.

"You mean you're not mad?" I asked hopefully.

"Oh, I'm still mad. But I can't be mad forever. I heard you up there on that StairMaster. It does sound like someone having sex." She spoke quickly, like she hated to be saying it at all.

I couldn't believe she was admitting I might not be such a jerk after all. After she'd left the bedroom, I'd gone to the StairMaster and tried it out, needing to understand how I could have been so stupid. The stepping motion was a pretty steady rhythm, but being the one on it, it seemed pretty ridiculous that I could have mistaken this sound for a creaking bed. I felt even more stupid after my little experiment, but now Di was confirming that from the first floor, it really could be confusing. The corners of my mouth started to curl into a smile, but Di stopped that in a hurry.

"That still doesn't mean you're right, Wil. You should have trusted me more than that. Had a little faith."

"I know. You're right." And she was right. After our past experiences with infidelity that really wasn't infidelity, we both had to learn to be a lot more trusting.

She walked past me into the hallway and I followed. We hadn't even got halfway down the hall when the doorbell rang. I opened it, and there was Trent, holding my son Teddy, half asleep in his arms.

"What's up, player?" He smiled at me with that devilish grin of his.

"I'm not a player. And where's my daughter?"

"Brenda's getting her outta her car seat." He handed me my son.

"Brenda? Who's Brenda?" I glanced at Diane.

"Don't look at me. When he left this house it was just him and the kids." Diane folded her arms across her chest and glared at my brother. "I done told you about bringing strange women around my children, Trent. Where'd you meet this one? At a gas station? Or was she hitchhiking?"

"Damn, Diane. That was cold." Trent shook his head. "But

for your information, she owns her own travel agency in Long Island. Matter of fact, she just got me two first-class tickets to Hawaii for my birthday. Those damn things are worth fifteen hundred dollars apiece."

"Oh, and I should trust someone stupid enough to give you free airline tickets with my children? Ha! You must be crazy." Diane shot Trent an evil look, pointing her finger in his face. "I'm not gonna tell you this again, Trent. Don't be bringing strange women around my children if you wanna spend time with them again." She pushed him aside and headed toward the van to get our daughter.

"Yo, player, wait until you see the body on this one," Trent whispered confidently. "Baby got back, front. Shit, she's got the whole damn yard."

He wasn't lying, either. When Brenda walked around the van behind Diane, I had to do a double take. She was wearing a skintight minidress that had to be at least one size too small and when she walked, everything important moved. She was a cute, thick sister with a cocoa face and a slamming body. For a second I was almost envious of my brother.

"Trent, aren't you gonna introduce me?" Brenda approached us, shaking her head playfully at his rude behavior.

"Oh, my bad." He placed his arm around her. "Wil, Diane. This is Brenda. Brenda, this is my brother Wil and my sister-in-law, Diane. Teddy and Katie's parents."

She shook Diane's hand, then I extended my hand, and she took it gracefully.

"Nice to meet you, Brenda."

"It's a pleasure. You have beautiful children," she replied with a smile.

"Why thank . . ." I never finished my sentence, because that's when I got a look at her teeth for the first time. Those damn things were going in four different directions, and believe me when I tell you at least two of them were missing. I swear, with that cute face and those messed-up teeth, she looked like somebody out of the Addams family.

"Wil." Diane nudged me back into reality, which was a good thing, 'cause not only was I still holding the woman's hand, but I was staring at her messed-up grill like she was on fire.

"Yes, Di?" I finally took my eyes off Brenda and looked at my wife.

"Why don't we go in the house so that we can put these kids to bed?" That's when I realized we were still on the front porch.

"Oh, yeah. That's a good idea. Trent, why don't you take Brenda in the den and make her a drink while Diane and I put the kids to bed?" I tried my best not to look at Brenda, 'cause if she opened her mouth I probably would have dropped Teddy trying to keep from laughing.

"A drink sounds good, big brother. Especially a free one. But why don't me and you put the kids to bed and let the girls fix the drinks? I got something I need to talk to you about."

I hesitated before answering. I knew he was going to curse me out about my rude behavior toward his date. Not that I didn't deserve it.

"Aw'ight." I waved. "Y'all come on in the house, 'cause this boy is falling asleep in my arms."

Diane handed Katie to Trent. He followed me into the house and up the stairs. Surprisingly, he didn't say a word until after both the kids were in the bed.

"Wil?" Trent tapped my shoulder as we walked toward the stairs. I sighed. I thought I was almost home free.

"Look, Trent, I know what you're gonna say. I'm sorry if I embarrassed you out there."

"Embarrass me? Embarrass me how?"

"You know. Staring at Brenda's teeth. I shouldn't have done that. I'm sorry. If you want, I'll apologize to her."

He chuckled. "Apologize? Apologize for what? Please, Wil, that girl knows she needs a good dentist. Why you think she's messin' with me?"

I had no idea what the connection could be between her crooked teeth and my brother. But knowing Trent like I did, I probably didn't want to know the answer. So I didn't ask.

"Well, if it's not about me staring at her teeth, then what did you wanna talk to me about?"

"Man, I wanted to know if you could lend me a hundred bucks so I could take Brenda out."

"A hundred bucks? Are you crazy? You already owe me three

hundred bucks from last month when you were short on your rent. If Diane knew I gave you money she'd kill me."

"I know that, Wil. And I'm gonna pay you back. Shit, I wouldn't even be asking you for this if I hadn't spent my last fifty on your kids at Chuck E. Cheese. Not that I'm complaining. You know I love them kids."

Damn, why'd he have to go there? I wasn't gonna give him shit. But now I felt bad that he spent his money on my kids. Trent was an ass, but if there was one thing I had to give him credit for, he was a good uncle. He'd do anything for my kids. I reached in my pocket and pulled out my wallet.

"I only got sixty on me."

He snatched the money outta my hand. "That'll do," he said before heading down the stairs. I looked at my empty wallet and a little voice in the back of my head whispered, *He got you again, didn't he?*

I sighed quietly to myself as I followed my brother down the stairs.

Trent and I walked into the den and found Diane sipping on a glass of wine.

"Hey, where's Brenda? She in the bathroom or something?" Trent looked around the room.

"No. She left in a cab about two minutes ago." Diane smirked.

"What?" Trent turned his head toward Diane. "Why'd she leave?"

"I don't know. Something about she had to get to her office and cancel your tickets to Hawaii."

"Cancel my tickets to Hawaii! She can't do that! I was gonna sell those tickets to pay my car note."

I wasn't sure yet what was going on, but my grinning wife obviously had some idea, and she was thoroughly enjoying herself. Poor Trent stood there looking like his whole world was coming apart.

"Oh, yeah," Diane said a little too gleefully, "and she told me to tell you to lose her number."

"She sure told you a lot, didn't she?" Trent snarled at my wife. "So, Diane, what the hell did you tell her?"

Di shrugged her shoulders and tried to look innocent. "I ain't tell her shit. All I did was answer her questions. That's all."

"Questions! What questions?" Trent was getting heated now. And to be honest, Diane was acting like a real ass. I didn't really think Trent would get stupid in my house, but I took a few steps toward my wife just in case he flew off the handle.

"She asked me if Wil was a dentist like you." Diane let out a laugh. She looked at me, but I declined to join in on her little game. Trent just shook his head. I guess he knew what the rest of the story would be. No doubt he was wishing he'd left the girl in the car when he dropped off the kids.

"And what did you tell her?" He tried to keep his voice under control but it was obvious he was not a happy camper.

"I told her that my husband ain't no damn dentist! And neither are you." Trent closed his eyes in anger. "Oh, yeah. She also asked me who this Michelle was that keeps calling you. It seems you completely forgot to tell her about your crazy baby momma."

Trent took a step toward Diane, then turned and walked toward the door. The tension in my shoulders relaxed just a bit, knowing this latest little confrontation was almost over.

"You know what, Diane?"

"What's that, Trent?" Diane smirked at him.

"You need to stop player hatin'." Trent didn't wait for a response. He just walked out the door and sped away in his Mercedes.

2

Trent

I was in the middle of a catnap when the phone rang. I let the answering machine get it, 'cause I had a pretty good idea who was calling. And I was right. It was Brenda, the fine ass travel agent with the messed-up teeth I'd been spending time with lately. She had some fucking nerve trying to call me now. Especially after she'd hung up the phone on me when I called her earlier. I tried to call back three times, but she kept hanging up. I know she was still upset about that shit Diane said but she wouldn't even give me a chance to explain. So now, as far as I was concerned, she could kiss my naturally black ass, 'cause I didn't have shit to say to her. I was just glad she didn't have a chance to cancel my tickets to Hawaii before I got over to Kennedy Airport to cash them in.

"Trent, you bastard, I know you're home! Pick up the phone!" Brenda's shrill voice came through my answering machine like a sonic boom. I figured by now she would have known I cashed in the tickets, but it sounded like I'd overestimated her. *"Trent, goddamnit! I want my tickets back! Do you hear me? I want my fucking tickets back, or . . ."*

I picked up the receiver. I hated when women made empty threats. "Or what? What the fuck you gonna do, Brenda?"

"Or I'm gonna come over there with a hammer and break every window in your fucking car! That's what!" Now that stopped my laughter cold. I'm not gonna lie, she had me shook. That wasn't no empty threat she'd just made. I could tell by her voice she was dead serious, and the last thing I wanted her to do was mess with my car. My Mercedes was my most prized possession.

"Now, Brenda," I stated calmly, "why you gonna go and

threaten my car like that? You know how much that car means to me." Besides that, I hadn't paid my car insurance this month.

"If you so damned concerned about your fucking car, then give me my tickets back."

I glanced at the pile of hundred dollar bills sitting on my coffee table. I'd gotten them from cashing in the airline tickets. No way was I giving back that money. I needed it to pay my past due car note.

"I'm sorry, Brenda, but I can't do that."

"I'm sorry too, Trent." Her voice was so polite it was eerie. But that was just the calm before the storm, because then she exploded. "If I don't get my money, I'm gonna fuck your car up!"

"I don't know what's wrong with you, but you leave my car outta this! You hear me? You touch my car and I'm gonna kick your fucking ass."

"Well, then you go ahead and kick it, 'cause I'm coming over there right now, you fake ass dentist."

"Fake ass dentist?" I repeated calmly.

"That's right, fake ass dentist. Your sister-in-law told me the truth about you. You ain't no dentist. You ain't even got a job, you lying bastard. What I should do is call the police on your ass."

"Go 'head. Call 'em." I laughed smugly. "But before you do, let me point out a few things to you. First of all, you gave me those tickets as a birthday gift. And I got the birthday card you gave me to prove it. So legally, I ain't gotta give shit back. And why you believing my sister-in-law anyway? How you think I pay for a Mercedes and an apartment overlooking Jamaica Bay if I ain't got no job?" There was silence on the line. "Did Diane explain that one to you?"

"No," she said weakly.

"Brenda, I'm a dentist just like I told you. You've seen my degrees and the state license on my wall. What did you think they were, fake?"

She was silent on her end as I got up off the sofa and walked into the second bedroom. I had turned it into an office. With my free hand, I wiped the dust from the glass framing the New York State dentistry license I had just mentioned to Brenda. It was hanging above my undergraduate and dentistry degrees.

"Well, what about this baby? I thought you told me you don't have any kids."

"Brenda, Brenda, Brenda, you are so naive. You saw me with my niece and nephew today at Chuck E. Cheese. Do I look like the kind of man who would hide his child from you or anyone else for that matter? I love children."

"But she said . . ." Brenda finally sighed.

"But she said what?" I asked her in irritation. "I told you at Chuck E. Cheese that Diane and I don't get along, didn't I? She's a hater, Brenda. A straight-up hater."

She muttered something that sounded like, "I'm sorry, Trent."

"Sorry about what? That you finally found a good man but you weren't woman enough to believe in him? You know what, Brenda? I can't tell you how disappointed I am in you." More silence. "You calling me up, threatening my car, walking out of my brother's house, embarrassing me. For what?" She had nothing to say. "Diane played you, Brenda. And not only did it cost you this relationship, but it cost you getting those teeth of yours fixed for free."

I hung up the phone with a satisfied grin. I was sure Brenda would call back, but next time she would probably be a little more humble. I was about to go back into the living room and finish my nap, but it seemed like the second I hung up the phone someone was knocking at my door. The first thing that came to mind was Brenda and her hammer. Had she played me? Was she outside on her cell the whole time? Was she gonna fuck up my car? Or had she already done it?

"Who is it?" I shouted as I ran to the window to check my car.

"It's Mrs. Wilson, Trent. I've come for your rent."

"Damn," I mumbled when I heard the voice of Viola, the three-hundred-pound, pain-in-the-ass wife of my landlord, Mr. Wilson. I knew I was gonna have to pay my rent soon, but I'd completely forgotten it was the first Thursday of the month, the day she came by to collect the rent money from those who hadn't made it to the rental office. Normally, when I didn't have her money I would try to duck her, but now that I'd opened my big mouth, she knew I was there. I walked to the door and put on a fake smile as I opened it.

"Hey, Viola. What's up?" I was as polite as I could manage to be considering Viola was the last person I wanted to see, other than Brenda.

"My husband sent me to collect the rent." Viola smiled as she stuck out her huge pawlike hand. I don't know who she thought she was fooling. It was nine o'clock on a Thursday night. Her husband was probably curled up with a bottle of gin, passed out on the couch somewhere.

"Damn, it seems like I just paid rent last week. Is it that time of the month again already?"

"Yep, it sure is." Viola grinned flirtatiously. She purposely brushed her extra-large breasts against my chest as she walked into my apartment. "So, do you have the rent money, or are we gonna have to work something out like we did last month? I don't mind giving you a few extra weeks to pay, Trent. That is, as long as you're nice to me."

My stomach started to do flips as I remembered just how Viola and I had worked things out last month. I had no problem sleeping with her to push back my rent a few weeks. I mean, she was big as shit, but she wasn't ugly or anything. And she had given me almost a thousand-dollar break on my rent. It's just that, well, Viola had a hygiene problem, a real bad hygiene problem. I swear, after I had sex with her it took three days to get her funky-ass scent off me. I felt like I'd been sprayed by a skunk. It was totally disgusting.

"Well, you got my money, or are you gonna give me some honey?" Viola kicked off her shoes and opened her arms, gesturing for me to come to her. She was obviously hoping I was broke. I took a step back, shaking my head. No way was I putting my nose through that again.

"I got your money right here, Viola." I practically ran to the coffee table to get the money from the airline tickets. "Here you go. Three thousand dollars."

I shoved the money in her hand. My past due car note was just gonna have to wait.

"Now, Trent, honey, you know you don't have to pay all this at one time. I know times are hard. I don't mind helping you out as long as you help me out once in a while. And, baby, I need some help right now." She started to lift up her skirt, and I turned my head with a grimace when I saw that she wasn't wearing any panties. I was definitely going to have to break out the air freshener once I got her ass out of here.

"I'm sorry, Viola, but I can't help you." I walked toward the door.

"Why not?" That was definitely not what she was hoping to hear. She truly looked insulted.

"Well, to be honest, I'm dating someone seriously right now, and I'd hate to start cheating on her this early in the relationship. You can understand that, can't you?" I opened the door and hoped she'd get the hint, but she stood her ground, staring out the window as she interrogated me.

"I know you ain't talking about that big ass woman with the messed-up teeth."

"No, not her. She's just a friend. I'm talking about the tall, light-skinned girl with the blond locks."

"Her?" Viola placed a hand on her hips and gave me a skeptical glance. "I thought she was your sister."

"Why would you think that?"

" 'Cause you told me that last month, right before we got our groove on."

"Well . . ." Damn. I hated getting caught in a lie. "She's not my sister. She's my girl."

"You sure about this? 'Cause Viola don't like to be lied to."

"Ain't nobody lying to you. And yeah, I'm sure. You got your money, Viola."

She slipped her feet into her shoes and I breathed a sigh of relief. It looked like she was gonna give up before she had to resort to begging. I waited by the door to see her out, but something out the window caught her attention and she started to laugh.

"Um, Trent? Isn't that your car that man's about to tow away?"

"Please, Viola. Ain't no one out there towing my car." I stuck my head out the door and almost had a heart attack. "Oh, shit! Hey! What the hell are you doing? Get away from my car!"

I could hear Viola's hysterical laughter as I took off for my car. The skinny ass brother hooking my car up didn't know it, but I was about to give him the ass whipping of his life. That is until a short, balding, overweight white man stepped out of the truck carrying a shotgun.

"Calm down there, fella." He didn't have to tell me twice as he raised his gun at my chest. I froze, raising my hands above my head.

"What are you doin' to my car?"

"What you think we doin'? We're repossessing it." The skinny brother laughed. "Unless you got the thirty-three hundred you owe Financial Credit."

I glanced evilly at the brother who had finished hooking up my car and was now standing next to his partner. "You like fucking over black folks, don't you?"

"No, I like fucking over anyone who don't pay their bills. I'm an equal opportunity hater, man." He laughed until his partner shot him a look.

"Look. We're just doing our job," the white man told me as he handed me a piece of yellow paper.

"Well, your fucking job sucks!" I looked down at the paper. "Look here. I don't even owe Financial Credit thirty-three hundred. I only owe them twenty-eight hundred."

"Not after you add in the towing fee, the repossession fee, collection fee and storage," the brother interjected happily. I ignored him and turned to the white man.

"Look, man, I know you gotta get something outta the deal. So what if I give you three grand? You think you can make this go away?"

The man with the gun looked at his partner, then turned to me.

"You give us three grand cash right now and we'll make sure this thing goes away."

"Hold on one minute, okay? I just have to get the money." The white man nodded and I ran over to Viola, who was just about to walk into the rental office. "Viola, sweetheart, I need to get that money back. So why don't you come back over to my house and we can discuss those terms you wanted."

She shook her head. "Thanks, but no thanks, Trent."

"What do you mean? I thought you said you wanted me to help you with your problem."

"I did, but that was before you got all high and mighty about cheating. As many women as you have running through here? Just 'cause I'm big don't mean I ain't got no pride, Trent."

"Come on, Viola," I pleaded.

I knew it would probably make me sick to my stomach, but I decided to use a desperate tactic. I whispered to her, "Remember when you asked me to go down on you last time and I told you I don't do that?"

"Mmm-hmm. I knew your ass was lying."

"I wasn't lying, but I'm willing to try it now. Come on, let's go back over to my place."

She smiled so I think I perked her interest. "You mean it? You're really willing to try it for me?"

"Of course I am." I tried to guide her toward my apartment. "I just need to get that money back so they won't repossess my car. Then I'm gonna eat you like a turkey on Thanksgiving Day." *That is, if I don't throw up first,* I thought.

Viola stared at me with an erotic smile. It was pretty obvious by her dazed look and heavy breathing that she was daydreaming about my head between her legs. I was sure that any moment she was going to hand me back my money and drag me to my apartment for some of her funky lovin'. But to my chagrin, she flashed the money in my face, then tucked it away securely in her bra.

"Viola, what you doing?"

She stepped into the rental office. "I'm gonna put this money in the safe, then I'm gonna take my ass over to the Benny's Bar in Hollis and find me a real man. One who appreciates a woman like me." She started to close the door. I stopped it with my foot.

"I appreciate you, Viola," I told her desperately.

"No, you don't. Only thing you care about is that car. Now get your foot out my door."

"Come on, Viola. I thought we said we were gonna help each other."

"We were. But I changed my mind. Like I told you before, I gots my pride." She slammed the door on my foot and I yelped. As soon as I pulled my foot out of the door, I heard the lock click. The repo men must've been listening, because I could hear them laughing as they got in the tow truck and pulled away with my car.

"Don't worry, baby," I mumbled as I watched my car drift from sight. "I'm gonna get you back."

Desperate, I reached into my pocket and pulled out my cell phone. I hit the numbers 6 and 9, then speed dial.

"Hi," a familiar woman's voice answered, "I'm unable to come to the phone right now but please leave your name, number and a short message at the sound of the tone, and I'll get back to you as soon as I can."

"Shit," I mumbled under my breath before leaving a message. "Look, it's me, Trent. I need to see you. It's important. Call me back on my cell. You know the number."

3

Melanie

Manhattan Proper was packed when I walked in around eleven o'clock. I was looking for Trent. He'd asked me to meet him at the small club on Linden Boulevard in Cambria Heights, Queens. I wasn't sure what he wanted, but he'd been calling my cell phone all night, leaving messages that he needed to speak to me as soon as possible. Usually, I would have called him right back, but I was at the hairdresser getting my dreads twisted and accidentally left my cell in my apartment. I didn't get his messages until I got home. My unavailability must have really pissed him off, 'cause his last message was downright indignant. He told me in no uncertain terms to make sure I brought my black ass right over to the club when I got home. So as usual, when Trent called I came running.

As I slid onto a bar stool, I smiled at Tim, the sexy almond-skinned bartender. He smiled back flirtatiously, wiping the area in front of me with one hand as he placed an apple martini, my favorite drink, on the bar with the other. Damn, he was cute, with his broad shoulders and tight round ass.

"What's up, Melanie?" Tim leaned over the bar with a seductive stare. If I didn't know better, I would have sworn he was gonna kiss me. If he hadn't already slept with my best friend, Desiree, I probably would have let him. I'd had a crush on Tim since the day we met. But as usual, Desiree spotted him first, and although she'd moved on, dealing with him would be crossing the line.

"Not much, Ti—" Some ugly-ass woman banged into my chair and I stared her down.

"Sorry," she whined. I glared at her, then turned back toward Tim.

"Damn, it's crowded in here for a Thursday night. What you giving out, two-for-ones or something?"

"It's always like this on Thursdays now that we have karaoke. Every wannabe singer in Queens is here. Especially after the word got out that some music executives from Arista Records signed a sister to a record deal last month." Tim tried to lean closer, and I sat back in my chair. "So what's up, Melanie? When you gonna let me take you out?"

"Never." I twisted one of my shoulder-length blond dreads around my finger.

"Why?"

"Don't play stupid, Tim. You know exactly why. Because you used to go with my best friend, that's why."

He looked like he was about to plead his case, but I cut him off.

"Look, you seen Trent? I'm supposed to meet him here."

Tim frowned as he pushed himself up from the bar. He'd made it quite evident in the past that he didn't like Trent.

"Yeah, he's out back on the patio. He's been looking for you."

"I figured that. He's not drunk or anything, is he?" I gave him a concerned look.

"Nah, he's fine. He looked a little agitated when he walked in, but he talked some stupid-ass woman into buying a bottle of Dom and he's been fine ever since."

"Thank God for small favors," I thought out loud.

I lit a cigarette, then picked up my drink as I turned toward the back of the bar. I spotted Trent through the small patio door. He was leaning against the fence, flirting with two sisters in their early twenties. I had to laugh. There was no question that if Trent was anything, he was a ladies' man. He had both those sisters mesmerized as he stood there profiling in his all-white attire. He looked like he belonged at one of P. Diddy's Fourth of July parties in the Hamptons. I could just imagine the bullshit he was telling those sisters. Of course you know there was no sign of the urgency that I had heard in his messages.

I watched Trent do his thing with the ladies while I finished my drink. Usually I would've just walked over with an attitude and interrupted his little conversation. But this time, believe it or not, he ended the conversation the second he spotted me at the bar. He just handed one of the women a business card, whispered something in her ear and headed my way. You should have seen the expression on her face when she glanced at the card. She looked like she wanted to run after him. So I know she must've been pissed off when she saw him approach me.

"Yo, where the hell you been?" Trent demanded.

"Nice to see you too, Trent."

I hated it when he did shit like that, no matter how cute he looked in his all-white outfit. But then again, Trent looked cute in anything he wore. He had one of those bodies that was made for clothes. My friend Desiree once said, "Trent don't wear clothes to look good, clothes wear Trent to look good," and she was right. Trent could wear a beat-up, old man suit from the thrift store, everyone else could be wearing designer suits, and he'd still be the best-dressed man in the place.

The funny thing is, Trent isn't this superfly pretty boy that you'd think he was. Don't get me wrong. He's not ugly, by any stretch of the imagination either. But he just isn't the type you'd expect to make women fall all over themselves. Trent's secret is the charming, almost regal way he carries himself. Not to mention his gift for gab. He can talk with the best of them. He's the type of man who could walk into a bar sober and as broke as a Tibetan monk, but when he walked out he'd be drunk and every woman in the place would swear he was the richest man they'd ever met.

"Melanie, did you hear me? I been tryin' to get in touch with you all night." This time Trent glared at me like he was scolding a child, and part of me felt like I was his child. Hell, he'd practically raised me. See, Trent's my older brother by six years and when my dad died, Trent was the one who looked after me. Most people think my eldest brother Wil's the one who kept our family together, but when Dad died, Wil was away at college. And since my mom was working two jobs to support us, I was left with Trent. Believe it or not, he never complained about having his kid sister hanging around. He actually made it his job to keep me outta trouble and teach me about life. It's just too bad he couldn't seem to do the same for himself.

"Mel, did you hear me?" he repeated himself for the third time.

"Yeah, Trent, I heard you. I was at Nu-Tribe getting my locks twisted. Now what's so important that you had to call me fifteen times?"

Trent slid onto the bar stool next to me, gesturing for Tim to bring him a Corona. He gave me this devilish smile as he placed his arm around my shoulder, and that made me nervous as hell. He always used that smile right before he was about to ask for something.

"Sis, I need you to do me a favor."

"What kinda favor?" I asked skeptically. Trent gulped down half his beer as soon as Tim placed it in front of him.

"Look, I want you to hear me out before you answer, okay?"

I removed his arm from around my shoulder because I knew that whatever favor he wanted, it wasn't gonna be in my best interest.

"Just get on with it, Trent." I exhaled.

"Aw'ight." He took a deep breath. "Sis, I need you to ask Wil to loan you four grand."

I paused, raising an eyebrow before I responded.

"Four grand! As in four thousand dollars? You're joking, right?" I started to laugh, but stopped abruptly when he didn't join in. I searched his face for some sign that this was just another one of his jests. But his face never gave me that sign, and neither did his words.

"No, Sis, I'm not joking. I'm dead serious."

"Let me get this straight. You want me to ask Wil to loan me four thousand dollars so I can give it to you?"

Trent nodded his head and this time I did laugh, but not because anything was funny.

"Are you fucking crazy? I'm not asking him that. You want the money, you ask him for it."

"Come on, Melanie," he pleaded. "Wil's not gonna give the money to me, but I know he'll give it to you."

"And what makes you think he's just gonna give me four thousand dollars?"

"He wants you to finish school," Trent explained. "All you gotta do is tell him you're gonna go back to school, and I bet he'll give you the money. Shit, he might not even ask you to pay it back."

"And what if he does? How can I be sure you're gonna give

me back the money? I love you, Trent, but you have a hard time paying back your debts. You owe me two hundred dollars already."

"I'll sign my car over to you," he told me desperately. Not that I believed him. "If I don't pay you back within three months, you can sell it to pay Wil." I guess he could see I was still skeptical, because he continued to plead. "Come on, Sis. I'm gonna pay the money back. I swear. You know I'd go homeless before I let you sell my car."

I shook my head pitifully. "You got this shit all planned out, don't you?"

He lowered his head, trying to avoid eye contact. "Well, yeah. Sorta."

"Well, I'm sorry to disappoint you, big brother, but I can't do it."

He obviously didn't expect me to say no 'cause he sat back in his chair, straight as a board. "Can't, or won't?"

"Both." My answer was stern.

Trent slammed his fist down on the bar. "Why not?"

"Because, Trent, I am going back to school, for real. I just borrowed tuition money from Wil. And on top of that, I'm sick of you trying to get over. You're thirty-five years old, and every time you get in trouble, either Wil or me gotta bail you out. When are you gonna grow up? This shit is ridiculous. And speaking of ridiculous, when are you going to go see your baby? Michelle told me you ain't gone to see that baby or given her any money yet."

"Damn, not you too. Melanie, I am not that baby's father! You gotta believe me on that. I am not that baby's father. Now stop trying to change the subject. I need that money. This is some serious shit." He placed both hands over his face, and I felt a momentary twinge of sympathy. Trent looked like he was gonna cry and I wasn't really sure why.

"What kind of trouble are you in, anyway?" I waited for his answer, but I didn't get one. We were interrupted by a tall, dark-skinned woman with flawless makeup and a boyish haircut. She was trying to step in between us.

"Excuse me. Can I get by?" I moved my feet so she could get to the bar, but she seemed more interested in Trent than she did in getting a drink. She must have seen our unmistakable family resemblance, 'cause she was taking a real chance on a beat down stepping between a sister when she was talking to a man.

"Hiya, handsome." She smiled flirtatiously, inspecting my brother from head to toe. "My name's Indigo. I was hoping you might buy me a drink so we can get better acquainted." Sister was bold if she was anything. She just didn't know who she was fucking with. A big butt and smile was not what my brother Trent was looking for.

"Buy you a drink?" Trent laughed for the first time since I'd seen him. "Are you out your mind? I ain't buying you nothin'."

The woman took a step back, looking both surprised and embarrassed by Trent's negative response. And I can't say I blamed her. But she didn't know that in Trent's world, things were the other way around. He didn't buy the drinks, women bought him drinks and a hell of a lot more.

"Did you hear this shit, Mel? She wants me to buy her a drink." Trent turned his attention to me, then back to her. "What the fuck you come here for if you ain't got no money?" Trent asked her viciously.

"Who said I didn't have any money?" she snapped with attitude. "I just wanted to get to kno—" She stopped herself in mid sentence. "You know what, just forget it."

"You already been forgotten." Trent smirked, about to continue his insults as she walked away. I had to grab his arm to stop him from tormenting the poor woman anymore.

"Trent, forget her. I wanna know what's going on. Why do you need four thousand dollars?"

He lowered his head and sighed. "So, how do you like those Mets?"

"What? You know I hate baseball. Stop trying to change the subject, Trent. I wanna know what the hell's going on. You're not gambling again, are you?"

Trent glared at me. "Who told you that? It was that big mouth Diane, wasn't it? She always talking about something she don't know nothin' about."

"All right, then, tell me what you need the money for."

"Well, to be honest . . ."

Trent's last words were interrupted when Tim placed fresh drinks in front of us.

"What are these for? We didn't order another round. We're not even finished with these." Trent pointed at his half-full Corona and my apple martini.

"Hey, look. If you too good for free drinks . . ." Tim reached to pull the drinks back.

"Free drinks?" Trent gave Tim a cynical glance, pulling closer the full bottle of Corona. "Who can say no to free drinks? So to whom do we owe the pleasure? I know it's not your cheap ass. You ain't bought a round of drinks since you started working here." Tim ignored him and pointed to the end of the bar.

"See the woman over there, looking through the karaoke book?"

Trent and I turned toward the woman, then glanced at each other with our jaws hanging open. It was the woman who'd asked Trent to buy her a drink less than five minutes ago.

"She bought us a round of drinks?" Trent asked in disbelief.

"Not just you. She bought the whole bar a round."

"What? Get the fuck outta here. That chick ain't got no money. She practically begged me to buy her a drink a few minutes ago." Trent laughed. "If I were you, I'd go ask that lady to see the cash before I started handing out free drinks, 'cause that bitch is broke."

"I doubt it," Tim said confidently.

"Aw'ight," Trent teased. "That's your ass, not mine."

"What are you, stupid? Don't you know who that is?" Tim glanced at us and we both shrugged our shoulders.

"Man, that's Indigo Jones."

"And . . . is that supposed to mean something? What is she, an entertainer or something?"

"No. Don't you read the newspaper?" Tim stared at Trent in disbelief, then turned to me. "You don't know who she is either, huh?"

"The name sounds familiar. But I really don't have a clue." Tim shook his head, and all of a sudden it came to me. "Wait a minute, Trent. He's right. She was on the news recently." I looked up at Tim, and he smiled. "She's the woman from St.

Albans who hit Lotto the day before she and her mother were supposed to be evicted. Didn't she quit her job to take care of her dying mom or something?"

"Yep, that's her. But she didn't quite hit Lotto. She won the Pick Five for a hundred grand."

"A hundred gran . . ." Trent choked on his beer. "You lyin', right?"

"No, I'm not."

Tim reached under the bar and pulled out a newspaper clipping. He handed it to Trent. My brother's eyes got wide as he read.

"I bet you wish you'd bought her that drink now, don't you?" Tim teased. Trent shot up his middle finger but never looked up from the article he was reading. Tim just laughed as he moved on to serve another customer.

Trent smoothed the article out on the bar as the two of us watched Indigo walk over to the karaoke machine and take the mike from the DJ. A few seconds later, she was standing in front of the whole bar, singing her ass off. No joke, she was singing so good she could've been on that show *American Idol*. And everyone in the bar let her know it by giving her a standing ovation. Everyone but Trent, that is. He was sitting at the bar, frantically shuffling through some business cards.

"What are you up to, Trent?" I was afraid I already knew where my brother's thoughts were headed.

"Nothin', but I don't think I'm gonna need you to ask Wil for that loan after all."

"And why's that?"

"'Cause I think Ms. Indigo Jones over there is the answer to all my problems."

"Is that so?"

"Yep. She's gonna help me get my car back from the repo man and pay off the rest of my bills, and . . ."

I cut him off. "Repo man? Your car got repossessed?"

"Ah, yeah." He didn't even look embarrassed.

"You wanted me to borrow money from Wil so you could get your car outta hock?" I never gave him a chance to answer. "I don't believe this shit. I thought you said you were gonna sign your car over to me if I got the money from Wil."

"I was, once I got it back." He looked right into my eyes. I was so mad, I wished my eyes could burn a hole right through his lying face. "Come on, Mel. Don't be mad. You know how I feel about my car."

"It's not how you feel about your car that I'm worried about. It's how you feel about me," I replied with attitude. "Besides, if you really cared about that car, you woulda paid your car note!"

I picked up my drink and I was about to walk away when this tall, gorgeous, athletic, Tootsie Roll–colored brother walked up. He was so fine, all I could do was stare at him with my mouth open.

"Yo, Trent, what's up? How'd everything work out for you at Chuck E. Cheese?" He stuck his hand out.

"Oh, man, it was beautiful! I swear, you musta saved me a c-note with those gift certificates the way those kids were usin' up those tokens." Trent slapped his hand. "I owe you one for that."

"Don't even worry about it. My sister Trina's the assistant manager over there. Ain't no reason to spend money if we ain't got to. Know what I mean?" Trent's friend smiled at me, and I felt like melting. He was so fine he was giving me goose bumps. "So who is this fine thing you with? Your new lady?"

Trent laughed. "Nah, man, this is my sister Melanie. Melanie, this is Prince." I stuck my hand out, and to my surprise and pleasure he took hold of my hand and kissed it. I don't think I've ever blushed like that before.

"It's a pleasure to meet you, Melanie."

"Oh, no, the pleasure's all mine." I tried not to giggle.

"You know, I love the way your blond locks highlight your golden brown skin." I knew he was running game, but it was game I was willing to listen to all night.

"Thank you," I whispered timidly.

"And your eyes. They're mesmerizing. What color are they?"

"They're hazel."

"No, you're wrong. They're beautiful," he replied. The two of us were locked in this incredible, electric stare, and he was still holding my hand until Trent interrupted us.

"What the fuck y'all think this is, *Love Connection*? Yo, dawg, that's my *sister* you tryin'a kick it to."

Prince let go of my hand immediately. I wanted to scream at

Trent to mind his own fucking business. Why was he so busy hatin', anyway? But I knew my brother, and nothing I said would have stopped him.

"Oh, I'm sorry, man, my bad. It's just that your sister's so *fine*." Prince stared at me as he spoke.

"Like I said, dawg. That's my sister. I know you don't want me rollin' up to Chuck E. Cheese all up in Trina's face, do you?"

Prince hesitated for a second, his eyes never leaving mine. "Nah, I don't. It was nice meeting you, Melanie."

He walked away before I could reply. I turned to Trent with fire in my eyes.

"Don't look at me like that. I told you about flirting with my friends."

"I'm not sixteen years old anymore, Trent. I'm a grown woman."

"Not around my friends you're not."

Trent got up from his chair without another word. He was headed in the direction of Indigo, who had just emerged from a small crowd, by the patio doors. I honestly felt sorry for her, 'cause she didn't know it, but her life was about to be turned upside down. I was tempted to go over there and tell her what Trent was up to, but one hater in the family is enough. So I finished my drink and headed for the door.

When I got outside the club, some fool had the nerve to scream my name like I wanted the world to know it. "Yo, Melanie! Melanie!"

I tried to ignore the voice until I looked up and saw the source. Prince emerged from a small crowd wearing a short red and black leather jacket, carrying a matching motorcycle helmet. It took me a few seconds to get myself together, because he looked even sexier than he did in the club.

"Yo, Melanie. You need a ride?"

I glanced at the entrance to the club just to make sure Trent hadn't followed me out.

"Sure, Prince." I smiled. "I could use a ride."

4

Trent

I had no idea what time it was when my bladder woke me up to go to the bathroom. All I knew was that it was dark outside and I was still tired. I tried to ignore the urge and go back to sleep, but there's nothing more irritating than trying to sleep when you've gotta pee. So I got up to relieve myself, then I went into the kitchen to get a drink. I hadn't even opened the fridge when the phone rang. I glanced at the Caller ID to find out who was calling and the number came up unavailable. I hesitated. Unavailable numbers at this hour of the morning usually meant surprises. I hated surprises, but I answered the phone anyway.

"Hello?"

"Trent."

Damn. This wasn't a surprise, this was a disaster. I should have gone with my first instinct and let the phone ring because I recognized the voice right away. It was Michelle, my ex-girl-friend, the only woman other than Melanie and my mother whom I ever really cared about. Michelle was my girl for almost ten years, and I never had as much fun with a woman as I did with her. Yeah, I'd cheated on her countless times throughout our re-lationship, but I'd never thought about settling down with any-one other than her. Hell, I thought she was my soul mate. At least I did until she ended up pregnant and tried to play me. That's when the fun and games were over and I had to kick her ass to the curb. I went through nine months of pregnancy with her, and that baby didn't look anything like me.

"What you want, Michelle?"

"What you think I want? I want some money. I want some Pampers. I want you to come see your son. You ain't come to see this boy since he's been born. He's almost eight months old now."

"Look, Michelle, I told you that's not my baby. He's too dark to be my baby. Now don't call here no more. Do you understand me?" I was about to hang up the phone when she exploded.

"Don't call you! Motherfucker, I'll call you whenever I want! Who the fuck do you think you're playin' with? I'm not one of these stupid bitches you be running game on. I'm Michelle, the bitch that had your baby. You better recognize. Now I need some money, Trent. And your baby needs a daddy!" I could almost see her head twisting as she spoke.

"I ain't giving you shit 'cause that's not my baby. Now don't call my house no more. How the fuck you get my number anyway?"

"Your sister-in-law gave it to me when she and your mother came over last week."

"What the fuck were they doing over there?"

"They came to see their grandson and nephew. Everyone knows he's your baby, Trent. Now if you don't wanna act like a father on your own, then I'll make you be a father. You ain't running around town driving no Mercedes and my baby ain't got no Pampers. I'll see you in court, motherfucker."

"Is that a threat? I know you didn't just threaten me."

"No. That's not a threat. That's a fuckin' promise. You made me carry this boy for nine months 'cause you wanted to be a daddy like Wil. Then you had the nerve to walk out the delivery room because you thought he was too dark. Fuck you! The least you coulda did was ask for a blood test."

"Wasn't no need for no blood test. I got eyes. I can see that baby don't look nothing like me."

"You one ignorant motherfucker, you know that? Now we might be light, but my daddy was black as coal. And so is *your* baby."

She hung up the phone with a loud click. I was tempted to call her back and put her in her place. I hated when anyone got the last word in an argument, especially a woman. But I decided to let shit die. Michelle knew the deal.

Remembering why I came into the kitchen in the first place I opened up the fridge and pulled out the orange juice. I took a long swig from the carton before I put it back, then walked into the living room. I was just lucky enough to catch the sun starting to peek over Jamaica Bay through my sliding glass door. Man, I tell you, it was one beautiful sight. I'd made a lot of mistakes in my life recently, but renting this place on the water wasn't one of them.

Once the sun was up I decided to head back to my bedroom. That's when I noticed my office light was on. I walked in to turn it off only to find Indigo, my new friend from the club, standing naked in front of the gold records on my wall. I'd replaced my dentistry degrees with the gold records after Brenda and I had our little falling out over the airline tickets. Little did I know how useful they would be for my newest *project*.

Indigo hadn't noticed I was there yet, so I stood in the doorway admiring her round, ebony-colored ass and shapely legs. Just the sight of her bare bottom made my nature rise. The first thing that came to my mind was that I should bend her over my desk and take her from behind. I was sure she'd be down for it. She was one hell of a sex kitten, and much more attractive than I had given her credit for in the club. Too bad she didn't have the brains to match.

I still couldn't believe she went for that vice president of Def Jam Records crap I'd thrown at her. It always amazed me how powerful something as simple as a business card could be. When I approached her in the club after her little karaoke performance, of course she didn't have a damn thing to say to me. She put her hand in my face and turned her head like I wasn't even there. It was pretty obvious she was still upset about the way I'd refused to buy her a drink. I knew I'd have to treat this situation a little differently to get her attention, so instead of running my usual bullshit I just handed her a business card and walked away. There was no need to make a scene. If I was lucky, she'd look at my card and maybe give me a call in a couple of days. Otherwise, I was pretty sure she was a regular at the bar, so I'd have to work up a Plan B and come back to try again. At least that's what I thought. But I couldn't have been more wrong, because I hadn't even gotten fifteen feet before she was tugging on my arm.

"You really work for Def Jam?" She studied my face. Maybe she was looking for signs that I was lying, but it didn't matter. I put on an Academy Award–worthy performance.

"Yeah, and?" I gave her this cold stare like it wasn't a big deal at all.

"So what's up? Why'd you give me this card?"

"What you think?" I glanced at my watch as if she were wasting my time. "I like the way you sing. I'm thinking about signing you up to a management contract."

"Really?" Her eyes got wide with excitement, but then quickly squinted with suspicion. "You serious? This ain't no line just to get some ass, is it?"

"Look, if I wanted some ass I would have bought you that drink earlier and we'd be halfway to my place by now. I don't have time for games, so either have a seat so we can talk business or move it along."

She glanced at the card again, then nodded. "Okay, let's talk, but this time you're gonna buy me a drink."

I agreed, and the rest is history. Two hours later we were on my couch making love.

"You know. That could be you someday if you work hard." I walked up behind her and wrapped my arms around her waist. She was fingering the frame of one of the gold records. I almost laughed. Women can be so damn gullible.

"You think so? You think I can really be like them?" She looked back at me with a smile full of wishes.

"Yeah, I think so." I gave her a reassuring kiss. "You've got more raw talent than half the people I've handled. I just wish you had a demo done, 'cause I'd really like for Russell to hear your voice when I meet with him next week."

"You said the same thing last night." She frowned. "We really need a demo, don't we?"

"Yeah, we really do." I gave an exaggerated sigh. "And we need one fast."

"Why can't we just go over to Def Jam and use their studio?"

"Like I told you last night, it's against company policy. I can't use our studio for an unsigned artist. I could get fired. And if I get fired, I can't help you."

"Well, why don't we use a private studio? I know you must know somebody with a private studio we can use."

"Sure, I know lots of people with studios, but they're not cheap."

"How much will it cost?" She was starting to sound desperate.

"More than you have, I'm sure." I let go of her waist and sat at my desk, drumming my fingers on the wood like I was thinking.

"I got money saved. How much is it—"

I cut her off. "Look, forget about the demo for a minute, all right? Maybe there's another way we can get your career started. Maybe we should start you off as a backup singer until you can get up enough money for a demo. I heard Alicia Keys is looking for backup singers for her new album. I can make a call."

"Backup singer! I don't wanna be a backup singer!" She was pouting now. "You said you were gonna make me a star."

"I am, but it's gonna take time. I can't talk to Russell without a demo. I'd get laughed outta the room."

"Look, Trent, how much is it gonna cost to do a demo?"

"I don't know. I could probably get it done for about four grand."

"Four thousand dollars? Is that all? I thought you were gonna say something like twenty thousand."

I laughed. "You act like you just got four grand lying around or something."

"I do." She kissed me, then ran into my bedroom.

I took my time straightening out one of the framed records before I followed her. No need to act anxious. When I finally sauntered into the bedroom, she was standing by my dresser going through her purse. A few seconds later she was sitting on my bed with her checkbook and a pen in hand.

"Who should I make the check payable to?" I was tempted to tell her just to make it out to *cash,* but I changed my mind when I saw it was written off a Citibank account.

I reached down and picked up my pants. I took out my wallet and handed her a business card. "Here, make it out to After Midnight Entertainment. These guys are good. They do a lot of work with Puffy."

Without hesitation she wrote the check and handed it to me.

"No offense, but you sure this check is good? These brothers are good but they're thugs, and if this check bounces, they're not coming to look for you, they're coming straight after me."

She reached her arms around my neck and pulled me on the bed. Then she shoved her checkbook in my face. "It's good. Look at my balance."

"Oh, my God!" I exaggerated my tone. "Where'd you get all that money? You rob a bank or something?"

"I hit the Pick Five about two weeks ago for a hundred thousand dollars." She smiled.

"Get the fuck outta here. You serious?" I raised my eyebrows, giving her a skeptical look.

She shook her head, kissing me again, this time even more passionately.

"Now, what's that for?"

"That's for not trying to scam me. I was so afraid you were gonna tell me to write that check out to you."

"I wouldn't do that," I told her, glad that I hadn't.

"I know that now, but I had my doubts a few minutes ago."

"So you thought I was trying to scam you?"

"Sorta. I wasn't really sure. I mean, I believed you at the club, but then when you told me your car was in the shop and you needed a ride home, I thought you were full of shit."

"You thought I was full of shit?" I faked a look of wounded pride.

"Yeah, but once we pulled in front of your apartment, I started to think that maybe I was wrong. I mean, this is one bad ass apartment. I don't know too many black people who can afford to live on the water."

"So that's what convinced you, huh?"

"No. To be honest, I wasn't completely convinced until I saw the gold records."

I had to hold back a laugh. Those damn gold records and professional plaques get 'em every time.

"So when are we gonna do the demo?" she asked.

"Well, today's Friday, and I have to get my car from the shop and make arrangements with the studio. How 'bout next Wednesday afternoon?"

"Wednesday?" she shouted. "That soon?"

"Yeah, I can do it on Wednesday. That is, if you're nice to me."

I kissed her and she kissed me back, reaching between my legs.

"Oh, I think I can be nice to you."

5

Wil

Monday morning I went to work early to look over the previous week's sales figures for my department. It turned out that leaving work early on Friday hadn't been the good idea I'd thought. First of all, I would've missed that whole stupid fight with Diane if I'd kept my behind at work. And secondly, I could've gotten the sales reports that are issued every Friday afternoon. I needed those reports so I could know who to chew out during my sales meeting later this morning. So instead of sleeping until seven, I got up at five and dragged my ass into the office to read the reports before the meeting. I'd been going at it, taking notes for over two hours when I heard a knock on my office door.

"Come in," I shouted.

I never looked up from my reports. I figured it was just my secretary Marge letting me know that she was at her desk if I needed her.

"Wil, you got a minute?" I took off my reading glasses and looked up from my reports. It was Jeanie Brown, the assistant director of human resources. The only black person working on the executive floor, other than a couple of secretaries.

"Hey, Jeanie? What's up?" I smiled.

Jeanie and I were friendly, but I still didn't like it when any of the big honchos from upstairs popped up at my door unannounced. It usually meant that someone was gonna lose their job. The last time Jeanie showed up at my door unexpectedly she arrived with pink slips and laid off ten percent of my staff. So I was pretty concerned when she didn't smile back at me.

"Wil, I've got a little bad news." Jeanie's cocoa brown lips curled into a frown.

I sat back in my chair, nonchalantly wiping away the sweat that was beginning to form on my brow. I gestured for Jeanie to have a seat and when she declined, I braced myself for the worst. I was no longer worried about her laying off some of my staff. I was concerned about being fired myself. Not that it should come as a shock if it happened. My department had missed our sales quota the last two months. Not by much, but we still missed and as the sales manger, the black sales manger I might add, that meant my head was the one that was gonna roll. The funny thing is, I'd been expecting bad news all weekend. I just never expected it would be losing my job.

"Okay . . . what kind of bad news, Jeanie?" I was trying to keep it together, not let my emotions get involved. It wasn't easy. I had a family to take care of.

"Well, Wil, I really don't know how to tell you this. Especially since I know how much you hate change, but . . ."

I stopped her because she was beating around the bush and that annoyed me. It was bad enough that the boys upstairs sent the lone sister to do their dirty work instead of coming to see me face to face like they do when a white manager is fired.

"Just spit it out, Jeanie. I'm a man. I can take it."

"Okay. Marge fell in the parking lot on Friday and broke her arm. It looks like she's gonna be out five to six weeks minimum. So I—"

"Hold up," I interrupted. "That's the bad news you had to tell me?"

"Yeah, what'd you think I came down here to do, fire you?" She let out a laugh but stopped it abruptly when I didn't join in.

"That's exactly what I thought." I gave her a serious look. "Jesus Christ, Jeanie, you know my department's sales are down. You scared the shit outta me."

"I'm sorry, Wil. But you don't have anything to worry about. The way things are going, your department's doing better than everyone else." She gave me an encouraging smile. "Have you seen the figures on Jonathan Goldsmith's department? If anyone needs to get fired, it's him. If you know what I'm saying."

We both laughed, because Jonathan Goldsmith was one of the executive vice president's sons and we both knew he would never be fired. Transferred maybe, but never fired.

"I'm not here to fire you. I'm just here to give you the bad news about Marge."

Her words finally sunk in, and I realized how important Marge, my secretary of five years, was to me. I'd been so damn paranoid when Jeanie first started talking I'd barely even thought about her real message. Poor Marge. She was in her early sixties, and I knew a broken bone was no joke for someone that age.

"Is she okay?" I asked.

"From what I could tell over the phone, she's fine."

"All right. I'm gonna have to give her a call after my sales meeting. See if there's anything she needs." I glanced at my watch, then shuffled all my reports into a folder. I walked around my desk and asked Jeanie, "So in the meantime, what am I gonna do for a secretary? You gonna transfer somebody over from another department?"

I gestured toward the door and we headed out of my office.

"Sorry, Wil. No one's available right now. We're gonna give you a temp until Marge gets back."

"A temp?" I stopped at the door and stared at her. "I don't have time to break in a temp. We're getting ready to go into the busy season. Why don't you transfer somebody from another division?"

"Wil, we just had a ten percent reduction of staff in every department. There is nobody we can transfer. You're just gonna have to make do with a temp."

She walked out of my office. I followed, about to protest, but that's when I noticed the large, very attractive sister sitting at Marge's desk. She smiled at me, and I straightened my tie self-consciously. If her work was as good as her looks, my department was going to be in good shape, 'cause this woman was fine.

"Wil Duncan, I'd like to introduce you to Maxine Graves. Maxine is going to be your secretary until Marge returns."

Maxine stood up, offering me a cup of coffee and a brownie. "Here you go, Mr. Duncan, light with three sugars, just the way you like it." I took a sip of the coffee and smiled at her.

"How'd you . . . ?"

"I hope you don't mind," she answered before I could even finish my question, "but I took the liberty of calling Marge. I asked her to give me a few hints on how to make our transition as smooth as possible. I may only be a temp, but I take pride in my work. Now you need to run along or you're gonna be late for your sales meeting." She motioned with her hand like a mother shuffling her kids off to school. I glanced at Jeanie, who was grinning from ear to ear.

"You heard the woman, Wil. You need to get going." Jeanie picked up a brownie from the box on Maxine's desk and laughed. So did I as I headed for my meeting. Ms. Maxine was going to do just fine.

By the time I finished my sales meeting, it was just about lunchtime. I didn't have any plans for lunch so I decided to grab a newspaper and head on over to one of the local restaurants. I liked to get away from the office crowd every once in a while, especially after tense sales meetings.

"Maxine, I'm going to lu—" I never finished my sentence, because when I walked out of my office, I was too mesmerized by the shapely beauty of Maxine's backside. She was bent over, picking up a file, and her tight black skirt was stretched across one of the finest asses I'd seen in years.

"Did you say something, Mr. Duncan?" Maxine quickly stood to face me. When we made eye contact, my high-yellow face turned bright red. I'm sure she knew why I was blushing, too, because she tugged at her skirt, grinning as she sat down at her desk. "Is there anything I can do for you, Mr. Duncan?"

"Ah, no. I just wanted to let you know I was going to lunch. I'll be back in about an hour."

"Okay. Well, you enjoy your lunch. I'm about to have lunch myself." She smiled, unwrapping what looked like a peanut butter and jelly sandwich.

"Maxine, is that what you're having for lunch? Peanut butter and jelly?" I eyed the sandwich as she picked it up.

"Yeah, that's what I'm having. I like peanut butter and jelly." She took a bite of the sandwich, then dropped it on her desk. "Oh, who the hell am I fooling? To be honest, Mr. Duncan, my son is probably sitting at day care eating tuna salad and drinking Diet Coke right now." She reached in her lunch bag and pulled out a container of chocolate milk with a disgusted look on her face. I couldn't help but laugh.

"It's not funny." She pouted. "I was in such a rush to get to work on time I must have mixed up our lunches."

"Look, don't get upset. Why don't you have lunch with me? My treat. It'll give us a chance to go over your responsibilities."

"But what about the phones? Who's gonna answer them?"

"We'll forward them to voice mail. Come on. You don't have to work nine hours straight. You're entitled to a lunch."

She smiled, pushing the childish meal into a trash can beside her desk. "All right, let's go."

Maxine and I ended up having lunch at Marino's Italian restaurant in the Village. We spent most of our lunch going over her responsibilities and my expectations of her job. It was busy season, and I wanted her to know that we'd be doing quite a bit of overtime in the next few weeks. She didn't seem to mind, and things were going remarkably well until she got up to go to the restroom. After that, things became a little uncomfortable. I had to struggle to keep my eyes from wandering down to her breasts. Don't get me wrong. She was dressed very professionally. It's just that a couple of the buttons on her blouse seemed to come loose after her trip to the potty, and from that point on, her cleavage was just begging me to take a peek. Thank God the conversation had moved from business to personal, because it was getting hard to concentrate.

"I really wanna thank you for buying me lunch, Mr. Duncan." Maxine smiled as she stabbed her salad with her fork.

"No, problem," I told her between bites of my lasagna. "So you said you have a son. Are you married?"

"Who, me?" She shook her head and laughed. "No. I think I'm destined to be an eternal bridesmaid."

"Why is that? You're a very attractive woman."

"Thank you." She lowered her head and blushed. "But if you'll excuse the expression, *these niggas out here ain't worth it*. Every decent man I've run into is gay, married or white."

"Wow, you sound just like my sister. She made almost the same comment the other day." I added, "So what about your son's father? No future there?"

"Let's not even talk about his sorry ass. He spends more time in jail than he does at home. And when he's home, he's drunk, and even worse, he's . . ." Maxine bit her lip and covered her face with her hands. When she looked back up at me, she had composed herself. "I'm sorry, Mr. Duncan. You don't need to hear about my problems."

"It's perfectly all right, Maxine." I patted her hand. "I'm surprised Marge didn't tell you that about me. I like to keep things pretty informal with my secretary. I find it makes for a more comfortable work environment."

"Really?" Her eyes lit up. "That's nice. I've never had a boss treat me as much more than a servant."

I'm sure she was exaggerating, but I meant what I'd said. I knew a few guys in my office who were real assholes when it came to their secretaries. I'd learned a long time ago that the better you treat them, the better work they do. So if Maxine wanted to talk to me about her man problems, I didn't mind listening for a while.

"So, your son's father, he's not abusive or anything, is he?"

"*Very.*" Maxine's eyes reflected her anger and hurt, and she abruptly changed the subject. "So, what about you, Mr. Duncan, are you married?"

I should be ashamed to admit this, but instead of just telling her, *Yes, I'm married,* I silently avoided the question. Unfortunately, as I remained silent, Maxine leaned a little closer, waiting for my answer. And the closer she leaned, the larger and more mesmerizing her breasts seemed to get.

"Mr. Duncan, you still there?"

"Ah, yeah. I'm still here." I forced myself to lift my eyes from her breasts to her face as I continued to avoid her marriage question. "Maxine, can you do me a favor? If we're gonna work together, don't call me Mr. Duncan. Everyone at the office calls me Wil."

"Okay, Wil, but everyone calls me Mimi."

"All right. Mimi it is." We both smiled and got back to our meals. For the time being, the issue of my marriage remained an unanswered question. That is, until my wandering eyes got me in trouble again.

"Um, Wil, is something wrong with my blouse? Do I have a spot on it or something? 'Cause you keep staring at it pretty hard." She reached up and closed the top two buttons of her blouse. My face immediately turned bright red, and it took a few seconds before I could reply.

"Ah, no, actually I was *admiring* your blouse," I lied, hoping that a compliment might defuse the situation. "I'd love to pick up something like that for *my wife*. You have excellent taste in clothes."

"You think so?" Now she was blushing, but the smirk on her face said, *I knew you were married.* "I picked this up at Ashley Stewart's in Green Acres Mall. They have the most phenomenal plus-size clothes in there. A girl could go broke in there." She stopped herself. "Oh, my goodness. I'm sorry. *Your wife* is probably a size six. I don't even know why I mentioned a plus-size shop."

"Size six," I laughed. "What would make you think that? For your information, *my wife* is a size sixteen, and she's been big ever since I met her," I stated with pride.

"Sixteen! That's my size." Mimi was grinning like she'd hit the lottery. "I must say, Wil, I'm impressed. Usually handsome men like you aren't attracted to us big-boned women. Y'all usually want them toothpick sisters that are always showing off their stomachs."

"Please, ain't nothin' a skinny woman can do for me but introduce me to her big friend," I joked. "I'm two hundred and seventy-three pounds, Mimi. How I look getting on top of somebody a hundred and twenty pounds? I might kill her ass. I need a woman with some meat on her bones."

Mimi waved her hand, grinning from ear to ear. "Wil, you are a mess. So how long you been married?"

"Ten years in three months," I finally confessed.

Mimi seemed to straighten up in her chair when she heard that.

"Wow, ten years with the same woman. These days, that's impressive. So, do you cheat?" The words came out her mouth so nonchalantly I wasn't sure if it was an invitation to fool around or an honest question.

"I beg your pardon?"

"I asked if you cheat on your wife." She looked me straight in the eye.

"No, I do not cheat on my wife, Mimi." I put some attitude in my voice for emphasis. She didn't know it, but after the incident with the stripper photos, cheating was a very sensitive subject in my marriage.

She lifted her hands passively. "Don't get offended. I had to ask you that if I'm going to be an effective secretary. I got fired from my last job because I called the wife by the mistress' name."

"Well, you don't have to worry about that, because I ain't got no mistress."

"Hmm, well I'm certainly glad to hear that." Mimi smirked naughtily to herself as if she'd just heard a private joke. I was just hoping the joke wasn't on me.

"Maxine! I knew that was you." A short, stocky man with schoolboy glasses and a receding hairline was now standing next to our table. How he got that close without either of us noticing him is beyond me. I guess we both must have really been into our conversation.

"Antoine!" Mimi jumped up and wrapped her arms around the man. She kissed him flush on the lips, and I think I actually felt a momentary twinge of jealousy. "What are you doing here?"

"I was about to ask you the same thing. I told Keisha that was you sitting over here in the dark."

"Keisha's here?" Maxine's smile became a look of concern.

"Yeah." He pointed toward a woman headed our way. Whoever she was, she was definitely related to Maxine, because except for the fact that the woman was a couple of shades darker than Maxine, the family resemblance was unmistakable. Not to mention the fact that the woman had the same phenomenal full figure.

"Girl, what are you doin' here? I thought you was supposed to start work today." The woman, an obvious motormouth, glanced at her watch. "Lord, I hope you ain't got fired on the first day because you was out here flirting with some man." She glared at me as if she were Maxine's mother.

"I ain't got fired, Keisha. Matter of fact, I'm having lunch with my boss." She turned her attention to me. "Wil Duncan, this my sister Keisha, who thinks she's my momma. And this is my incredibly handsome brother-in-law, Antoine."

"It's nice to meet you," I told them as we politely shook hands.

"It's nice to meet you, too, Wil. So what's up with you and my sister?"

Maxine gave her sister a don't-go-there stare, but her sister ignored it. Keisha placed her hand on her hip and waited for my answer. When I made eye contact with Antoine, he just looked away.

"Nothing," I replied, trying to remain polite. "This is your sister's first day at work, and I asked her to lunch to discuss her responsibilities around the office. Completely professional, you see?"

"Yeah, but for how long? Handsome man like you. I bet she'll have you in bed by the end of the night."

"Keisha!" Antoine yelled, grabbing her by the arm. "Look, we need to go back to our table."

I was in shock as I watched them hurry away from our table. I turned to Maxine and said, "I think it's about time we got back to the office."

Maxine glanced at me, then angrily in the direction of her sister. "I'm sorry, Wil. Sometimes my sister gets a little out of hand."

"Don't worry about it. I have a brother who acts the same way."

6

Melanie

Prince pulled in front of my building, and I reluctantly let go of his sculpted waist as I stepped down from his motorcycle. When we left Manhattan Proper we went and had a late-night break-fast at a diner. Then he took me on the most romantic ride down Ocean Parkway in Long Island. I hadn't had that much fun since my high school prom. We sat and talked on the beach for what seemed like forever. I took my helmet off and set it on the back of his bike.

"Shit," I cursed softly as I glanced at my watch.

"What's wrong? You got a curfew or something?" He pulled his helmet back and flashed a gorgeous smile at me.

"No, I just never expected to get home at seven o'clock in the morning. I gotta be at work in two hours."

"So take the day off. We can go back to my place. Spend the day together." He smiled as he gestured for me to get back on the bike. "The night doesn't have to end like this, Melanie."

I took a step toward him, then stopped dead in my tracks. His words, although enticing, had just made this the most awkward moment of the night. Awkward because for the entire night, we hadn't so much as kissed. Now was the moment I had to decide whether I was gonna be a lady and take my ass upstairs to my apartment, or be a slut and go home with him. I was seriously leaning toward the slut scenario, especially after snuggling up next to him on that vibrating motorcycle for five hours. The only problem was, I liked Prince. I liked him a lot. He was funny and smart. He was the kind of guy I wanted to be with five years down the road. So acting like a slut was probably not the best way to guarantee a long-term relationship with him.

"Maybe some other time, Prince. I really need to get to work." I held my breath as I stepped back.

"You sure? I was thinking we could ride down to Atlantic City. A friend of mine works at Bally's Grand. I could get us a room overlooking the ocean."

"That sounds great, but I think I better take a rain check." *I also better take my ass upstairs before I change my mind,* I thought.

"Aw'ight." He sighed. I could see the disappointment on his face. "So what's up? You think I can get your number?"

"I'd be disappointed if you didn't." I reached in my bag for a pen and paper, then I jotted down my cell phone number for him. When I handed it to him, he leaned over and kissed me. No tongue, just a kiss. But what a kiss it was. I felt like I was floating. He had the most incredibly soft lips I'd ever felt, and by the time our lips parted, I was inches away from jumping back on that motorcycle.

"I'll call you," he whispered.

"Okay," I replied with a sigh, hoping it would be soon. I watched as he slid his helmet down over his head, then forced myself to head toward my building. I could almost feel his eyes staring at my hips as I walked the fifteen feet to the doors. So of course you know I swayed those hips enough to keep him hypnotized. I concentrated on my movements to keep myself from thinking about the horizontal movements I really wanted to be doing.

Calm down girl, I kept repeating in my head. *You're doing the right thing. He's not gonna wanna buy the cow if he's gettin' the milk for free.*

I slid my key into my door and prayed that my best friend and roommate, Desiree, had already left for work. The last thing I wanted was for her to see me sneaking in the house at this time of the morning. Especially since I was still a little confused about why I was coming in at that hour myself. Unfortunately, just as my luck would have it, Desiree was dressed in her waitress uniform sitting at the kitchen table, smoking a cigarette and writing in her journal. I'm sure if I'd waited ten more minutes, I would've missed her. Then again, if I had waited another ten minutes I doubt I would've been heading into my apartment at all.

"Well, well, well. Look what the cat done dragged home. Where you been? I thought your ass was in bed." Desiree gave me a devilish grin as she closed her journal. I didn't even bother to respond. I just walked over to the kitchen counter and poured myself a cup of coffee, yawning the whole time.

"What's wrong, hooker? Tired from a long night out on the track?" Desiree laughed teasingly.

All I could do was suck my teeth as I playfully snapped back, "Who you callin' a hooker, ho?"

I grabbed a cigarette from her pack, lit it, and took a long drag.

"I'm calling you a hooker. You the one who ain't come home last night. And don't be tryin' to play like you was baby-sitting for your brother Wil, 'cause he called here last night lookin' for you." She took a drag of her cigarette, leaning forward as she released the smoke. "So where were you last night?"

I so wanted to tell Desiree where I was or what happened last night. I wanted to tell her every detail. I mean, she's my best friend, and that's what we do, share our most intimate secrets. But I knew if I told her about what a good time I had with Prince, we'd both be late for work. I couldn't afford that, 'cause today was payday, and a sister was broke.

"Look, Dez, we'll talk tonight, okay? I promise, I just have to get outta these soaking wet panties and take a shower, or I'm gonna be late for work."

"Wait a minute! Soaking wet panties?" Desiree screamed. "Ah, hell no, Melanie. You ain't leaving me hanging!"

I took a sip of my coffee, then headed to my room with a sigh. I should've known the second I said anything about wet panties that Desiree was gonna be right on my heels. I could hear her rush out of her chair as I entered my room. I slipped out of my wet panties and the rest of my clothes and tossed them in the hamper. By the time I turned around, Desiree was standing in my doorway lighting another cigarette.

"All right, who is he and what's he look like? And don't you leave out one detail. I ain't had a man in three months, and I'm living my sex life through you until I find one." She sat on my bed.

"Look, Dez, aren't you gonna be late for work?"

Desiree glanced at her watch, then sucked her teeth. "Yeah, and? Don't worry about me. I'll get to work when I get there. Now stop playin' and tell me about last night."

Her eyes never left mine.

"You're really not gonna let me get outta here unless I tell you, are you?"

"No." She crossed her legs and smiled at me.

Ah, what the hell, I thought. I was gonna be thinking about it all day, anyway. I took my robe off the back of my closet door and slipped into it. Then I sat on the bed next to my friend.

"Okay, what you wanna know? And don't be writing this shit in any of those damn journals of yours." My voice was full of the excitement I felt, and so were Desiree's eyes as she leaned closer.

"Who was he, and where were you last night? Oh, yeah, and did you get some?"

"Gurrrrlll, his name is Prince. And he is so fine!" I had to take a deep breath as I reminisced. "He's the kinda brother a sister could take home on a cold winter's night and never need a blanket."

"For real! What's he look like?" Desiree got all up in my face. I closed my eyes and an image of Prince standing in front of me, wearing his motorcycle jacket, appeared in my head. Just thinking about him made me squirm around in my seat.

"Come on, Melanie. Stop playing!" Desiree's agitated voice interrupted my little fantasy. "What does he look like?"

"Oh, I'm sorry, Dez." I opened my eyes. "He's about six-one, with these broad, sexy shoulders. You know who he reminds me of?" I sat back, smiling, because I knew she was gonna flip when I told her.

"Who? Who?"

"Morris Chestnut."

"Morris Chestnut?" Her eyes got real wide. "You lying . . ."

I shook my head. "No, I ain't. He could be his brother."

Desiree got real quiet for a few seconds. I wasn't sure if she believed me or not, but just the chance that Prince might look like Morris Chestnut must have been eating away at her. She thought Morris Chestnut was the finest man in the world, and jealousy was written all over her face as she fell backward onto my bed.

"Damn. So where'd you find him?" she finally asked. "This the first I'm hearing about this Morris Chestnut look-alike."

"Believe it or not, he's one of my brother Trent's friends. I met him last night at Manhattan Proper."

"Trent introduced you to one his friends?" Desiree sat back up skeptically. She knew my brother.

"Well, sorta. He introduced us, but he told Prince to stay away from me."

"So how'd y'all hook up?"

"When I was leaving the club, he offered to give me a ride home on his *motorcycle*."

"He's got a motorcycle?" That was another detail that was sure to make her envious. "Wait a minute. Manhattan Proper closes at three o'clock. It's quarter to eight. Where the hell y'all been for five hours?" She stared at me for a few seconds, putting together the pieces of what she believed. "Oh, Melanie, you fucked him, didn't you? That's why you in here changing your panties!"

"No, Desiree, we didn't. But I had a mind to. It was just too soon."

"Too soon? Please, it's not like you ain't never gave a man some on the first night."

"I know, but this guy's special."

"He's that special?" She sounded skeptical, and I couldn't really blame her, with the kind of losers we'd been meeting lately.

"Desiree, do you believe in love at first sight?"

"I guess . . . I never really gave it much thought."

"Well, I have, and the minute I saw Prince, I knew he was the guy I wanted to have kids with."

Desiree looked like she couldn't believe what I was saying, and I could barely believe it myself. I wasn't the kind of woman to fall head over heels, especially on the first night. But there was something about Prince that left me wanting all of him, forever.

7

Trent

I pulled in front of the shabby-looking storefront bar on Merrick Boulevard and smiled. As Ice Cube would say, "Today was a good day." I had my car back, I'd just gotten five hundred dollars and my dick sucked by this stupid ass chick who thought I was a stockbroker. To top that off, I was about to get paid again, because I was picking up Indigo and we were headed to Atlantic City. I was paying for the hotel room but I'm sure once I pretended to lose all my money at the tables she'd pick up the slack and hand over a couple'a grand so I could continue to have fun. So yeah, today was a good day.

Knock! Knock! Knock!

I looked out my car window and my contented smile disappeared at the sight of Jasper's toothless grin. Jasper was the right-hand man to my mentor, Big Mike Wilson. Mike owned 718, the small lounge I was parked in front of. Jasper ran the bar while Mike, a former member of the early eighties one-hit-wonder rap group called the Supreme Team, ran a rinky-dink music studio in the basement. He tried to make it seem like he was helping struggling rappers get a break, but Mike wasn't fooling me. He might have helped a few brothers break into the industry, but the truth was that Mike wasn't doing anything different from me. He was beating people out of their money. Almost everyone who came in there couldn't rap or sing worth shit, but Mike would take their money and encourage them to make as many demos as possible. Mike's famous line was, "I can make you famous."

"Yo, Trent! Mike wants to see you inside. He just finished that girl's demo."

"Yeah, aw'ight. Tell 'im I'll be right there." Jasper stepped away from the car, and I took a few seconds to get myself together. I had to make sure my clothes and hair were right. Image is everything, especially when you're gonna be around a guy like Big Mike Wilson. When I stepped out the car, Jasper was waiting for me by the entrance to the bar like I was some little kid who might get lost. I ignored him and walked inside where I was greeted by Indigo and Big Mike's new flavor of the month, Beverly, sitting at the bar.

"Trent!" Indigo shouted.

She jumped up from her seat and ran over to me, wrapping her arms around my neck before kissing me square on the lips.

"Thank you!" Kiss. "Thank you! Thank you! Thank you!" Kiss, kiss, kiss.

"Wow, I guess things musta went pretty well, huh?"

"Did they." She sighed. "You gotta hear my demo. I sound better than Alicia Keys. Beverly thinks we should cancel our trip to AC and go meet with Russell Simmons this week."

"Is that what Beverly thinks?" I glanced over at Beverly and rolled my eyes. She was always getting into shit that was none of her business. I for one was gonna be glad when Big Mike found another piece of ass.

"Uh-huh, what do you think?" Indigo gave me this pleading look, and I knew that after we returned from Atlantic City I was gonna have to cut her loose. Not that I wanted to. She was actually a pretty decent girl and way more generous than I would have expected. And by the way she was falling for me, I could probably milk her for another five or ten grand. It's just that she was so damn worrisome and now that her demo was finished it was obvious she was gonna drive me crazy about meeting Russell Simmons. Shit, the only thing Russell and I had in common was that we were both from Queens.

"I think it's a great idea, only I just found out Russell's out of town till next week. Besides, I wanted to let some other people listen to your demo while we were out of town. See if they can write some songs that'll fit your range."

"Big Mike said I had better range than anyone he's ever worked with. He said I was the type of singer he'd love to work with. That he could make me famous. Didn't he, Beverly?" She looked over at a smiling Beverly, who nodded.

Oh, great. That was all I needed. I was trying to figure out ways to tell her I was wrong, that she doesn't have a career, while Mike and Beverly were telling her she's the next Whitney Houston. What the fuck was their problem, anyway?

"Big Mike said that, huh?"

"Uh-huh." She smiled.

"Well, that's great. Where is Big Mike, anyway?" Indigo shrugged her shoulders, and I glanced at Beverly.

"He's in his office. He's waiting for you," Beverly replied.

"I'm sure he is." I walked to Mike's office door and opened it. Big Mike, a handsome, clean-shaved, brown-skinned man was sitting behind an old metal desk, talking on a cell phone. He gestured for me to sit down, but the empty chairs were covered with electronics and paperwork.

"Just move some of that shit, Trent. I'll be right with you," he told me as he continued his conversation. My eyes traveled around the shabby room while he finished his call.

"Hey, Trent. Sorry about that." We stood and grabbed each other's hands in a brotherly hug, then sat back down. Mike offered me a cigar, which I gladly took. He only smoked expensive cigars. "So what's up? You got something for me?"

I tossed an envelope on his desk. He opened it and counted the contents with a smile. "Five hundred, just as we agreed."

He picked up a manila envelope from his desk and handed it to me. "There's two demos in there."

"Cool," I told him as I stood.

"Hey, Trent. You got a minute? I wanna talk to you about a couple of things."

"What's up? Why you look so serious?" I sat back down, giving him my full attention.

"I didn't wanna tell you this earlier in front of Indigo, but Beverly and I seen your girl Michelle at IHOP this morning."

"Jesus, not you too, Mike. What the fuck is it about this fucking girl? Does she have everyone under a spell? Look, Mike, I don't fuck with Michelle no more, okay?"

"Please, man, you know you love that girl. Trent, I been knowing you for most of your adult life. I've never seen you as happy as when you're around Michelle. You can't see it, but she the one."

"No, Mike, Indigo's the one. She's the one with the money, remember."

"Well, you might wanna rethink that, 'cause, man, Michelle was looking good as shit when I saw her. And believe me, money can't buy you love. Besides, what you gonna do, run out on your kid? You might have everyone else fooled but I know you better than that. You love kids, Trent, and that little boy of yours is cute as hell. You can't deny that one, can you?" Mike laughed but I didn't join in.

"Yeah, I can. 'Cause he ain't mine."

Mike leaned back in his chair, eyeing me strangely. "Please, Trent, I don't know who you think you foolin', 'cause that boy looks just like you. You both got them round Charlie Brown heads." His comment pissed me off and I leaned forward, pointing my cigar at his face as I stared him dead in the eyes.

"Yo, Mike, let's get something straight. That's not my baby, aw'ight. I don't know what the fuck Michelle told you, but that bitch is lying."

"Hold up, man." Mike sat back in his chair, the expression on his face very serious. "There ain't no need to call the sister a bitch. She ain't even tell me that was your baby. I came up with that assumption on my own."

"Well, then you need to stop assuming shit."

"You're right, I should." He hesitated, smiling as he sucked on his cigar. "Besides, it's probably that guy she was with anyway. He sure was acting like he was the baby's daddy."

"Guy? What guy?" Mike's words hit me like a ton of bricks. Could Michelle be seeing someone? I know it seems selfish but I never even imagined her messing with another guy. Not this soon. Damn, she'd only had the baby eight months ago. "What guy, Mike?"

"You know who I'm talking about. That guy." Mike snapped his fingers like the person's name was right on the tip of his tongue. "That pretty boy nigga who had a baby with LaTisha Jones. Damn, what's his name? Ron, Rich or Raymond . . . damn, I know it starts with an 'R.'"

"You mean Ray? Ray Jenkins!" My eyes bugged outta my head.

Mike smiled, nodding. "Yeah, that's him. That pretty Ray."

I took a deep breath, trying to hold back my emotions. The thought of Ray Jenkins fucking Michelle made every muscle in my body tense up like a rubber band. Ray was one of Wil's best friends and probably the biggest player in town. I hated him with a passion. Ever since we were kids, every woman that I ever wanted seemed to want Ray. Every woman except for Michelle. And now if Mike was right, he'd gotten her, too.

"What the fuck she hanging around that nigga for? He's a player!"

"And you're not a player?" Mike laughed. "I think I've heard it all."

"I'm sayin', though. That nigga Ray's just gonna hurt her."

"And you didn't? You just denied the girl's baby, Trent."

"That's 'cause the baby ain't mine. I didn't mean to hurt her. She was just trying to cramp my style."

"Oh, so walking out on a sister when giving birth, that's not gonna hurt her? That's just cramping your style."

"Don't try to make this about me, Mike. This is about Michelle hanging out with Ray and being a ho. She needs to keep her ass home and take care of that baby. I know she don't want me to come over there."

"Come over there and do what? You just said you don't fuck with her no more. What you gonna do?"

"Look, Mike, I was with that girl for ten years. I'm not gonna just let a guy like Ray fuck her over."

"Look at you, man. You're jealous. You still feelin' her, ain't you?" I shook my head, but Mike wasn't having it. "Yeah, you do. But I think you're right. I think you need to go over there and talk to her before it's too late. Before your son is calling that brotha 'Daddy.'"

8

Wil

I stomped into the bathroom around five-thirty in the morning and turned on the cold water in the shower. I'd just had an argument with my wife. An argument about the one thing we never argued about—*sex*. In ten years of marriage, I can't ever remember Diane spurning my advances. Hell, even when she was on her period she found some way to take care of my needs. But that all changed about two months ago, and I for one was sick of it. I was so sexually frustrated I felt like I was going to explode at any minute, like I was some oversexed teenager. Lately, all I had to do was think about getting some and my manhood would swell up like a balloon. And with Mimi and her low-cut blouses around, that was happening more than I wanna admit. I stepped into the cold shower and sighed thankfully when I felt the swelling between my legs begin to subside.

"Wil?" Diane called from outside the shower. I smiled. Maybe the guilt trip I laid on her a few minutes ago had worked, maybe my sexual drought was about to be over. I turned off the water and stuck my head out the shower curtain, hoping that she'd decided to join me.

"Yeah."

"Telephone." She shoved the portable phone in my face with an ice-cold glare.

"Who is it?" I asked, glancing at the phone with a little concern. I wasn't used to getting calls this early in the morning.

"I don't know. She wouldn't give me her name."

"She?" I repeated in confusion.

"Yeah, *she*." Diane sneered sarcastically. She shoved the phone in my face again. This time I took it nervously. I didn't have a clue who was calling but whoever it was had terrible timing.

"Hello?"

"Wil." The voice was low, but it sounded like my new secretary. But how the hell did she get my home number? And why didn't she give her name to Di?

"Mimi, is that you?"

It sounded like the caller said "yes," but I couldn't be sure with Diane yelling, "Who the fuck is Mimi?" in my ear.

"Can you hold on a second?" I covered up the phone and glared at my wife, whose lips were poked out like she was about to go off on me. "Just a minute, Di. Calm down and I'll tell you about it when I get off."

"I'm not gonna hold on a minute. I wanna know who the fuck that is!" She folded her arms.

"Don't start, Di. I told you, I'll talk to you after I get off the phone."

Di stopped harassing me momentarily, but I knew I was gonna catch hell later. Especially after I ducked back behind the shower curtain to continue my conversation with Mimi.

"Mimi, is everything all right?"

"Wil, I'm sorry. I didn't mean to get you in trouble. I should have known not to call so early. I just didn't know who else to call."

"Don't worry about it. You didn't get me in trouble. We were already fighting before you called. Now what's goin' on? You sound like you've been crying."

She sighed, as if whatever she wanted to say was just too painful. "It's not important. I just wanted to know if you'd give me a ride to work."

Mimi's request took me by surprise. In all the years Marge had been my secretary, she'd never called me at home, especially this early in the morning. When I first heard Mimi's voice, I was a little concerned. A guy can get in a whole bunch of trouble with his wife over a phone call like this. And after meeting her crazy sister at the restaurant, this early morning phone call made me wonder for a second if there was some truth to what Keisha had said about Mimi.

But when Mimi asked for a ride, I relaxed a little. Mimi seemed like a nice enough woman, just trying to make it as a single mom. And I had given her my little speech about thinking of me as a friend, not just a boss. I guess she was just in a bind, and took my offer of friendship a little further than I would have expected. But as I considered her request, I realized it would look pretty bad for me to refuse to give her a ride after I'd offered her my friendship. I'd look just as bad as all those other bosses who'd mistreated her in the past. Di would just have to get over her jealousy, 'cause I was going to stand by my word. Besides, I needed her to be at work today.

"Sure, Mimi, I can give you a ride. What happened to your car?" I don't know what I said, but the crying started again.

"My son's father . . . *sniffle* . . . he tried to beat me up . . . *sniffle, sniffle* . . . and took my car . . . *sniffle* . . . last night."

"Jesus Christ! Are you serious? Are you all right?"

"I'm fine, except for a few bruises. But he took my pocketbook, too. I don't have any money to get to work. That's why I need a ride."

"Don't worry about work. Did you call the cops?"

"No, are you crazy? He'd kill me if I called the police on him."

"You gotta call the cops, Mimi! You can't keep letting him get away with this crap. Next time he might kill you." I had to take a deep breath. I was getting upset.

"Look, Wil, I don't wanna argue with you. I just need a ride to work. Okay? Can I just get a ride, please?"

I didn't wanna argue with her, either. I just wanted her to see the light. "Sure, Mimi, I'll give you a ride. Where do you live?"

"Not too far from you. Do you know where Rochdale Village is?"

"Yeah, my sister lives in building four."

"Okay. I'm in the next circle. Building seven."

"Aw'ight. I know where that is. Why don't you meet me in front of your building at eight?"

"Sure, I'll see you then."

"Hey, Mimi?"

"Yes, Wil."

"If he comes back, call the cops."

"I'm not calling the cops, Wil, but I'll call you."

I hung up the phone with a long exhale.

"Jesus, Wil, what the hell have you gotten yourself into?" I pulled back the shower curtain and almost slipped and fell in the tub when I realized Diane was still standing there.

"Yeah, Wil, what the hell have you gotten yourself into? And who is Mimi?"

When I saw the look on her face, I instantly felt a migraine coming on. "Mimi's my new secretary."

"New secretary? I thought you said your new secretary's name was Maxine. Not Mimi. Mimi sounds like a stripper's name." She twisted her lips as she tilted her head. "What's going on, Wil?"

"Nothin's going on, Di. Her name is Maxine, but everyone calls her Mimi." I was about to tell her about Mimi getting beat up, but she cut me off before I could speak.

"If nothing's going on, why the hell wouldn't she give me her name?"

"I don't know. She's got some problems. Her boyfriend beat her up and took her money."

"So why the hell is she calling you and not the police? Don't she have family?"

"We're friends, Di. She needed someone to talk to about her problems."

"I don't give a damn if she needed to tell you where she stashed fifty million dollars. You tell that secretary of yours, don't be callin' my house at five-thirty in the morning refusing to give me her name. Do we understand each other, Wil Duncan?"

She glared at me until I nodded my head. "Yes, Di. I understand."

"You know what, Di? Just forget it! I'm going to a diner to get something to eat. I'll see you when I get home." I hung up my cell phone and immediately ripped off the hands-free device I was wearing. I was pissed the fuck off. Diane had just informed me that there was no rush for me to come home, because she wasn't feeling well and dinner hadn't been made. Now don't get me wrong. I wasn't pissed about dinner. There were plenty of nights she's called and told me to get something on the way home. I was pissed because she made it very clear that she was headed for bed and that when I got home she didn't want to be disturbed. After what happened this morning, I took that to be just another excuse not to have sex with me. Any other time, she would've been whining for me to get my ass home so I could take care of her and watch the kids.

"Wil, are you all right?" Mimi's voice startled me out of my thoughts. I'd completely forgotten she was in the car with me. I was headed to Rochdale Village to drop her off when Di called.

"No, I'm not all right."

"I didn't think so. You haven't said a word to me since we got in your car. And you just hit me with your headset." She was holding my headset loosely in her right hand.

"Oh, I'm sorry, Mimi. I'm just a little preoccupied. Family problems."

"I hope it's not about this morning." She placed her hand on my knee. "I don't know what the hell I was thinking about, calling your house at five-thirty in the morning. And the Lord knows I should've given your wife my name. I can just imagine what she must think of me."

"Well, let's put it this way. I don't think you're going to be invited over for dinner anytime soon. But you're not the problem, Mimi. We were arguing way before you called. Our problems are a lot deeper than you not giving her your name."

"Really. What's going on? Is there anything I can help you with?"

I glanced at Mimi and smiled a naughty thought. "Sure. You wanna be my wife's surrogate?" I said it as a joke, but after it came out my mouth, I'm not so sure it sounded that way.

"Excuse me? What did you say?"

"Nothing. I was just playing." My face became flush.

"Well, you gonna stop playing and tell me what's going on at home, or what?" She gave me this look that made me lower my head.

"I don't know, Mimi. It's kinda personal."

"So was my son's father beating my ass, but I told you *that*. Aren't you the one who told me that we're friends? And that a friend is someone who listens to another friend when they have problems?"

"Yeah, I guess I did say something like that, didn't I?"

"Yeah, you did. And you listened to my problems this morning. Now it's my turn to return the favor. Besides, it's always good to get a woman's perspective when it comes to these things. Maybe you're not looking at this right."

She made a good point. A damn good point.

"Mimi, you gotta promise me you're not gonna tell anybody about this." I glanced at her as I said it. "We work in a very small office, which my wife used to work in. She's still got a lot of friends whom she talks to every day. So you gotta keep this between you and me."

"You don't have to worry about that. I don't talk to those people in the office. Now stop stalling and get whatever's bothering you off your chest. It might make you feel better."

"You're probably right." I took a deep breath before I continued. "God, I don't even know where to begin. I guess it all started about two months ago when my wife stopped having sex with me."

"She stopped having sex with you?" Mimi raised an eyebrow, making me more than a little self-conscious. "Why?"

"I honestly don't know. That's the million-dollar question. If I knew the answer to that, I probably wouldn't be so stressed out right now." I let out a disgusted sigh as I pulled in front of her building.

"Now let me see if I understand this. Your wife just cut you off for no reason? You weren't having any problems in the bedroom, were you? I mean, she was being satisfied, wasn't she?"

I gave her an insulted look. "Mimi, up until two months ago, my wife and I were having sex four times a week. And most of the time she was the one who initiated it. So I don't think she was having a problem with my performance. I'm a very attentive lover."

"Is that right?" I must have embarrassed her, because she started to blush.

"Maybe she just doesn't think I'm attractive anymore."

Mimi turned her head and gave me the once-over with her eyes. "Please. I doubt that. You're a very handsome man, Wil, and don't act like you don't know it. I'd probably like you a little better if you grew a mustache, but I'd jump on you if you were single."

Now I was the one who was blushing. I never imagined that Mimi might think I was that attractive.

"Well, if it isn't the sex or my looks, then what is it? Why won't she make love to me?" I wondered out loud.

"Don't get offended, but have you ever given any thought that maybe your wife is having an affair? It could be another man. I mean, maybe she's getting from someone else what she used to be getting from you."

I slammed my hand down on the dashboard as hard as I could. Just the thought of Diane being with another man had my blood pressure boiling. "I'm not gonna lie, Mimi, the thought did cross my mind. I mean, Diane loves sex. I can't see her just stopping for no reason."

"I know I wouldn't," Mimi confessed.

"You really think she's having an affair, don't you?"

"Well, I don't really know her, Wil, but I wouldn't put it past her. The truth is, women can be slick. Much slicker than men. And if I were you, I'd be careful." She gave me this sad look as if she were delivering bad news. "I've been home alone taking care of my son, like your wife is doing. It can get real boring. You crave adult attention. After a while, the UPS and the grocery man start to look good. Heck, I even started calling the chat line and using the Internet when my son's father wasn't home."

"Oh, my God, Diane's always joking about how fine our mailman Joe is."

"Maybe she's not joking," Mimi replied in the most serious of tones.

I was so upset my hands were shaking. I felt like I was gonna cry.

"Hey, relax. It's gonna be all right. We're just speculating. We don't know if she's cheating or not. And if she is, I'll be right here to support you." Mimi reached over and took hold of my hand. "Hey, why don't you come on up for a drink? I'll fix you dinner."

"That sounds good, Mimi. Real good." I looked over at her and smiled. She was a good friend and easy to talk to. Kinda like Diane was before we had those problems a few years ago. I never realized how much I missed having a woman to talk to till now. "You really think she could be cheating on me?"

"I'm really not sure, Wil. Come on, let's go upstairs so we can talk about it some more." She tugged at my hand.

"Mimi, you just don't know what me and this woman have been through. I would do anything in the world for her. Why do you think I work all the hours I do? I want to make sure she's taken care of, you know what I mean?"

"I know. I wish it were me," it sounded like she mumbled.

"Excuse me? I didn't quite make out what you said."

"Oh, I said, maybe that's the problem. Maybe you were so concerned about the material things that you forgot the little things that made her wanna make love to you in the first place. When was the last time you sent her flowers?"

"I'm embarrassed to say it, but it's been a while. Probably when she stopped working last year." Mimi placed her other hand over mine, and in a comforting gesture began to rub my hand between hers. "Maybe you're right, Mimi. Maybe I have neglected Di. We almost got divorced a few years back because she thought I was cheating. I'm not gonna jump to conclusions. I need to sit down and talk to my wife." I pulled my hand back from Mimi's, realizing we were getting a little too comfortable.

"Well, that's not exactly what I'm trying to say. I mean, she could be cheating. I wouldn't rule it out if I were you."

"I have to rule it out. I love my wife."

"You do?"

"Yes, I do," I replied, kind of surprised by her question. "Thanks for the dinner invitation, Mimi. Maybe one day me and my wife will take you up on it. But for now I gotta go home. I've got a lot of making up to do."

"Well, let me give you my number just in case things don't work out and you wanna talk." She reached in her handbag and pulled out a pen and paper, jotting down her number. She handed it to me, then surprised me by leaning over and kissing me square on the lips. "I'm here for you, Wil. You can call me anytime."

9

Melanie

"How 'bout another round on me, ladies?" Tim smiled at Desiree and she eyed him seductively as he refilled our drinks for the third time.

"You tryin' to get me drunk so you can take advantage of me, Tim?" Desiree picked up her glass and winked at him flirtatiously. "Because if you are, it's working."

Tim's smile remained as he walked to the other side of the bar to help another customer. If I didn't know it before, it was pretty damn obvious now that they both planned on leaving together. Desiree nudged me with her elbow and I shot her an evil glare.

"What the hell is wrong with you? Didn't I tell you that fool tried to get with me last week?" I was too through.

Desiree rolled her eyes. "Please, Melanie. Stop trying to play Mother Teresa. I know Tim ain't shit. But I'm not trying to marry him. I'm just trying to get my swerve on."

"Get your swerve on? You gotta be kiddin' me. You really gonna give him some after he tried to talk to me?"

"Why I gotta be giving him some? Why can't I be gettin' some?" She sucked her teeth. "It's been over three months since I had some, Melanie! Three months," she repeated. "I can't take it anymore. I need some dick. I need some dick bad. So I might as well make sure it's some good dick. And I know Tim got some good dick. You should see the things I've written about him in my journal." She gave me this pitiful, deranged look that begged me to understand.

"Fuck it!" I threw my hands in the air. "It's your life. If you wanna make a fool outta yourself, then by all means, go right ahead. Just don't come crying to me if he plays you." I pulled my last cigarette out of the pack and lit it.

"Look, don't be coming down on me because you're pissed off at the world and feeling sorry for yourself."

"I'm not pissed off. And I'm damn sure not feeling sorry for myself," I snapped.

"Please, Melanie. You goin' through them cigarettes like they're breath mints and you got a hot date."

"So what? I smoked a few cigarettes. That doesn't mean anything." But I knew it did and so did Desiree.

It was a well-known fact that the only time I smoked more than a couple cigarettes a day was when I was upset with a man. I was now on my second pack, which had been full when we left the house. So you can imagine just how upset I really was. It had been over two weeks and I hadn't heard one word from Prince. I hated to admit it, but he'd played me. Thank God I didn't give him any ass, 'cause instead of just feeling sorry for myself I'd probably be in therapy somewhere. God, I hated men and their fucking lies. If they're not gonna call, I just wish they'd just say they're not gonna call. I mean, if you're not gonna use it, why even ask for the number?

"Fuck that nigga Prince, Melanie. He ain't the only dick on the block."

I looked up at my friend, who I know was trying to comfort me, but was doing a horrible job. "No, but he's the only one I want."

I lowered my head, fully prepared to wallow in my self-pity, but was forced to lift it again when I felt the stinging pain of Desiree slapping my arm.

"Oh, my God, Melanie! Look over there. Look!" Desiree kept slapping my arm repeatedly as she pointed across the bar. I knew she must have been pointing at some cute guy, which was the last thing I was interested in at the moment, so I tried my best to ignore her. But she wasn't having it. She grabbed my arm and squeezed it so hard I dropped my cigarette.

"Goddamnit, Desiree, look what you did. That was my last damn cigarette." I pulled my arm free with a scowl.

"Don't worry about that. I got a whole pack in my purse." She reached in her bag and handed me a cigarette without even looking in my direction. "God, did you see him? Isn't he fine?"

"I don't know," I told her as I lit the cigarette. "I wasn't looking. I don't give a damn about these sorry-ass guys in here."

"You will when you see this one. Look over there. Look! Isn't he fine? Now I know what you meant by love at first sight, 'cause that's my future husband."

I looked in the direction she was pointing and gasped. The man she was talking about was none other than Prince, and Desiree was right. He was looking good, all decked out in a double-breasted white sport coat with a black turtleneck and slacks.

"All right now, put your tongue back in your mouth, 'cause I saw him first." Desiree had opened her compact and was busy fixing her makeup. I know I should have told her right away that the guy she was fawning over was the guy I was agonizing over, but she was so excited, I didn't wanna pop her bubble. Not yet, anyway.

"What about Tim?" I finally muttered.

"Please. Why settle for hamburger when you can have steak?" She tugged on my arm. "Come on, I gotta go to the bathroom and straighten out my hair before I meet my future husband."

"But . . ."

"Ain't no buts. Come on. And stop looking at him like that. He's mine, remember? I saw him first."

On that note, I followed her without a word. When we arrived in the bathroom I knew I had to tell her who her future husband really was, but she was talking a mile a minute.

"Oh my God, Melanie! Did you see him? Did you see him? That man is so fine. I don't give a damn if he's got a woman or not. Hell, I don't care if he's married. I gotta get me some of that tonight. Mmm, mmm, mmm. He is too fiiiiine."

She was so excited, I don't think she even noticed I hadn't spoken a word. Finally, she stopped babbling long enough to apply her lip gloss, and spotted me in the mirror with my arms folded across my chest.

"What's wrong with you?" She placed her hand on her hip and glared at me in the mirror. "Look, I know you ain't mad because I seen him first." She turned around. "Come on now, Melanie, you the one who made up that rule. Whoever sees a man first gets first crack at him. Besides, I thought you was still stuck on that nigga Prince."

"Desiree." I sighed. "That is Prince."

Her jaw almost hit the ground.

"What! You lying?"

"No, I'm not."

"That fine ass nigga out there is Prince? The same Prince you went out with two weeks ago?" I nodded and she kept on talking. "The same Prince you been waiting to hear from?"

"Yep, that's him."

"Damn! Why the fuck didn't you tell me? If you made me fuck up with Tim, I'm gonna kick your ass." She rushed out the bathroom and I followed. A few minutes later, she seemed to have forgotten about Prince and was busy flirting with Tim again.

I just wish it had been that easy for me. For twenty minutes, all I could do was stare at him. I was tempted to get up and approach him, but I didn't want him or his friends to think that I was sweatin' him. Especially after he played me the way he did. So I sat there, frozen in my seat, staring, smoking Desiree's cigarettes, and feeling sorry for myself. I should've never let Desiree drag me in here in the first place. I know she called herself trying to cheer me up by taking me out to dinner and all. And we did have a good time at Bronx BBQ over by Green Acres mall, but when she suggested we stop by here for a drink before heading home, I should have refused. I knew Prince hung out here. I also knew I wasn't ready to confront him.

"Hey, you all right?" Desiree grabbed my hand when I reached over to take another cigarette. "Look, you better take your ass over there and talk to him, 'cause you ain't gonna smoke up all my cigarettes."

"Please. What the hell am I gonna say to him?" I snatched her pack off the bar.

"How 'bout 'Why didn't you call me, nigga?'" She got a smile out of me for the first time.

"Now you know damn well I'm not gonna say that to that man. That is not my style."

"Well, it's mine. You want me to talk to him?"

"What're you gonna say to him?" I asked inquisitively.

"I don't know," she replied. "You know me. I'll think of somethin'."

"That's what I'm afraid—" I hadn't even finished my sentence when she jumped off her bar stool and was halfway across the dance floor, headed for Prince. A few seconds later, my heart was in my mouth and Desiree was in Prince's face. Not long after that, she was pointing in my direction and the two of them were staring at me. Whatever was said after that was brief, because Desiree was walking back toward me in no time.

"Well, what did he say?" I asked nervously.

Desiree sighed, so I knew whatever news she had wasn't good. "I don't know how to tell you this, Mel, but he said you're full o' shit."

"He said what?" I jumped out my seat and glared at him across the bar. I was about to walk over there and give him a piece of my mind, but I hesitated when I realized he was glaring back just as hard as if I were the one who'd wronged him.

"Calm down, girl. Ain't no need for a scene." Desiree guided me back to my seat.

"No, I won't calm down, Desiree. I waited two weeks for that man to call me. And he's got the nerve to say I'm full o' shit? Fuck him! What else did he say?"

"His exact words were, 'Don't come over here talkin' about that chick Melanie 'cause she's full o' shit. If she didn't want me to have her number, she should have just said so.'"

"Shoulda said so? What the fuck is he talkin' about? I gave him my number."

"He told me you gave him some bogus shit." Desiree tried to hide a smile, probably because we were known for that kinda shit. But I wasn't smiling. I was heated. I knew I'd given him the right number.

"Prince is the one who's full o' shit."

"Well, that's not what he said, and he's sitting over there waiting for an apology."

"An apology! Well, I hope he don't wait too fucking long, 'cause I ain't got shit to apologize for."

"Look, Mel." Desiree could probably tell from the number of curses I was shouting just how angry I was, and she tried her best to calm me down. "Why don't you go over there and talk to him? He seems like a nice guy. Maybe you did write the number down wrong. That man is too fine to lose over a mistake."

"Please, Desiree, stop trying to defend his ass. I ain't write shit down wrong. I know my phone number. Can't you see he's tryin' to play me? That nigga got game."

"Yeah, but . . ."

"But what?"

"But that man is off-the-charts fine. Maybe you should go over there and talk to him. I mean, you ain't gotta apologize. Just talk."

"Talk to him for what? So he can run some more game? No, thank you. He ain't no different than the rest of them no-good men I've fucked with, Desiree. He just got a prettier face. If you want him, you can have him. I ain't got time for games. I'll see you back at the house."

"Not tonight you won't. I'm going home with Tim, remember." She smiled from ear to ear.

"Yeah, whatever." I finished my drink in one gulp, then picked up my purse and headed for the door. I'm not gonna lie, I was hoping Prince would follow so I could talk to him outside in private without Desiree's knowledge. I even waited outside for him for ten minutes, but he never came out.

10

Wil

Diane and I walked up to the hostess of Legal Seafood in Huntington, Long Island, holding hands. We were dressed cleaner than the preacher and his wife on a Sunday morning, and all eyes in the restaurant were upon us. Diane was wearing this red strapless dress I loved because it accentuated all her full-figured curves in just the right way. I was wearing my dark-blue, double-breasted pinstriped suit with my matching gangster-style hat.

I'd asked my sister, Melanie, to watch the kids so I could take Diane out to dinner. After talking to Mimi, I was convinced that my intimacy problems with Diane were not all her fault. Maybe I had been working too hard lately. Like so many married couples, we'd neglected the little things that had made our relationship so special in the first place. Not that Diane ever complained, but she had mentioned that we never seemed to go out anymore without the kids. And that shit Mimi mentioned about stay-at-home moms being bored and using Internet chat lines really scared the shit outta me. So I figured a little dinner at a fancy restaurant, a couple'a tickets to a comedy club and a token of my affection from Zales, and I might just get back in her good graces.

"Hi, my name's Wil Duncan. I have an 8:30 reservation."

The hostess looked in her book, then smiled. "Right this way, Mr. Duncan." She picked up two menus and gestured for us to follow her. She escorted us to a small candlelit table in a corner. Diane and I settled into our seats and held hands across the table.

"Wil, this place is lovely."

I glanced around, nodding my approval. "Yeah, it is nice, isn't it? Sure beats the hell outta Ghetto Seafood."

"Ghetto Seafood?" My wife gave me a strange look.

"Yeah, that's Trent's nickname for Red Lobster."

"Why's that?"

"He said if you ask a black or Hispanic person to name two seafood restaurants, most of them can't name but one. And that's always Red Lobster. Thus the name Ghetto Seafood. To the average black person, Red Lobster is a five-star restaurant."

Diane laughed. "You know, as much as I hate to admit it, he's right. If you say you're going to Red Lobster, everybody black gets excited."

"Does that include you?"

"You damn right. I love me some Red Lobster."

Diane and I both laughed as the waitress came and took our order. When she finished, we handed back our menus and I reached across for Diane's hand again.

"Di, can I ask you a question?"

"Of course. What do you wanna know?"

I lowered my head, slightly embarrassed. When we first were married, Diane and I used to talk all the time about everything and anything, but since the marital problems we'd had a few years ago, talking wasn't that easy for us. I guess that's why Mimi and I had become so close. I really needed a woman to talk to. I just wish it could be my wife.

"Do you still find me attractive?"

Diane gave me this where-the-hell-did-that-come-from look as she took a sip of her wine.

"Of course I find you attractive. I've never met a man I've been more attracted to, Wil." She looked me directly in the eyes. "What's this all about, anyway? I hope it's not about the other night. Look, I'm sorry. I just wasn't in the mood."

"No, it's not about the other night," I lied. But it had everything to do with the other night. And every other time the past two months she'd made an excuse not to make love to me.

"If it's not about the other night, then what is it about?"

I held her hand a little tighter and leaned in a little closer. "I just wanted to know if you were happy with me. I mean, I've started to grow this mustache, and you haven't even noticed it."

She cut me off with a frown. "Yes, I have. I was just afraid if

I said something you might shave it off. I've been trying to get you to grow a mustache for years, remember? I think it's sexy." She winked at me.

"You do?" I raised both eyebrows, grinning. Her words made me feel like a man again. God, I loved my wife so much. And it was nice to spend quality time with her away from the kids. It really did make me appreciate her. After my conversation with Mimi the other day, I was starting to realize just how far apart we'd actually grown.

"Oh, and by the way, I'm very happy with you, Wil."

"Really?"

"Really." We both smiled.

"I know this is a little late coming, but I have something for you." I reached in my pocket, then handed her a jewelry box. "I was gonna give this to you on our anniversary, but I wanted you to know how much I love you now."

Diane opened the box and her eyes were as wide as they could be. "Oh, my goodness, Wil. I don't know what to say. It's, it's beautiful."

"Here, let me put it on you." I took the box from her hand and placed the diamond bracelet around her wrist.

Diane leaned over and kissed me. "I may not say it enough, but I love you, too, Wil Duncan."

After we had dinner, Diane and I made our way over to Governor's Comedy Club. The comedians weren't big-time, but those white boys were funny nonetheless. One of them even made fun of my gangster hat. All in all, we had a really good time and the night wasn't even close to being over yet. Or that's what I thought until I pulled into the parking lot of the Kew Motor Inn.

"What are we doing here?" Diane looked up at the motel, then looked at me with this expression that almost looked like fear.

"I thought it might be nice to get a room here and reminisce. I mean, it's the first place we ever made love. And we haven't been here in years." I leaned over to kiss her, and she pulled back.

"We can't do this, Wil," she stated flatly.

"Why not?"

"Well . . . I know I should have told you before, but I didn't wanna ruin our night."

"Tell me what?"

"Well." She paused like she was searching for an answer, or dreaming up an excuse. "I've been cramping ever since we left the restaurant. I think I'm about to start my period."

"Oh, really?" She nodded her head and I sat back in my seat. Skepticism was written all over my face. I wasn't about to call my wife a liar, but something was seriously wrong with her story. Diane's cycle was like clockwork, and she wasn't supposed to get her period for at least a week and a half.

"Well, that's okay. I already paid for the room. Why don't we just go upstairs and cuddle?"

"I don't wanna cuddle. If I start cuddling with you, I'm gonna wanna do something. And I don't wanna get all worked up if I'm not gonna get some."

"So what are you trying to say? You wanna go home?"

"Yes, that's exactly what I'm trying to say," she answered matter-of-factly.

"This is fucked up, Diane."

"Look, Wil, I'm sorry, all right? I can't help nature. Why don't you try being a woman for a while?"

"Why don't you try being a wife," I mumbled as I backed out of the parking lot. I glanced at the diamond bracelet I'd given her earlier and wished I could take it back. *God, why can't she just be like Mimi?*

11

Trent

I walked into 718 around midnight and had to do a double take when I saw my brother Wil, Mr. Family Man, sitting at the bar. I was early for a meeting with Big Mike so I figured since he was there that I'd get him to buy me a drink. Hell, if he was drunk enough and his friends weren't around, I might even try to get him to loan me a few dollars. Wil could be quite generous when he had a few drinks in him.

"What's up, player? What you doin' on this side of town?" He glanced my way and shook his head, giving me the impression that I was the last person he wanted to see.

"I'm drinkin'. What's it look like I'm doing?" He threw back what was left of his drink, then glared at me with contempt. He musta been fighting with Diane 'cause that's the only time I've ever seen him drink scotch. He's usually a rum and Coke man.

"I thought Diane didn't let you hang with the boys anymore." I looked around for that little motley crew of his, but none of them were around.

"For your information, Diane doesn't make decisions for me. What do you want, Trent? I'm fucking busy." Yeah, he was fighting with Diane all right.

"Damn, what's got your panties in a bunch? That wife of yours not giving you any?" I slid onto the bar stool but his ice-cold stare shut me up.

"What the fuck do you want, Trent?"

"Look, man, I just saw you sitting over here alone so I thought I'd come over and see what's up. Have you seen Mel? I been tryin' to get in touch with her all week."

"Yeah, she's been staying over my house the last couple'a days. She's having another one of her crises over some guy." He gestured for Jasper to refill his glass.

"Uh-huh, that's what I wanna see her about."

"What you drinkin', Trent?" Jasper asked as he refilled Wil's drink.

"Let me have a shot of Henny and a Corona. And put it on his tab." I pointed at Wil with a grin.

"Don't do that, 'cause I ain't gonna pay it," Wil snapped at Jasper before turning his attention to me. "I ain't buying you shit till you pay me the three hundred and sixty dollars you owe me."

"I'ma let you lovebirds figure this out." Jasper nodded as he walked away.

"I want my money, Trent."

"Well, um . . ." I had enough money in my pocket to pay Wil right then. It's just I'd had my eye on these Italian loafers and this designer suit. And to be frank, me looking good was way more important than me paying Wil back. "I know I owe you a couple'a dollars but you don't have to get indignant about it. I'ma get it to you."

"Yeah, right. When?" He picked up his drink and glared at me. His glassy eyes looked like they could burn a hole right through me.

"Soon, real soon," I told him confidently.

Wil gave me this smirk I was sure was going to be accompanied by sarcasm, but before he could speak we were interrupted by a woman's voice.

"Excuse me. I think you're in my seat."

I turned toward the voice and there was this big, red-boned sister smiling at me like there was no tomorrow. I had no idea who she was, but for a big girl she was sexy as hell. She kinda reminded me of a larger version of Jackee when she was on 227. Not only was she sexy, but she looked and carried herself like she might have money, too. A romp in the sack with her just might be worth my time. A brother did have to eat and pay his bills.

I eyed the sister from head to toe. All I had to do was figure out what type of man she'd be interested in and I'd be straight. Shit, I had a business card for every situation. I just needed to figure out if she was the doctor/dentist type, or did she want a self-employed man, like a contractor or a jeweler. From her looks, I figured she was probably the executive type, and that was a good thing, because I'd just put up my law degree plaques before I left the house.

"I'm sorry, good-lookin'. I didn't know this was your seat. Why don't you let me buy you a drink and make it up to you?" I slid off the stool and extended my hand, smiling like a Cheshire cat. "My name's Trent. Trent Duncan, *attorney at law.*" I handed her a business card, then bent over to kiss her hand. Wil grabbed my arm and pulled me away from her.

"He ain't no damn lawyer, Mimi. He ain't even got a job."

I wanted to smack Wil's ass for hating, but then something occurred to me.

"How'd you know her name? Do you two know each other?" I straightened up, rotating my head back and forth between the two of them. It was obvious now that this Mimi woman hadn't been smiling at me at all, but at my slick ass brother. "Well, do you two know each other?"

There was a silence between them. Finally the woman gave me this who-the-hell-are-you look.

"That's your business because . . . ?" she asked sarcastically.

"Because I'm his brother," I answered back.

"His brother?" Her face became flush as she swallowed hard, glancing at Wil. Either I was imagining things or something was up between these two. Her reaction was too contrite. It also told me that she knew he was married. I must admit, though, I'm surprised Mr. Goody Two-shoes would do something like this. I always thought he worshipped the ground Diane walked on. Not that I gave a shit. If he was getting a little on the side from Ms. Thing, then so be it. That bitch Diane had been hating on me for years so she deserved it. Besides, his little indiscretion could be my pot of gold.

"So, do you two know each other?" I repeated.

"Yeah," Wil finally replied. "We know each other. We work together. Mimi's my secretary."

"Is that right?" I raised an eyebrow, grinning the entire time. "Y'all working mighty late, aren't you?" Wil's eyes got small. It was obvious he was worried about what I might say, and he was right. "What's up, bro? You gonna give her a little *dick*-tation tonight?" I started to laugh until Wil put his finger in my face.

"Yo! You may not have any respect for me, Trent, but you're gonna have some respect for my friend. You hear me?"

"Yeah, I hear you. Now get your hand out my face." I pushed his hand aside.

"I think it's time for us to go, Mimi. Why don't you wait for me at the door? I wanna talk to my brother for a minute."

"All right," she told him in this overly concerned voice. She walked toward the door.

"You sure do like them big-boned ones, don't you, player?"

"I keep telling you I'm not a player. And she's just a friend, Trent. Do you understand, a friend?"

"Sure she is." I sat back on my stool. "So, let me ask you a question. Does Diane know you're out with this friend?"

He didn't answer and I smiled.

"Look, man, you ain't got anything to worry about from me. I can keep a secret. Shit, I get amnesia when I'm drunk. Think you could buy me a couple'a drinks before you and your *friend* leave? A couple'a drinks will go a long way toward my amnesia." I leaned forward and smirked. Wil pulled out a twenty and placed it on the table. I cut my eyes at him, shaking my head. "Now, Wil, you know it takes a hell of a lot more than twenty dollars to get me drunk."

Wil rolled his eyes as he pulled out a hundred dollar bill, slapping it on top of the twenty.

"That should be enough to make you forget you were even born."

"You know what, Wil? I think you're right. I can't remember when my birthday is to save my life." I laughed again as he walked away, then I shouted his name. "Hey, Wil!"

He looked back with a scowl. "What, Trent?"

I winked at him. "Don't do anything I wouldn't do."

Twenty minutes after Wil left I was sitting in front of Big Mike Wilson's desk with my feet up, drinking cognac and smoking a cigar. I had no idea what I was doing there. I was just hoping it didn't have to do with my ex, Michelle.

"So, Mike, what's up? Why the cognac and the cigars? What you want, man?"

Mike puffed on his cigar twice. "Well, Trent, I wanna talk to you about a couple of things."

"I hope it ain't nothing to do with Michelle 'cause I'm about sick of her."

"Look, you know I never try to get in your business, but Beverly and I was talking, and—" I cut him off. The last thing I wanted was to hear what Beverly had to say about anything. That wench never graduated from high school but was an authority on everything. If it wasn't for that fine ass body of hers I'm sure Mike wouldn't even be talking to her.

"Talking about what?" I sighed.

"You and this girl Indigo."

"What about us?"

"You've brought a lot of sisters around here over the years. Some of them you're just screwing and some you're hitting up for cash."

"I'm hitting them all up for cash, Mike. What's the point?"

"Well, you might not wanna do that to this one." He gave me a serious look.

"You know what, Mike? I'm outta here. I do not need any self-righteous speeches today." I got up outta my seat and took a step toward the door.

"Hold up, Trent. You're not understanding me." He stood and placed his hand on my arm. "This girl's not like the rest. She's . . . she's special."

I pulled my arm free as I spun around to look him in the eyes.

"Special? Please." I let out a laugh. "What you saying, Mike? You wanna tap that ass? Well, by all means, my man, do it. Just don't get in my way. I can probably get another ten grand outta her."

Mike shook his head adamantly. "Nah, man, it's nothing like that. You think I'd be talking to Bev about it if I just wanted to tap that ass?"

"I don't know what you would do. Hell, Beverly might want some, too. Truth is, right about now you're confusing the hell outta me. I mean, what's the big deal, Mike? We've been doing business for years. Why all of a sudden you sticking your neck out for this chick?" My voice was agitated.

"The big deal is this is the first one you've brought by worth sticking my neck out for. Indigo can sing, Trent. I mean she can really sing. I sent her demo out to a few people and they all wanted to know if I'd signed her. With a little fine tuning, she could make it, make it big." His eyes were wide and for the first time in our conversation, I could feel his passion.

"You're serious, aren't you?"

"Man, I've never been more serious in my life. Trent, this chick could be the ship we've both been waiting to come in."

"How?"

He handed me the papers he was looking over. "Get her to sign this contract. That way I can start to shop her demo legally. After that it's just a matter of time."

"Wait a minute. This thing says you're gonna be her manager. And your cut is fifteen percent. If you're managing her what the hell am I gonna get outta this?" It sounded like good old Mike was trying to give it to me in the wrong end.

"You're gonna get a hell of a lot more than me."

"How's that?" I asked skeptically.

"By marrying her."

"Marrying her? Are you fucking crazy?"

"Why not? You already told me you don't give a shit about Michelle. Besides, if you marry her before she signs a deal, you get fifty percent of everything she makes. That's the law, my friend. Plus you get a salary as her road manger and you control her career."

"I don't know about marriage, Mike."

"Trent, this chick is gonna make at least a million dollars with her voice. How the hell you gonna tell me you're gonna turn down half of that?" I looked at the seriousness on my friend and mentor's face and the only thing that came to mind was, *he has a point.*

12

Mimi

I arrived at work about thirty minutes early, with a cup of
Dunkin' Donuts cappuccino for myself and a cup of their regular
coffee just the way Wil liked it. I'd even picked up some bagels
and his favorite doughnuts. My momma always said the way to
a man's heart was through his stomach. But just in case she didn't
know what the hell she was talking about, I unbuttoned the top
three buttons of my blouse before I entered the office. A little
cleavage never hurt when it came to winning a man's heart, either. And there was no man I wanted more than Wil.

"Breakfast." I walked into his office with a smile.

Wil lifted his head and took off his glasses. His smile bright-
ened my day, and it was obvious he was glad to see me. I was
just praying that smile was for me and only me. The last thing I
needed to hear was that he got some from his wife after he
dropped me off last night. Shit, he could have gotten some from
me if he hadn't been so stubborn and refused to come up to my
apartment. I must have tried every trick in the book, except coming outta my face and telling him, "Let's go upstairs and fuck,"
but he still wouldn't budge.

"Hungry?" I whispered.

His eyes went straight to my breasts and I sighed thankfully.
It was evident by his stare that he hadn't gotten anything when
he went home. I sucked in a little air to make my breasts appear
larger. *God, I wish he would just reach out and touch them.*

"Hungry?" I repeated.

"Starved."

"Well, what would you like?" His eyes were still glued to my
breasts, and when I sat down in the chair in front of his desk it
felt like he leaned closer. I wasn't sure if I should offer him a
doughnut or a titty sandwich. But when a man gives you this

much attention you have to offer him something. So I arched my back and stuck out my chest a little more. Then I lifted my arms in a long stretch. I'm sure by the way his eyes were bulging that it must have looked like my breasts were gonna pop out my blouse. His face was beginning to become flush and a single bead of sweat rolled down his forehead. Lowering my arms, I teased him with my words. "Which one would you like?"

He lifted his head in stuttering confusion. "I'm . . . I'm not quite sure what you mean."

I pointed at the doughnuts. "Which doughnut would you like? I made sure to pick up some Bavarian cream. They are your favorite, aren't they?"

"Ah, yeah, they are," he replied, obviously still a little confused. "You know, Mimi, you never cease to amaze me. How do you always seem to know what I need?"

"Isn't that what a good . . . secretary is supposed to do?" I wanted to say "wife" but I controlled myself for now.

"Yeah, but you go way beyond the regular duties of secretary."

Yeah, and I'm ready to go further than that whenever you are, I thought.

"I'm just doing my job, Wil."

"No, you're being a good friend, Mimi. I know I thanked you last night, but I really appreciate you meeting me at that bar then. I really needed to get a woman's perspective about what's going on at home. I don't know what I would've done without you."

"Neither do I, Wil. But like you said, I'm your friend. Whenever or whatever you need, I'm gonna be there for you. And I do mean whatever you need."

"I'm starting to see that." He smiled. "I'm really starting to see that."

I took a bite of a jelly doughnut and purposely let the filling run down my lip. Then I waited until Wil was watching and licked it up sensually with my tongue. He took a deep breath that seemed to take forever for him to release. Encouraged by his reaction I lowered my head and naughtily sucked out the remaining jelly from the doughnut. When I finally lifted my head, my lips were covered with jelly. Of course, I licked it off in the same sensual manner that I'd done before. Wil's face turned three shades of red, and not only were there several beads of sweat running down his face, but he was squirming around in his seat so much I thought he was gonna fall out of it. From that moment on, I knew it was just a matter of time before I would have Wil substituting his favorite Bavarian cream doughnuts every morning for some Mimi pie.

"Phew." He wiped his brow. "Is it me, or is it getting hot in here?"

"It seems fine in here to me." I watched him wipe away some more perspiration. "So, how's everything at home? Did you and your wife sit down and talk last night?"

"Hell, no." He frowned. "I should have gone back to your house and had that drink like you asked me to."

I turned my head away from him and mumbled under my breath, "You would have gotten a lot more than a drink."

"Did you say something?"

"Oh, no, it was nothing. So what are you gonna do about your wife, Wil?"

"I don't know. I just wish she would talk to me. I just wish I knew what the hell was going on."

"You know, Wil, after seeing what you went through last night, I'm starting to think she's fooling around."

"I hate to admit it, Mimi, but I'm starting to think the same thing. All I need is some proof and I'm outta there."

"Well, I hope you find something soon 'cause what she's doing to you is wrong." I glanced at my watch, then stood up. "Oh, my goodness, it's nine o'clock. I gotta get to my desk and start answering the phones."

"Wow, is it nine already? I gotta get to my sales meeting." He rummaged through some folders while I picked up the leftover doughnuts and bagels before leaving his office. Of course, I gave him a little extra sway of my hips before sitting down at my desk.

"I'll see you in about two hours." He smiled as he walked past. "We still on for lunch?"

"Wouldn't miss it for the world." I smiled as he disappeared down the corridor. The second he was fully out of sight I placed the doughnuts on my desk and I flipped through my Rolodex and picked up the phone.

"Hello, Rosedale Florist? I'd like to have a dozen roses sent to 176 234th Street but they have to be delivered after six this evening."

"We charge quite a bit extra for that service, ma'am."

"Oh, I don't mind paying extra for that service," I replied. I gave him my credit card information and what I wanted the card to say and hung up the phone just as Jeanie Brown walked up to my desk.

"Hi, Maxine."

"Hi, Ms. Brown. Wil's not here. He's at a sales meeting."

"Oh, that's okay. I didn't just come to see him. I came to see you, too."

"Come to see me why?" *God in heaven, please let this woman tell me they're gonna hire me permanently.*

"Maxine, Marge just called me, and it looks like her arm healed faster than the doctors thought it would. She's gonna be coming back to work on Monday. So Friday's going to be your last day in this department." I felt like I was gonna faint.

"But, but I thought she was gonna be out for three months. It's only been five weeks."

"I thought so too. Evidently the break wasn't as bad as they first thought. But don't worry, we have someone leaving the executive floor this week on maternity leave. You can have that position if you'd like. She's gonna be out a lot longer than Marge was."

"I don't wanna work on the executive floor. I wanna work with Wil!" Jeanie took a step back. That's when I realized I was out of control. "I mean, Jeanie, me and Wil work well together. Why can't Marge go to the executive floor?"

"Because you're a temp and she's been working this desk for five years. It's her job, not yours. Do we understand each other?"

I took a short breath. "Yeah, I understand."

"Good. I'll let you know about the job upstairs later this week." She was eyeing the Dunkin' Donuts box. "You don't mind if I have one, do you? I have such a sweet tooth." I wanted to say *Hell, no. You can't have shit, bitch, if I can't have the job I want,* but instead I just smiled, nodding. She lifted the cover to the box, then jumped back like she'd seen a roach.

"Oh, Jesus Christ. What are you trying to do, kill me?" She sighed, covering her mouth with her hand.

"Something wrong?"

"You've got sesame seed bagels in there." She took another step back.

"Yeah, and?" I gave her this strange look.

"I'm severely allergic to sesame seeds. For me they are like the kiss of death."

"Really? Well, why don't you try one of these brownies my sister made? No sesame seeds in them." I took the top off the box of brownies I brought for Wil's afternoon snack.

"Oh, those do look good, don't they?" She reached in the box and took out a brownie square, biting into it. "Mmm, these are delicious, Maxine. Can I have another?" She reached in the box and took another, smiling at me before getting back to business.

"Thank you so much, Maxine."

"You're welcome," I told her, hoping that I'd just earned a few brownie points toward staying in sales with Wil but I couldn't have been more wrong.

"By the way, Maxine, your blouse is wide open. I know you're single but we have a lot of married men around here. Especially now that you're gonna be working on the executive floor. We wouldn't want to give them or their wives the wrong impression, would we?"

"No, we wouldn't." I reached up and buttoned my blouse, giving her the finger when her back was turned. That bitch didn't know who she was fucking with 'cause I was not going to the executive floor. I was staying right here in sales with Wil, and I meant to achieve that by any means necessary.

13

Melanie

I walked up the steps to Trent's apartment and lit what must have been my twentieth cigarette of the day before I knocked on the door. I was still depressed over Prince and it didn't seem like that was gonna disappear anytime soon. I was hoping Trent would cheer me up with some of his silly ass stories about his women. But to my surprise it wasn't him that answered the door. It was a dark-skinned woman, about my height with a short natural hairstyle, and she was wearing the robe I'd given Trent for Christmas. She was pretty and looked familiar, but I couldn't place a name with the face to save my life. It was hard to keep track of all Trent's women, since he went through them so fast. Whoever this one was, she must've had some money, 'cause Trent rarely had women over before five o'clock on a weekday. That's because most of his women were at work so they could help him pay his bills.

"Hi, I'm Melanie, Trent's sister. I think he's expecting me."

"Yeah, he is. Come on in. I'm Indigo. I think we met at Manhattan Proper a few weeks ago." She extended her hand and I shook it, still unsure of just who she was. "Remember? I asked your brother to buy me a drink and he refused, acting all stink."

"Oh, yeah. I knew you looked familiar." I smiled politely as I walked past her into the living room. "I guess you got him to buy you that drink after all, didn't you?"

"Now that you mention it, I guess I did." She laughed and I joined in, although I wasn't laughing at her joke. I was laughing at how stupid she was. I knew Trent was up to something that night, but I never imagined he'd be able to pull Indigo after the way he'd treated her. It never ceases to amaze me how stupid we women can be when it comes to men. I couldn't wait to hear what BS Trent had run on her. Whatever it was, she went for it hook, line and sinker 'cause I was pretty sure she was the one who gave him the money to get his car outta hock.

"I see Trent's got a new sofa."

"Yeah, he kept whining about how uncomfortable his old one was so I went out and got him a new one. It's leather."

I ran my hand over the smooth, white surface. It wasn't just leather, it was Italian leather. This thing must have cost her a fortune. Damn, this woman was looking stupider by the minute.

"What happened to the other one?" If she said he threw it out, I was not gonna be happy. Trent hadn't had that sofa more than a year, and he knew mine had so many holes that Desiree and I had to lay a sheet over it whenever we had company.

"It's in storage. You want it?" Trent walked out of his bedroom wearing a pair of boxers and a T-shirt. He was holding his head like he had a headache or a hangover but he still looked like he was about to pose for an underwear commercial.

"Yeah, I want it," I snapped as I walked over and gave him a hug.

"Aw'ight. Then it's yours," he whispered, holding me tight. "So what's this I hear you playing games with my man Prince?" He let out a laugh.

I let go of his waist and pushed him back. "Is that what he told you? That I was playing games?"

"No. But he was pretty upset. What's going on, Mel?"

"Your boy Prince ain't shit. That's what's going on." I was giving him attitude like it was all his fault.

"Well, I told you to leave my friends alone, didn't I?" His voice was sharp, so I didn't answer. Trent shook his head and sat on the sofa.

"I don't wanna hear that I-told-you-so crap, Trent." I was trying to hold back my emotions.

"Com'ere, Melanie." He patted the cushion next to him and I sat down, feeling like a child about to be lectured. "So what's up? You really like Prince, don't you?"

I glanced at Indigo. No way was I washing my dirty laundry in front of a complete stranger. I guess Trent must have sensed it.

"Hey, baby, can you give us a minute?" Indigo didn't reply. She just walked back to the bedroom.

"So what's up with Prince, honestly?" Trent sat back on the cushion.

"I don't know. We went out and I was feelin' him."

"So why ain't he shit? He didn't try to take advantage of you or anything, did he?" Trent's eyes got small.

"No, nothing like that. But he's just like every other man I know, including you. He's a fucking liar."

"Fucking liar!" he repeated. "That's a pretty strong statement, little sister. You sure you can back that up? I mean, I'm a liar. I admit it, but Prince . . . ? That doesn't sound like him."

"Obviously we're not talking about the same guy. What did he tell you, anyway?"

"Well, we actually had two conversations." Trent sighed. "The first one was a couple of hours after you and him took that motorcycle ride." I gave him this stunned look. I was surprised he knew about that ride. "Yeah, he told me about that. He also told me that he was feelin' you too, and that he was sorry if I didn't approve but he wanted me to know that he was gonna keep seeing you."

"He said that?"

"Yeah, and that's when I told him if he came within ten feet of you, I was gonna fuck both his sisters."

"There you go hating again. Is that the reason he never called me?" If he said yes, I was gonna slap him.

"I doubt it. 'Cause he said he didn't give a damn if I fucked his momma. He wasn't gonna let an opportunity to be with someone as special as you slip away. He said he never felt like this about anybody. And then he said some crap about us being brothers-in-law one day and I'd understand then."

I couldn't help it. I was grinning from ear to ear.

"Don't get all happy. He left here about an hour ago pissed off like a motherfucker. It seems a certain blond-dreaded sister named Melanie sold him a dream with no intention of waking his ass up." Trent chuckled. "Mel, why you give my man a bogus number? I know I told you to stay away from him, but you ain't had to do him like that. I mean, the brother does like you."

"Like I said before, Trent, he's a fucking liar. I gave him the right number." Trent gave me a look of disbelief. "I know you don't believe him over me?"

"You wanna know something funny, Mel? I do believe him over you."

I lost all expression in my face. "What? Oh my God. This nigga got game. I can't believe you, Trent. You know I wouldn't lie to you."

"I didn't think so until . . ." He reached over to the end table closest to him and picked up a piece of paper. He handed it to me. "You remember this?"

I unfolded the paper. "Oh, shit!" It was the piece of paper I'd given Prince. Only it had a wrong number written on it. I'd reversed two of the digits. "How the fuck did I do that?"

"I don't know, but I think you owe the brother an apology." I looked up at Trent, embarrassed. "He's a good man, Mel. And he really does like you. If I was a chick, I'd go for him."

"I don't have his number."

"I do."

"So you don't mind if I talk to him?"

"No. Just don't be stupid about it. He's a good brother, but he's still got a dick." Trent smiled, picking up the phone. He dialed a number, then handed me the receiver.

"Peace." I almost dropped the phone when I heard Prince's voice.

"Prince?"

"Yeah."

"This . . . this is Melanie."

There was a silence before he spoke. "What's up, Melanie?"

"I wanted to apologize for giving you the wrong number. It wasn't done on purpose."

"I know. Your brother told me."

"He did?" I glanced at Trent. That was the first unselfish act I'd seen him do in ten years.

"Yeah. He told me you have dyslexia and that you have a problem transposing numbers from time to time." I could kiss Trent right then, even if the thing about dyslexia was a lie. "I just don't know why your girl acted that way."

"You mean Desiree? How'd she act?"

"Never mind. It's not important. Look, I got tickets to Def Jam Poetry tomorrow night at the Garden. Think you might wanna go?"

"Hell, yeah!" I shouted until I saw the expression on Trent's face. "I mean, sure I'd like to go."

"How about I meet you in front of your building at say, six o'clock?"

"It's a date."

"Good. I'll see you tomorrow night." He hung up, and I handed the phone back to Trent, who was smiling from ear to ear.

"So now that I've done you a little favor, you think you can do one for me?" I knew it was too good to be true.

"What kind of favor?"

"I need you to talk to your girl Michelle about this baby shit."

"What you want me to talk to her about?"

"I want her to stop telling everybody that's my baby. And tell her to stop calling these fucking talk shows. That bitch has entirely too much fucking time on her hands."

"Talk shows? What talk shows?"

"She's calling all these motherfucking talk shows and they're driving me crazy. First it was Maury Povich trying to get me on his show to do a paternity test. Then it was Ricki Lake trying to get me on her show. What's next, Jerry Springer? I'm about to change my cell phone number." I couldn't help it. I bust out laughing.

"I don't see a damn thing funny, Melanie."

"Why don't you just call her? She probably just wants you to come see the baby."

"I ain't calling her. And I ain't going to see no damn baby. That's what I want you to do."

"Let me ask you a question, Trent. Do you really think she's going to all this trouble because that baby's not yours? Why don't you just go and get a blood test? 'Cause I'm not gonna lie, Trent. That baby looks just like you. Ask Momma."

He glanced at me silently for a few seconds. "Look, Mel, you gonna go talk to her or what?"

"Let me think about it, okay? So what's up with you and Indigo, anyway?"

"I'm thinking about asking her to marry me."

I slapped his arm. "Stop playing, Trent. She's gonna hear you."

"I ain't playing."

"Yes, you are," I told him adamantly.

"No, I'm not, Mel."

"Look me in the eyes and say that."

He got up in my face and stared at me. "I'm thinking about asking her to marry me."

"You're serious, aren't you?"

He nodded his head. "Yep."

I lifted my hand and felt his forehead. "You feeling all right? You don't have a fever or anything, do you?"

He pulled my hand down. "I'm fine."

"No, you're not."

"Yes, I am."

"You sure? 'Cause first you tell me it's all right for me to date your friend Prince and now you're telling me you're getting married. Those are sure signs that you must be sick."

"So I'm sick because I finally found someone I might wanna settle down with?"

"Settle down with? For how long? Until the money runs out? A hundred thousand dollars isn't a lot of money, Trent. Especially with your taste."

"Yeah, baby sister, but a couple'a million could last a lifetime." He smirked and I knew he was up to something.

"A couple of million? I thought she only hit the Pick Five for a hundred grand."

"She did, but she's about to hit the music lotto for a whole lot more."

"What are you talking about, Trent? You know what, I'm not really sure I wanna know. Look, I gotta go, anyway. I've gotta get ready for my date." We both stood and walked to the door. I kissed him on the cheek and opened the door.

"So what's up? You gonna go see Michelle for me?"

"You need to go over there, Trent. Not me."

"Mel, if I go over there, there's gonna be nothing but drama," he said.

"All right. Let me think about it."

"Yeah. Have a good time with Prince tomorrow. He's a good brother. But lemme give you one piece of advice before you go. Watch your back, 'cause your girl Desiree, she ain't really your girl."

"What's that supposed to mean?"

"Just watch your back, Mel."

14

Trent

I was sitting on the living room sofa flipping through the morning talk shows when Indigo came up behind me and wrapped her arms around me and kissed me on the neck. I reached back and I could feel that she was still naked. She must have just read the poem I'd left on the pillow next to her. Well, I didn't exactly write the poem. I got it off the Internet, but she didn't need to know that.

"Good morning." I turned my head toward her, and she kissed me passionately.

"Morning. Thanks for the poem. I didn't know you wrote poetry." She climbed over the sofa and sat in my lap.

"There's a lot of things you don't know about me." *A whole lot,* I thought as I kissed her.

"I can see that," she replied. "Did you mean it? Did you really mean what you said? That you're falling in love with me?"

"I told my sister yesterday that I think I'm already in love with you, Indigo. It's just hard for me to admit with us being together for such a short time. Truth is, I wasn't looking for this. And I'm afraid I might get hurt."

"I know how you feel, but I already know I'm in love with you." Her smile gave away her emotions. She really was in love with me. And if that were true, now was the time for me to put to rest this Russell Simmons crap. It was time to tell her the truth.

"Indigo, I have to tell you something," I started reluctantly. "Something that's probably not gonna make you very happy." I leaned over to kiss her and she pulled back.

"What? Don't tell me you're married. Please don't tell me you're married." She looked pissed off already.

"No, I'm not married. Not yet, anyway."

"Not yet? What's that supposed to mean?"

I smiled, squeezing her hand a little tighter, then looked in her eyes. "It means I've found the right woman. I just haven't had a chance to ask her to marry me yet." A smile widened across her face and I kissed her lips gently.

"God, you sure know how to make a girl feel good. But if you're not married, what's the bad news?"

I took a deep breath, letting it out slowly for effect. "Actually, I've got some good news and some bad news. Which would you like first?"

"Give me the bad news." She sighed, bracing herself on my lap.

"Okay, Russell doesn't like your demo."

She closed her eyes briefly, and when she opened them they were full of tears. "I thought it was something like that. Well, it was good while it lasted. At least I have my demo . . . even if it did cost me four thousand dollars."

"Hey, did you forget I said I have some good news, too?"

She didn't even look like she cared. "Okay, Trent. What's the good news? I might as well hear something good this morning."

"Just because Russell doesn't see your talent doesn't mean Big Mike and I don't see it." I lifted her off my lap and wiped away her tears. "I love you, Indigo, and I have faith in you. I told you when we first met I was gonna make you a star and I meant it. So I'm gonna quit my job at Def Jam and work exclusively on your career. I even talked Big Mike into managing you."

She sucked up her tears and attempted a smile. "You'd really do that for me?"

"I got no choice. I'm in love with you. Oh, and there's one other thing."

"What's that?"

I bent down on one knee, taking a long deep breath. I couldn't believe what I was about to do and the more I thought about it the harder it became. So I tried to just spit it out.

"Indigo . . . Indigo . . . will you . . . will you marry me?"

Her eyes were as wide as silver dollars and she clutched her chest. "Are you serious? You really wanna marry me?"

"Yeah, if you'll have me. I know I don't have a ring right now, but we can go looking for one this week."

She glanced down at my face. I think she was trying to read my eyes to see if I was sincere. Whatever she was looking at must have convinced her because she said, "Yes, yes, Trent. I'll marry you." She wrapped her arms around my neck and I scooped her up, carrying her into the bedroom.

Two hours later, Indigo and I had just had some of the most hair-raising sex I'd ever had. Sweat was dripping over both of us and I didn't wanna move.

Shit," I mumbled, slowly raising myself outta bed. I'd never had a phone installed in my bedroom because women had a habit of calling just when you had another woman in bed. I swear, it was like radar. And there is nothing that says guilty more than not answering a phone that's ringing less than three feet away from you.

"Don't answer it," Indigo whispered, grabbing my arm. "I don't want you to move."

"I got to. It's probably Mike." She released my arm and I kissed her before heading for my little office to answer the phone.

"Hello."

"Trent Duncan, please," a man on the other end said in a very official tone. If I didn't know better I would've thought he was a bill collector. But thanks to Indigo I wasn't behind on any of my bills.

"This is Trent."

"Hi Trent. My name's Rueben Michaels."

"How can I help you, Mr. Michaels?"

"To be honest, I was hoping I could help you."

"Is that right? Well I don't know you, so how you gonna help me?"

"How about by giving you a thousand dollars?"

"A thousand dollars! You're gonna give me a thousand dollars. What type of scam is this?" I glanced at my Caller ID, thinking it was probably one of my boys trying to play a trick on me. But It was a 202 number, so I knew whoever it was had called from D.C. "Look, who the fuck is this? How'd you get my home number?"

"This isn't a scam at all. I'm the producer for BET's *Two Sides To A Story* show."

"*Two Sides To A Story*! Ah, hell no! What y'all want with me?"

Whatever it was, I was sure it had something to do with Michelle. That girl just wouldn't quit. *Two Sides To A Story* was the BET version of *Ricki Lake* and *Jerry Springer,* only worse, 'cause no relationship ever left that show intact. When I watched it the other day, they had this show on infidelity where they set this brother up by putting this fine ass naked woman in his hotel room. Then the next day they showed the videotape of them having sex to his wife. Can you imagine? Now you know she flipped. But the fucked-up thing is if you'd seen his ugly ass wife, you woulda went for the woman in the hotel room, too. What the fuck did they expect?

"Well, we're doing a show on deadbeat dads. And your child's mother, Michelle, called and told us about how you walked out of the delivery room."

"Ah, hell no! First of all, that's not my baby! Secondly, I'm not a deadbeat dad. If that baby were mine, I'd be taking care of him. But he's not mine."

"So why don't you come on the show? We'll give you a paternity test and you can prove you're not the father. Settle this thing once and for all. Give your side of the story."

"What, do you think I'm stupid? I know what time it is. I get on your show and prove I'm not the baby's father and you gonna have some other reason to embarrass me. I ain't stupid. I watch your show."

"It's not like that," he insisted.

"Yeah, right. Look, I'm not going on your show, aw'ight?"

I was about to hang up when he said, "What if we pay you five thousand dollars?"

"Five grand! You're willing to pay me five grand to come on your show?"

"We sure are." I could see that motherfucker smiling through the phone.

"Ah, hell no! Now I know I'm not going on your show, 'cause if you're willing to pay me that five grand, there's more to this than meets the eye." On that note, I hung up, deciding that it was time for me to pay Michelle a visit.

15

Wil

"Well, tell her I hope she feels better. Take care of yourself, Jim."
I hung up the phone and looked across the dinner table grimly at
my wife. My kids had already eaten and were watching TV. Di
and I were supposed to be having a conversation about our relationship but as usual, the second I think she's about to open up
to me, the kids call us, somebody knocks on the door or the
phone rings. This time it was the husband of my secretary Marge
calling.

"What is it, Wil? What's the matter?"

"That was Jim St. John. Marge fell down the stairs going into
her apartment building."

"Oh, my God. Is she all right?" Diane's face was full of concern.

"Yeah, Jim says she's all right, but she broke her arm again."
I frowned.

"Jesus, I love Marge, but is she clumsy or *what*? Every time
you turn around she's falling down and breaking something."

"No. Jim said this time she was pushed. Some woman was
running out her building trying to catch a cab and accidentally
pushed her down the stairs."

"Oh, no." Diane frowned. "Does that mean your *friend*
Mimi's still gonna be your secretary?"

"Probably." Diane's voice was filled with contempt and it was
obvious Marge was the least of her concerns, but a small smile
came to my face when I thought about how nice it would be to
continue working with Mimi.

"I'm glad you're happy about it." Diane rolled her eyes.

"What is your problem with Mimi, anyway? I mean damn,
Di. The woman apologized for calling the house so early. What
else do you want from her?"

"I just don't like her, Wil," she told me adamantly. "There's something about her that just makes me uncomfortable."

"Oh, my God." I threw my hands in the air. "What are you talking about? You've never even met the woman."

"And I don't want to."

"How can you say that, Di? That's so closed-minded."

"I'm not closed-minded, Wil. I just think this woman is trying to get with my husband."

"Where the hell is this coming from?" I mean, shit, other than the phone call that Mimi had already apologized for, what reason did Di have to be so suspicious?

"I'm not stupid, Wil. You've changed ever since this woman started to work for you. Growing a mustache, buying new cologne, working overtime. You don't even hang out with your friends Kyle and them anymore."

"Oh, ain't this some shit! I don't hang out with them because you don't want me to. You're the one always complaining about me being out too late when I'm with them. And as far as work is concerned, it's our busy season. I always work overtime during busy season. You know that. You used to work for the company."

"You just don't get it, do you?"

"No, you don't get it. The reason I grew a mustache and bought new cologne is to impress you. Just like I took you out to dinner and bought you that bracelet the other day. I want this to work, Diane. I'm just trying to get things back to where they were, so we can be happy."

"You sure you're not doing it outta guilt?" She stared at me with contempt.

"Guilt! Are you crazy?" I threw my napkin on my plate. She'd hit a nerve. "The only one who should be feeling guilty around here is you. You haven't had sex with me in months, Diane. Way before Mimi even started working for me. So let's not talk about fucking guilt, 'cause if you do, start with yourself, sister." I was livid.

Just then the doorbell interrupted our conversation.

"I'll get it," Diane said, obviously looking for a reason to change the subject. I don't think she expected me to come on so strong.

"No, I'll get it!" I raised my voice and she froze in her seat. "You put the kids to bed, 'cause we have a lot to talk about tonight." I got up from the table without another word and walked to the door, agitated. When I opened it there was a guy holding a big bouquet of roses.

"Can I help you?"

"I've got a delivery for Diane Duncan."

"I'll take it." I signed for the flowers and carried them into the kitchen. I placed the vase on the table wondering who had sent my wife roses. I was tempted to open the card but I knew I'd be wrong if I did, so I waited for Diane. I must have sat there for twenty minutes before I realized she wasn't coming down. Finally, I picked up the vase and went upstairs. Diane was dressed in her nightgown, about to go to bed. It looked like she'd been crying.

"Are you gonna tell me what's wrong with you?" I asked with probably a little less feeling than I should have.

"Nothing's wrong, Wil. Who was that at the door?"

"The florist. Someone sent you flowers."

"They did? Who?" Diane's voice kind of perked up as I handed her the vase.

"I don't know. Open the card." She placed the vase on her dresser and smiled at me. Did she think I'd sent her the flowers?

"Oh, that's sweet."

"What's sweet?"

"This card from the mailman." She handed me the card.

> *Thanks for everything. You make*
> *coming over to deliver the mail worth-*
> *while. I can't wait until tomorrow.*
> *See you then. XOXOXO*

"What the fuck is the mailman sending you roses for? And what did he mean, thanks for everything? He can't wait till tomorrow? XOXOXO!"

"Oh, he's probably just talking about the Christmas envelope I gave him. You know people in this neighborhood are cheap. We're probably the only ones who gave him anything and he's grateful."

"We only gave him twenty-five dollars. He spent more money on having these roses delivered than you put in the envelope." Something was not right about this, and Diane was acting nonchalant about the whole thing.

Diane shrugged. "You know mailmen get around. Maybe he knows the florist?"

Maybe he knows a hell of a lot more than I know, I thought.

"What's up, Diane? What's going on with you and the mailman?" The look on my face said whatever my words didn't.

"Don't go there, Wil. Don't you jump to conclusions. I'm telling you I don't know why that man sent these flowers."

"Don't go there? Why shouldn't I go there? Isn't that what you're doing with Mimi? You think I'm fucking Mimi, don't you Diane? Well, if I was, could you blame me? My wife hasn't given me any in two months and the postman's sending her flowers. What's wrong with that picture?"

She lowered her head. "I only said I thought Mimi was trying to get with my husband. I never said I thought you were fucking her." Diane crossed her arms over her chest. "But while we're on the subject. Do you find her attractive? Is she pretty, Wil?"

"Yeah, she's pretty but—" I never got to finish my sentence.

"I knew it! That's why none of my friends would tell me what she looks like!"

"Please. Don't read more into this than there is. Ain't nothing going on between me and my secretary, all right?"

"And that must bother the hell out of you, don't it?" She gave me that same contemptuous look she gave me before. "You think I don't notice that little twinkle in your eye whenever her name comes up? You wish you could get with her, don't you? Be honest, Wil!"

I took a deep breath to calm myself. "You want me to be honest, Diane? Okay, I'll be honest. There is a woman I wanna get with. Her name is Diane Duncan. She's my wife. I wanna get with her. You think you can help me with that?"

She looked like she wanted to say something but instead she burst into tears.

"Jesus Christ, Diane! What the hell is going on?"

"Just go 'head and fuck her, Wil, okay? Just fuck her and get it over with. At least that way I won't have this shit on my conscience anymore." She grabbed the flowers and left the room without saying another word.

"That's right, Diane," I yelled after her when the initial shock wore off. "Walk away! Walk away with the flowers from your boyfriend!"

I sat down on my bed and actually felt some tears run down my face. I loved Diane. I loved her more than life itself, but it appeared as if we were at the beginning of the end because she'd just admitted to having a guilty conscience, which meant she had or was having an affair.

A few minutes later I got up and went downstairs. I had no idea where Diane had gone, but her van was in the driveway so I knew she was still home. I didn't bother to look for her. I grabbed my jacket and headed out the door. When I got in my car my first instinct was to call Mimi. But after the things Diane said, my own conscience was bothering me because if I called her she might invite me over and if she invited me over . . . well who knew what could happen. So I dialed my best friend, Kyle Richmond, instead. We'd talked about my attraction to Mimi several times and each time he'd warned me to stay away from her. With me finding out Diane was cheating on me that was easier said than done. But if anyone could stop me from doing something crazy it was Kyle. Unfortunately, he wasn't home so I decided to drive over to the Roadhouse Bar and have a drink to calm my nerves.

It took me over an hour to get up the courage to get out of my car and knock on Mimi's door. I probably would have never done it at all if it wasn't for the liquid courage I drank over at the Roadhouse Bar. She'd given me an open invitation to stop by anytime but I'd never taken her up on it. I guess deep down I knew if I did, I'd be compromising my marriage. But now with everything that had happened with Diane and the mailman, I wouldn't be compromising anything that she hadn't already destroyed.

"Who is it?" Mimi's voice just seemed to get sexier every time I heard it.

"Hey, Mimi. It's Wil. I hope I'm not disturbing anything."

She opened the door right away with a smile a mile wide. "Wil? What are you doing here?"

"I just happened to be in the neighborhood. But I see you've got your coat on. If this is a bad time I can . . ."

"Don't be silly, Wil. Come on in. I've always got time for you." She took off her coat, gesturing for me to come in. I kissed her on the cheek and walked in. "Matter of fact, I was just thinking about you."

"Well, I hope it was good thoughts."

"I can say this much. I've never had a bad thought about you, Wil," she said sweetly, pointing to the sofa where we both sat down. "Can I get you a drink or something?"

"If you have some scotch I'll take some straight. If not, I'll take a beer."

"I think I have a little scotch." She walked over to the entertainment center and pulled out a bottle and two glasses.

She sat down and poured the drinks. "So what's up? What brings you to Rochdale? Visiting your sister?"

"No, I was just riding around town and needed somebody to talk to. So I thought I'd stop by."

She handed me a glass. "Well, you know I'm always here for you. What's on your mind?"

I swallowed most of what was in my glass in one gulp, then turned to her. "You were right about my wife. She is cheating on me."

"Oh, God, Wil. I'm so sorry to hear that. Are you okay?" She reached up and rubbed my back with one hand and refilled my glass with the other.

I stood up, taking another long gulp of my drink, trying to contain my emotions. "No. No, I'm not aw'ight. I'm hurt and I'm pissed. I can't believe she's done this to me. To us."

"Well, you have a right to be upset. What happened?"

I started to pace in front of her, sipping what was left of my drink.

"My wife got a dozen roses sent to her from her lover this evening."

"Get the fuck outta here!" Mimi's eyes were wide with surprise and she sat back, stunned, in her chair. "Who was it? Someone you know?"

"The fuckin' mailman. Can you believe it? I knew she was talking about that son of a bitch too much."

"Oh, Wil, I'm so sorry. God, it's just so hard to believe. Then again, I can't say I'm that surprised. She was displaying all the signs." She stood up and hugged me. "So what are you gonna do? Are you gonna leave her?"

"I don't know. I'm so confused I can't even think right now."

"Wil, you can't stay with her if she's gonna treat you like this. I mean, I know you love her but she's playing you. You said yourself if you found proof you were going to be outta there."

"You wanna know the funny part?" She nodded. "She suggested that I should sleep with you."

"She said what?" Mimi's mouth hung open.

"She probably feels so guilty about her own shit. Guess it would make her feel better if I was sleeping with you. You know, she doesn't want to be the only unfaithful one."

"But why me, Wil? She's never even met me. Why would she say me?"

Mimi looked genuinely confused. I knew Diane had been wrong about Mimi trying to get with me. But she was at least close to the mark when she said I was interested in Mimi.

"My wife thinks I have the hots for you."

Both Mimi's eyebrows shot up like rockets, and it looked like she was trying to suppress a smile. "So, do you?"

"Do I what?" I looked away. I knew what she was asking, I just didn't wanna answer.

"Do you have the hots for me?" Her smile almost made me melt.

If I said yes, I could be opening up a whole new can of worms. But the way I was feeling about my wife right now, maybe it couldn't hurt. If Mimi and I did end up sleeping together, it wouldn't be any worse than what Diane had already done to our marriage. "I know I shouldn't say it, but yeah. I do."

"Really? So why haven't you acted on it?"

"Well . . ." I was about to explain to her that being attracted and acting on it aren't nearly the same thing, especially when you're married. I could look all I wanted, but up until Di got the flowers, I always thought I could work things out in my own marriage before I had to go elsewhere. Now I wasn't so sure what I was going to do. So I was going to let Mimi know where things stood between us now that my attraction was out in the open, but my ringing cell phone interrupted the conversation.

"Hold on a second." I reached for my phone.

"Hello."

"Wil." It was my friend Kyle.

"Yeah, Kyle."

"Lisa said you called when I was out, so I called your house. Diane told me what's going on. You all right?"

"Yeah, I'm all right."

"Where you at, bro? You're not with your secretary, are you?" I guess Diane really had told him about everything, including her suspicions.

I glanced at Mimi before I lied. "Nah, I'm not over there."

"Good. Why don't you meet me at the Roadhouse before you do something stupid and lose your family?"

His words were a quick dose of reality. I was so angry at Diane that I wasn't thinking straight. If Mimi had said the word, I would've been in bed with her in a New York minute. But Kyle's words reminded me that I at least owed my family the effort to work this out. "All right. I'll be there in ten minutes." I hung up.

I could see Mimi still wanted an answer to her question. But she wasn't gonna get one now. I needed to talk to my boy. Sort things through. If I had talked to him first I never would have come over here.

"Look, Mimi, thanks for the drink, but I gotta go." I put down the glass.

"You sure? You never answered my question." She looked disappointed.

"I know. But I can't deal with this right now, Mimi. I have to get my shit together and decide if this marriage is gonna last." I turned and walked toward the door. She followed me and opened it.

"You know what, Wil? I think the real reason you never acted on your feelings is because you were afraid of what my answer would be." She placed her hands on my shoulders. "Well, this is what my answer would be." She pulled my head down toward hers and kissed me. My mouth opened for her tongue, and we stood in her doorway making out like two horny teenagers. I guess Diane was right after all. Mimi did like me.

16

Mimi

I had just taken a quick bath and dried myself off before rubbing White Diamonds lotion all over my body. Once I was all lotioned up I slipped into a sheer black negligee and posed in the mirror. I looked pretty damn good if I did say so myself. Usually I spend over an hour in the bathroom preparing myself for bed, but tonight I cut things short because I had company waiting for me in my bedroom. God, just the thought of getting some was making me moist. So I hurried into my bedroom.

"Sorry to keep you waiting." I smiled bashfully, striking another pose as I entered my bedroom. He was still lying naked in the same spot I had left him. I dimmed the lights, trying to shake off the nervousness I was feeling. When I finally calmed down I walked over to the CD player and hit the "play" button. A few seconds later Alicia Keys's "Falling" filled the room. Swaying erotically, I made my way over to the bed.

I had never been much for foreplay so I decided to take matters into my own hands. Reaching across the bed, I gently took hold of him, rubbing my thumb along his smooth, mushroom head. Little Wil was much bigger than I would have given him credit for, and all I could do was smile as I ran my hand along his long, thick shaft. He was the kinda brother a big-boned sister loved, because he had enough dick to hit it from the back or let you climb aboard and ride it from the top.

I climbed over top of him, positioning him right between my legs. Taking a long, deep breath, I closed my eyes and slid downward onto him. I couldn't help it. I moaned his name for the entire building to hear when he hit the bottom. Now that's what I call some dick.

I must have hit the right buttons, 'cause he was jumping around like a man on a mission. I rode him for the better part of twenty minutes, and I'm not ashamed to say I screamed his name quite a few more times. I'd always been a very orgasmic woman, but the way he was moving around inside me had taken me to new heights. I was on the verge of busting one of those once-every-blue-moon super nuts but unfortunately the phone rang, breaking my concentration.

"Damn it! Hold on, baby," I whispered, but he wouldn't stop and I really didn't want him to. I had to answer the phone, though, because it was probably my sister, Keisha, or her husband, Antoine. They were watching my son, Tyrell. I hadn't checked in with them since I went to pay Miss Marge a visit. I was on my way to pick him up when Wil knocked on the door. After that I completely forgot about everything else. So reluctantly I slid off him and ran into the kitchen to answer the phone, praying that he would still be in the mood when I returned.

"Hello?"

"Mimi?" It was my sister, Keisha, just like I thought.

"What you want, Keisha? Is Tyrell all right?"

"Yeah, he's fine, and what you mean what do I want? I thought you was coming to get this boy."

"To be honest with you, Keisha, something came up and I had to run out. Do you really need me to come get him right now?"

"No, it's too late now. He's in the bed 'sleep with Tony. Just bring some eggs and bacon in the morning when you come over."

Thank God, I thought.

"Maxine, you all right? You sound like you've been running or fighting. Oh, Lord. Harris isn't over there, is he?" Harris was Tyrell's father.

"No, he's not. I haven't heard from him since he brought my car back the other day." I hesitated for a second, because I wanted to tease my sister and tell her what was going on. She was a pain in the ass, but we were close like that. "But if you must know, Mrs. Keisha, I'm about to hang this phone up and finish getting my groove on. Bye!" I hung the phone up and before I could count to five it was ringing again.

"Hello?"

"Maxine Natasha Graves, don't you hang this phone up like

that without telling me who's over there." I loved it when I had her dangling on a string. "Now who is it?"

"If I told you, you wouldn't believe me, anyway."

"Dear Lord, it's your new boss, isn't it? What's his name? Wil?" Keisha exhaled through the phone. I let my silence be my answer, but my grin was so big she could probably see it through the phone. "Mimi, what is wrong with you? Aren't you ever gonna learn from your mistakes?"

My smile turned upside down. "What do you mean, what's wrong with me? I thought you liked Wil."

"I did until I found out he was married."

"Who told you that?" I hated when Keisha snooped around my business. Unfortunately she made a habit of it.

"Don't act like you didn't know. Antoine told me he saw Wil's wedding ring when he dropped you off last week."

"Okay, yeah, I know he's married, but so what? He's gettin' a divorce."

I could hear Keisha sigh skeptically. "And you believe him?"

"Yeah," I said weakly. "Why shouldn't I?"

"What are you, the stupidest woman in Queens? Damn, Mimi, didn't you learn anything after what happened with Philip? Leave these married men alone."

"I don't wanna talk about Philip, Keisha."

"Okay, then, let's talk about this Wil. He told you he was getting a divorce?"

"No, but I know he is. Trust me, Keisha. His wife's a real bitch. You know, she won't even have sex with him. As fine as that man is, she won't have sex with him."

"I can see why, if he's fooling around with his secretary. She's probably worried about catching something. Are you using protection?"

I got silent. I never even thought about using protection.

"Oh, my God. Maxine, this is not a good idea. That man is going to hurt you."

"No, he's not, Keisha! His wife is the one who's gonna be hurt. He's going to love me. And you're wrong. This is a good idea. I never felt like this about anyone before. You should see the way he looks at me. The man wants me and I want him. Why shouldn't we be together?"

"Because the man's married, Maxine. That's why."

"So what? You never know. Maybe his wife will have an accident and die like Philip's wife." The line went silent for a second and I was afraid she'd hung up.

"Don't play, Maxine. That's nothing to play with. You hear me? People don't just have accidents."

"That's not what the Nassau County D.A. said," I told her confidently.

"Maybe, but you still didn't get Philip, did you?"

"Fuck you, Keisha."

"Look, have you been taking your medicine? Maybe I should call Doctor Stanley."

"Will you stop with this medicine shit? I'm sick of you always trying to tell me to take my medicine. I don't need that medicine. I'm not sick. I'm just in love. God, why can't you stop hatin' and just be happy for me?"

"I'm not hating, Maxine. I'm worried. I'm worried that you're making more out of your relationship with Wil than it is. I'm worried that your mind is playing tricks on you like it did before, and you're confusing a one-night stand with a long-term commitment."

"I don't wanna hear that shit. If you don't have nothin' good to say then don't say nothin' at all."

I hung up the phone and walked back into the bedroom, shutting the door. I could hear the phone ringing in the background, then Keisha's voice on the answering machine begging me to pick up. I wasn't about to go back and answer it. I had shit to do. I was still horny and was hoping Wil was, too. Unfortunately, he was far from being turned on. He was lying on the bed motionless, probably pissed off that I just jumped up without a word. I walked over to the bed and shook him.

"Wil, come on, baby. Get up. I'm sorry. Momma wants some more."

He didn't even budge. Damn, I should have never left him turned on like that. I should have just handled my business and called my sister back later when we were finished. At least then I wouldn't have to go buy new batteries. I looked down at the new lifelike vibrator that I'd affectionately named Little Wil and threw it across the room.

My sister was right about one thing. I needed to take my medication, because my mind was playing tricks on me. For a while there I thought I was with Wil and not some battery-operated rubber toy. I still don't understand why the real Wil left me to go be with his friend after the way I kissed him. I mean, damn, it was obvious he liked it. Didn't he understand that we were meant to be? That I was sick of playing with toys and wanted the real thing?

No, it wasn't his fault. I couldn't blame this on him, not after the way he kissed me tonight. It was his wife's fault. She was the one who was in my way. As long as she was in the picture he'd never be able to concentrate on us without worrying about her. So it was time to take her out the picture. I walked over to my dresser and picked up a photo of Wil and his wife that I'd stolen from his desk. I ripped the picture in half so that the two of them were separated. First I taped Wil's half to my mirror, then I took out a lighter and lit his wife's half on fire.

Watching her disappear into flames I whispered, "Good-bye, Diane. I'll take good care of Wil and the kids."

17

Trent

It had been a long time since I'd been to Michelle's house in Hollis, Queens. It felt strange walking up her steps and knocking on the door, because at one time I had a key. Back then I came and went as I pleased and nobody questioned me.

"Who is it?" Michelle's mother asked through the door.

"It's Trent, Mrs. Williams. Is Michelle home?"

"Who?" she yelled back.

"It's Trent!" I repeated a little louder.

"That's what I thought you said!" The door flew open after a few more seconds, and there was Michelle's mother, Rita, holding a black cast-iron frying pan.

"What the fuck do you want, you no good piece o' shit? If you don't get off my steps, I'm gonna bust your head wide open!" Rita spat angrily, backing me down the steps as she waved the frying pan. Both her tone and her attitude surprised the hell outta me because Rita and I had been real close after Michelle's father died four years ago. Hell, I paid for his funeral. Well, at least this married woman I was messing with did. The way Rita was pointing and flaring at me with that frying pan, you woulda thought she wanted me dead. Then again, maybe she did. I guess she didn't take very well to me leaving her daughter in that delivery room alone that night.

"How you doing, Mrs. Williams? How has life been treating you?" I tried to act polite as I backed away from her. I mean, after all, she did have a reason to be upset with me. But I was coming over there to get all that straightened out. So that she and everybody else would leave me alone.

"Don't you, 'how you doing' me, you son of a bitch. Not after what you put my baby through." She swung the frying pan and hit the railing on the steps. It echoed loudly, and I was glad she'd connected with the steps instead of me.

"Now, Mrs. Williams, why don't you put down that frying pan before someone gets hurt?" I had to jump away in a panic as she swung again. "Someone like me!"

"Git your ass off my property!"

I scrambled to her gate, opened it and ran through. I closed the gate behind me just in time. Rita stood on one side huffing and puffing while I stood on the other side, watching the frying pan.

"What you doing here, Trent?" She was trying to catch her breath.

"I came to see Michelle. Is she home?"

"What you want with her? I'm not gonna let you break my baby's heart again. You hear me?"

"I'm not trying to break her heart, Mrs. Williams. Honest. I'm just here because she asked me to stop by." Rita glanced at me skeptically. It's funny, now that she stopped trying to beat my head in with that frying pan, I could see Michelle in her mother. Rita was an attractive woman to be in her fifties and she and her daughter both had the same hazel eyes that attracted me to Michelle in the first place.

"You know, Trent, I used to like you. I used to like you a lot. But what you did to my baby in that delivery room was the coldest thing I've ever seen. Your own momma talks bad about you."

"Well, Mrs. Williams, I'm sorry you and Momma feel that way. But Michelle knows the deal. She knows that baby's not mine."

"That baby's name is Marcus and he is your son." I could see the anger in her eyes as she tightened her grip on the frying pan. So I took a step back, keeping myself at arm's distance from her. "Go on and get outta here, Trent, before I knock you in the head with this thing. Michelle don't need you. You already said the baby ain't yours. Besides, she's got a new boyfriend now and a new life."

"I need to see Michelle, Mrs. Williams," I told her defiantly.

"I'm not letting you on my property."

"Then call her out here. What I got to say won't take long." I guess she could see I wasn't going away easily, because she turned toward the house and yelled, "Michelle! Michelle! Get out here!"

"Damn, Momma, you ain't gotta yell. You gonna wake up the b —" When Michelle poked her head out the doorway she stopped dead in her tracks, then pointed. "What's he doing here?"

Rita looked at her daughter, then turned to me. "He said you told him to stop by."

"No! I told him to come see his son. And that was almost a month ago."

"He just told me Marcus isn't his son." Rita twisted her lips as she rolled her eyes.

"Yeah, well, Momma, Trent says a lot of things but we both know he's *full o' shit*. Now come on up here and watch Marcus for me while I talk to his daddy."

"Don't you come on my fucking property! You hear?" Rita waved the frying pan at me, then walked toward her daughter, trying to shove it in her hand. "Here, if he lays one foot on my property, knock his ass out. And don't let him leave without giving you some money."

"I don't need that, but don't worry. He gonna give me some money," Michelle stated flatly before she approached me.

She might not have come near me if she'd noticed the way I'd been staring at her ever since she poked her head out the door. And the closer she got the more I couldn't keep my eyes off her. I hadn't seen Michelle in over eight months and just the sight of her brought back feelings I'd been trying to suppress. I felt like a little kid. There was something about that girl that just did things to me. Like Big Mike said, "You know you love her." I guess deep down, I really did.

"What the fuck do you want, Trent? And why you staring at me like that?" I guess she did notice.

I took a breath, trying to retain my cool composure. "I forgot how pretty you were, Michelle. Motherhood agrees with you."

She sucked her teeth. "Yeah, well I wish fatherhood agreed with you. Did you bring any money for your son?" She placed one hand on her hip and the other one out like she wanted me to put money in it. She really was insistent on this son crap, wasn't she? "I brought some money to take you out. Why don't we head over to Ghetto Seafood? They're having Lobsterfest."

"Nigga, please!" She sucked her teeth. "I got a man. And he's about to come over here and take me out to City Island, not some cheap ass Red Lobster. Now, can I have some money for your son?" She stuck her hand out again.

"You're not going out with that chump ass Ray, are you?"

"The only chump I see is the one who's not taking care of his baby. Any idea who that could be?" She smirked.

"Michelle, Ray is just using you."

"Please, Trent. Let's not talk about using people. You used me for years."

"I ain't use you," I replied adamantly.

"Yes, you did, Trent. You cheated on me our entire relationship. I was just too stupid to see it. Love will do that to you sometimes."

"Michelle, I never cheated on—"

"Don't, Trent. Don't!" She lifted her hand, cutting me off. "You know the one thing you find out about a relationship once you break up with someone, Trent?"

I just stared at her. I didn't answer 'cause I didn't know what the fuck she was talking about.

"Dirt! You find out all the dirt. All the dirt nobody wanted to tell you because they didn't wanna hurt your feelings or didn't think you'd believe them or didn't wanna get involved because they didn't think you cared. The funny thing is, even though you're broken up with the person, it hurts even more because you realize how stupid you were."

"Michelle, I never cheated on you. Them people out there are just hating. And I'm telling you, that nigga Ray, he's gonna fuck you over. He's no good."

"Well, at least he brings Pampers when he comes by. I don't see you with anything in your hands."

"I don't give a damn how many diapers he brings over!" I pointed a finger at her. "I'm not gonna let him fuck over my girl!"

"Your girl?" Her eyes got wide. "I'm not your girl! I stopped being you girl the day you walked out that delivery room."

"You're always gonna be my girl, Michelle." I took a step closer to the fence and stroked her face gently. She leaned her head in the direction of my hand. She always loved when I stroked her face. "I love you, Michelle. And you know you love me. Don't you?"

A smile flickered across her face but she quickly replaced it with a frown. "Trent, I . . ." She hesitated before continuing. "I just want you to take care of your son."

I didn't reply but I did exhale purposely, showing my frustration with her mentioning her kid.

"You should see him. He looks just like you."

"Too bad he don't look like you. 'Cause you're beautiful." I reached out and touched her face again. This time she moved her face away.

"Stop trying to flirt with me, Trent. I want you to see your son." Michelle turned toward the house. It was very obvious now that I wasn't the only one who was getting frustrated and impatient with our present conversation. "Momma, bring Marcus out here!"

"Michelle, I love you. But you know that baby's not mine."

"I'm sick of fighting with you about this, Trent. Take a look at him, then tell me he's not yours."

Rita came out the house carrying what was not such a little boy over her shoulder. I know he was eight months, but for some reason I thought he would be much smaller. Even from a distance, he wasn't as dark as I thought he was. He was more the color of a caramel than the chocolate bar I'd expected. I still hadn't seen his face until Rita handed him to Michelle, glaring at me the entire time.

"Marcus, this is your daddy." Michelle turned him toward me and I had to do a double take. That boy looked just like me. I mean he was the spitting imagine of the baby picture my mother kept on the mantel in her house.

She was right; there was no doubt about it, he was my son.

I glanced at Michelle and she smirked. "I told you he was your son."

18

Melanie

Desiree walked into the apartment at about 8:30 in the morning carrying one of her journals. I was sitting on the couch in my bathrobe, and I smiled at my roommate as she came through the door. She definitely didn't return a smile as she plopped down on the couch next to me. She took out a pack of cigarettes and offered me one.

"No thanks. I quit."

"You quit?" She looked at me and I smiled contentedly. "What the hell are you so happy about?" she asked with a pout on her face. She'd been over Tim's house the last couple days and didn't know I'd gone out with Prince last night.

"Oh, I've got my reasons." My smile widened as I thought of each and every one of them. "So what's up? What brings you home so early? Tim kick you out?" I thought I was joking, but Desiree's glare told me maybe I'd stumbled on the truth.

"Did he call here or something?"

"No. Was he supposed to?"

"Melanie, I almost went to jail a few hours ago."

"Why? What happened?" I leaned forward.

"Well, first of all, I knew something was up because after he got some this morning Tim kept asking me if I was ready to go home. He never asks me that. Usually I gotta drag his ass outta the bed or take a cab home. But he got dressed in a flash, talking about, 'Are you ready? Let's go.' Well, you know me. I took my damn time then, but he kept insisting."

"So what happened? He had a girl coming over there, didn't he?"

"Mmm-hmm. And *girl* is right. That bitch couldn't have been more than nineteen. And had the nerve to be pregnant, too." Desiree exhaled.

"Dammmmn, is it his baby?"

"It must be, 'cause that motherfucker asked me to leave. Can you believe that shit? That nigga had the nerve to ask me to leave."

"Get the fuck outta here. You lying?"

"Next time you see him, look at the scratch on his face and tell me if I'm lying." She tried to look strong but I could tell by her eyes that she was really hurt.

"You all right?"

She burst into tears and I wrapped my arms around her neck and hugged her.

"I really liked him, Mel. I was trying not to, but I was really starting to like him." Translation, *she was falling in love with him*. Something I warned her not to do. Desiree fell hard for guys fast. If you could make her come, you could make her fall in love. It was that simple. Desiree couldn't distinguish the difference between good sex and love.

"It's all right, Dez." I rubbed her back as she continued to sob. "It's gonna be his loss. He's the one who's gonna wish he had you."

"Hey, Mel?" Both Desiree and I looked up as Prince walked in the room and stopped abruptly. "Oh, excuse me. I didn't hear anyone come in." He was buttoning up his shirt. In a heartbeat, Desiree sat up and wiped away her tears.

"It's all right." I smiled. "You remember Desiree, from Manhattan Proper, don't you?"

He acknowledged her with a nod, then turned his attention back to me. "I'm about to leave, but I hope you don't mind, I straightened up your room and made up your bed. We kinda knocked some things around."

"We did, didn't we?" I glanced at Desiree who was just staring at Prince like he was the last steak in the supermarket. But that was okay. She could look as much as she wanted as long as she remembered that particular piece of steak belonged to me.

He bent over and kissed me. "I'll call you tonight, okay?"

"Sure." I got up and walked him to the door where he gave me a passionate kiss, igniting memories of last night. My God, last night. I don't think I'll ever forget last night.

We'd just returned from Russell Simmons's Def Poetry Jam

and what was supposed to be a good night kiss had turned into me being pinned against my front door with him grinding up against me until I was near orgasm. I was at that awkward stage again where I had to either send him home or invite him in.

I wasn't about to make the same mistake I'd made before. I whispered in his ear, "Would you like to come in? I have very nosy neighbors."

He nodded his head as he delicately blew in my ear, sending little tremors down my spine. He kissed me again and I reached for the door handle. We slowly backed into my apartment, not once breaking the seal of what I could honestly call the most passionate kiss of my life. The second the door was shut I could feel his strong hands slide under my skirt, lifting me up into the air. His hands were smooth and soft and I loved the way they felt against the bare skin of my ass and thighs. *Thank God for the person who invented thongs.*

"You are such a good kisser," he murmured as his tongue slid up and down my neck.

"You're not so bad yourself," I whispered, wrapping my legs around him.

He carried me to the sofa and I moaned, arching my back when his fingers gently caressed me through the thin cloth of my thong. He laid me down on the sofa. I looked up at him in almost disbelief. I was about to make love to arguably the finest man I'd ever seen. I was so excited I was shaking as I watched him unbutton his shirt, letting it fall to the floor to expose his perfect bare chest. I couldn't wait to suck on his small, protruding nipples. Guys never admitted it, but they loved that shit. And so did I.

He reached down and took hold of my right ankle and gently slipped off my red pump. Then he surprised me by sucking each one of my toes. Now, I've heard Desiree talk about shit like that, but you can't really appreciate it until you've had it done. He repeated the same thing with my other foot, then ran both his hands up along my legs and hips until he reached my waist. Gently he took hold of both my skirt and panties and slid them down past my ankles, exposing what made me a woman. He moved in between my legs and I took a deep breath, expecting him to lick me. But he bypassed my lower half to take hold of the lapels of my shirt. Then without a second of hesitation, he pulled them apart, popping all six buttons off a sixty-five dollar blouse. At that moment, I didn't give shit about that shirt.

Within seconds he'd released both my swollen breasts from my bra and was running his tongue around the outer edges of my nipples. Before I knew it he'd pressed my breasts together and had both my nipples in his mouth at the same time, driving me crazy. By this time I was moaning so loud I didn't care if the entire building heard me. I needed to release something that had been cooped up in me for months. I gently guided his head down between my legs, praying that he wasn't one of those brothers who didn't believe in oral sex. Fortunately he wasn't, and in no time his soft tongue was running along my clit sending waves of indescribable pleasure throughout my body.

"Don't stop, baby! Please don't stop! I'm about to commmm-mmmme!" He had me climaxing so hard the only parts of me on the sofa were my feet and head. And when the laws of physics finally made me collapse on the sofa I was shaking uncontrollably.

I can't begin to explain how good that felt. And that was only the beginning because as I savored the pleasures of my orgasm, Prince, unlike any other brother I'd been with, patiently held me in his arms until I recuperated. When he knew I was ready for more he slid off the sofa and stood in front of me. I watched him unbuckle his pants, letting them slide to his ankles. He stepped out of them and as he stood before me, the view was purely magnificent. Not only did he have the finest face I'd ever seen, he had the body to match. The only thing I needed to see now was what those sexy ass red boxers of his were covering up.

He must have read my mind because he didn't waste any time pulling them down and taking a step closer to the sofa. I didn't wait for an invitation. I acted just like I was AT&T. I reached out and touched someone. Prince wasn't huge, but he was big enough to do the job. And just like everything else about him, even his dick looked perfect. It was smooth and perfectly proportioned. The thing I liked about it most was that he knew how to use it.

Kneeling down on the floor, he slid in between my legs, kissing every spot of my body from my belly button to my upper lip. When his tongue slid into my mouth, his dick slid inside me, too.

The combination of his tongue and his dick made me close my eyes and moan, "Ooh-la-la," as his rhythmic strokes brought me closer and closer to my second orgasm.

"That's it, baby. That's it! Just a little bit more," I encouraged. "I'm about to come, boo. Please, please come with me!"

I don't know if he was some sort of expert or something, but he reared back and hit a spot I'd never felt before. That shit felt so good it started an orgasm that left me helpless to do anything other than close my eyes and clutch onto his back. I held on to Prince for what seemed like eternity.

"Melanie!" Desiree snapped me out of my reminiscent fantasy, waving me over to the sofa. I closed the door after I watched Prince step onto the elevator, disappearing behind the closing doors. I smiled when I looked over at the sofa, 'cause I knew exactly what Desiree wanted.

"Melanie! Git your ass over here and tell me what the hell is going on. I thought you two weren't speaking." I walked over to the sofa and sat next to my girlfriend with a big grin. I couldn't wait to tell her every detail of what was without question the most wonderful night of my life.

19

Trent

I pulled in front of Michelle's house, and I knew there was gonna be trouble the second I saw her and that son of a bitch Ray standing on her porch, all hugged up like they were on *Love Connection.* Just the sight of him touching her pissed me off beyond belief. I'd been stopping by to see Michelle and Marcus almost every day for the past two weeks, but this was the first time Ray was there when I showed up.

I'd been trying to get Michelle to dump his ass so that we could get back together, only she wasn't having it. At least she was acting like she wasn't having it. There were plenty of times I caught her checking me out or smiling affectionately when I was playing with the baby. The last few times I was over she wouldn't even let me leave without giving her a hug. I think deep down she wanted us to be a family. And to be honest, I was starting to want that, too. I think she was just keeping Ray around for a while so that I wouldn't get too sure of myself. I bet if I showed her enough interest, she'd lose that brother in a heartbeat.

The only thing I was concerned about was that she might find out about my engagement to Indigo. I hadn't even told my mother about that, and I was a little sorry I'd mentioned it to Melanie. Not that she would blow me up on purpose, but you never know when someone's gonna slip up.

When I stepped out my car, Ray spotted me right away. That bastard had the nerve to smirk at me, then kiss Michelle like she needed CPR and he was trying to resuscitate her. At first I thought Michelle was in on his little game, but by the time they finished slobbing each other down I was standing three feet away and she jumped like hell outta his arms when she saw me.

"Trent! What are you doing here? I thought you weren't coming by till later." She was nervous.

"I was in the neighborhood and thought I'd stop by. What's he doing here?" I pointed at Ray. "I don't want this nigga around my son, Michelle."

"Trent, why you tripping?" She cut her eyes at me.

"Yeah, Trent, why you tripping?" Ray smirked again. "I'm just here to see *my* girl." He reached out and pulled Michelle closer to him, looking way too self-satisfied. I wanted to slap that smirk right off his face, but Ray was kinda nice with his hands and I didn't wanna write a check my ass couldn't cash. I wasn't scared of him but I damn sure wasn't gonna start nothing physical. I'm a lover, not a fighter.

"Your girl?" I glanced back and forth between the two of them. I was hoping Michelle wouldn't embarrass me.

He bent over and kissed her forehead. "Yeah, my girl. Isn't that right, boo?"

Michelle smiled at him weakly. It was obvious she was not comfortable with this situation at all. "Marcus is inside with Momma, Trent. Why don't you go inside? Ray's just about to leave." I nodded my head and stepped toward the house. I could've started something, but he was the one about to leave and I was the one she was letting in the house.

"Hey, Trent," Ray called to me. I turned around and faced him as he continued, "Glad to see you're no longer an absentee father. I'm proud of you, man."

He gave me that smirk again. He'd said that shit to impress Michelle, but his words meant more. Much more. What he really meant was, *glad to see you back, nigga. 'Cause now I can get this good pussy without having to take care of your sorry ass kid.*

"Thanks, Ray." I wanted to punch him in his head. "I'm just trying to follow in the footsteps of a great father like you. How many kids you got now? Is it six, or is it seven? I keep getting confused. Matter of fact, didn't LaTisha Jones just have a baby by you? Dammmmmn, that makes eight kids, doesn't it?"

"Eight!" Michelle snapped, her head in his face. "I thought you said you only had two kids."

"I do, Michelle." He shook his head adamantly, glaring at me. "That nigga's lying. LaTisha ain't had no baby by me."

"Look, man, don't get upset with me. You know how shit gets misconstrued on the street. We can always call LaTisha and find out the truth, can't we? You know LaTisha, don't you Michelle?"

"Yeah, I know her." She shot Ray an evil look and he swallowed hard. "Maybe I should give her a call when I get in the house." It's a good thing Ray didn't have a gun or my ass might've been dead.

"Don't worry, Ray. Maybe it's this other triflin' ass nigga I know." Now I was the one smirking.

"Triflin'? Nigga, I'll kick your ass." He took an aggressive step toward me. I took a step back.

"See, Michelle? See?" I continued to instigate. "Is that the kind of man you want around *our* son? Always trying to settle things with his fists."

"No, that's not the kinda man I want around my son. Ray, relax. You started this by calling him an absentee father. I told you to stay outta my business." Michelle spoke calmly, trying to soothe his ego even though she was obviously blaming this shit on him. That's just what I'd hoped she'd do, but I never expected him to flip on her.

"What? I know you not taking his side. After what he's put you through? You the trifling one. He's coming over here like he's king shit. Where was he when you needed him? Nowhere to be fucking found. I was the one helping you out."

"You don't have to throw it in my face, Ray. I know you helped me. But Trent's my son's father and you're gonna respect him or you gonna have to bounce." Her voice wasn't so calm now.

"Respect him? For what? He don't respect me. And he damn sure don't respect *you*! I bet he didn't tell you he was engaged, did he?"

Uh-oh! This nigga was about to blow me up!

"Engaged?" Michelle spun around and I knew I was in trouble. "Who are you engaged to, Trent?" I couldn't answer. I was too busy trying to figure out how Ray knew.

"Yeah, he's engaged. He engaged to some chick that hit the Pick Five." It was time for quick thinking and drastic measures.

"Is that true, Trent? Are you engaged?" Michelle looked hurt. I know what she was thinking. I'd been with her for ten years and never even brought up the subject of marriage.

"How the fuck can I be engaged when I came over here to ask you to marry me?"

"Yeah, right. Get the fuck outta here," Ray snapped with a laugh.

"Oh, yeah? Well, I got the ring in my pocket. I was just waiting to talk to Michelle in private."

"Stop lying. Where's the ring, then? Let me see it," he challenged.

I reached in my pocket and pulled out the ring that I'd just purchased less than an hour ago. It was supposed to be for Indigo. I'd promised her she'd have a ring on her finger tonight. "Right here." I opened the box and walked toward Michelle.

"Oh, my God, Trent. It's beautiful. Can I see it?"

I handed her the box.

"Is this for real? Do you really wanna marry me?"

"He don't wanna marry you. He just don't wanna see us together."

Ray was right about that. I didn't wanna see them together, but there was one thing he didn't know. Hell, I didn't even know it till recently. In my own crazy way, I was in love with Michelle.

"Trent, do you really wanna marry me?"

I nodded my head, then said some things I didn't even know I'd been feeling till right then. "Look Michelle, I know I fucked up. But you and me, we got history. And we got a son who deserves to have a mother and a father who share the same last name. This chump's not gonna offer you that. Are you, Ray?"

We both turned toward Ray who had this stupid ass look on his face. "Michelle, this nigga's trying to trick your ass."

"Maybe he is, Ray. But he's right about one thing. My son needs a family. You said yourself you're just trying to take this one day at a time." She paused and took a long look at me, then at Ray. "Look, I know you gotta go to work. Why don't you give me a call during your break? I need to talk to Trent alone." She didn't kiss him. She barely hugged him before she walked toward the house. She was still holding Indigo's ring. "Trent, you coming?"

"Yeah, baby, I'm coming." I wanted to smirk at Ray as I walked in the house. But reality set in. If Michelle accepted my proposal, I was in trouble. Big trouble. 'Cause not only was I gonna be engaged to *two women,* but I was one ring short and I'd promised Indigo I'd have her ring tonight.

20

Wil

I'd been sitting in my car about two blocks from my house for the past couple hours, waiting for the mailman. I'd spent the night at my boy Kyle's house at his insistence. We'd stayed up talking about Mimi and Diane most of the night. He thought I needed to cool off, then go home and talk to my wife. I think he was afraid that if I left his house last night I was going to go back to Mimi's and sleep with her. After the way she kissed me, and the resentment I was feeling toward Diane, he was probably right. So I left my friend's house this morning determined to confront both my wife and her lover about their affair.

I finally spotted the mailman in my rearview mirror pushing his little cart down the block. The first thing that came to my mind was why the hell was Diane fucking with him. He wasn't all that. Yeah, he had a handsome face and curly hair like he was from Trinidad or something, but he was short and skinny. Nothing like I expected. I'd always been under the impression Diane liked tall men, like me. If she was going to cheat, I'd think her dream man would be a mixture of Denzel Washington, Billy Dee Williams and Michael Jordan all in the same body, not this little nothing of a man I was looking at.

My cell phone rang and I lifted it up off my seat, never letting my eyes leave the rearview mirror and the postman.

"Hello?"

"Wil." It figured it was Diane.

"What, Di?"

"Where are you? I called your office and your *secretary* said you hadn't come in yet. And Kyle said you left his house three hours ago." How the hell did she know I was at Kyle's?

"What's wrong, Diane? Worried that I'm going to double back on you and catch you in the act with your little boyfriend?"

"Wil, he's not my boyfriend. I barely know the man."

"Yeah, right. Whatever. Now all of a sudden you don't know him. Did you forget you admitted it last night? Did you forget he sent you flowers?"

"No, I didn't. Look, we gotta talk. Can you come home?"

"I'm about to do something, Diane."

"Well, when you finish whatever you're doing, can you come home so we can talk? It's important, Wil."

"Sure, Diane. When I finish what I'm doing I'll definitely be home to talk to you."

I hung up the phone and placed it back on the seat just as the mailman passed my truck. I started it up and pulled up next to him. I was driving the same speed he was walking, and when he headed up a walkway to deliver the mail I stopped the truck and waited for him to continue down the block. After we repeated this for about four or five houses his nervousness was all over his face. Not that I cared. That was his problem. You don't fuck with a man's wife and let him find out about it.

"Hey," I yelled, rolling down my truck window when he stopped at the sixth house. "You know who I am?"

"Did you say something to me, sir?" That motherfucker had the nerve to be polite.

"Yeah, I said something to you! Do you know who I am?" I pulled the truck over to the side of the road. He walked up nervously to the car and looked in.

"No, sir. I don't know who you are."

"Oh, you don't? Well let me introduce myself." I jumped out the car and sprinted around to the sidewalk where he was standing. "I'm the motherfucker whose wife you're fucking!"

"Oh, shit!" He no longer looked nervous, he looked scared as he took two steps backward. He reached for the can of Mace he had attached to his belt. But he was so scared I easily knocked it out of his hand. My next move was a right hand to his face that knocked him to the ground, spurting blood all over both of us.

"Please, mister, don't hurt me. Your wife was coming on to me. I didn't even know you were still together until last week. She told me you were separated."

"Separated, my ass! I'ma separate your head from your neck

if I find out you been fucking with my wife again! Do you hear me?" I kicked him in his ribs. "I said do you hear me?"

"Yeah, I hear you, Mr. Reynolds!" He was curled into the fetal position. "I'm sorry. I won't mess with her no more."

"Mr. Reynolds? My name ain't Reynolds." I pulled my foot back again.

"I'm sorry. Please don't kick me again," he pleaded as he tried to squirm away from me. "I thought you had the same last name as Ruth."

I was about to say, "I do," when a very frightening thought hit me. He'd just called Diane, Ruth and me, Mr. Reynolds. I had a neighbor who lived five houses down whose name was John Reynolds and his wife's name was Ruth. This motherfucker might not be talking about my wife at all. Then again, maybe he thought he was a playboy and was screwing all the wives in the neighborhood.

"Who else's wife are you fucking around here? You know, I gotta lot of friends in this neighborhood. You could get your ass kicked every day."

I pretended like I was gonna kick him again and he screamed his answer in anticipation of the blow. "Nobody! I'm not fucking with nobody else's wife. Just Ruth. I'm sorry, man! I'm sorry!"

"You liar! I bet you fucking with half the wives in the neighborhood." I kicked him again, but not as hard as before.

"I'm not lying. I swear!" he cried out.

"What about my friend's wife, Diane Duncan over on 234th Street? Do you know her?"

"Yeah, that's the lady with the two kids. She's always planting flowers in her yard."

"What about her? You fucking her?"

"Hell, no! She's too big for me." I kicked him again for calling my wife fat.

"So why did you send her flowers last night?"

"I ain't send her no flowers. I swear to God. Tell your friend, I ain't send her no flowers. I got enough trouble dealing with your wife." The desperation in his voice made me believe him. But if he didn't send the flowers, who the fuck did?

"Stay away from my wife," I told him with very little enthusiasm. "You hear me?"

"Man, I'm not fucking with that lady no more. I'm gonna change my route and everything. I don't care what she says."

"You do that!" I jumped back in my truck, praying he didn't write down my plate number or something.

21

Mimi

"Damn it!" I slammed the phone down on my desk in frustration. I'd been trying to get in touch with Wil ever since Diane called this morning, but every time I called his cell it went straight to voice mail, which meant he'd turned it off. But why? Was it his wife he didn't wanna speak to or was it me?

It had to be Diane. She'd probably been blowing up his phone. His voice mailbox was full and Wil's the type who always checked his messages. I bet he didn't even go home last night after he went to see his friend. Why else would she be interrogating me on the phone? She was trying to find out if he'd been to work or if I'd heard from him. Well, she wasn't getting any info outta me even if I had some. I bet she was pulling her hair out, trying to figure out where the hell those flowers came from, too. *Lord, Mimi girl, sending those flowers to her house was a stroke of genius.*

It's too bad Diane didn't know who she was fuckin' with. If she did, I'm sure she woulda packed up her shit and headed for the hills a long time ago. People who get in my way always seem to have accidents. And that stupid-ass, fast-healing Marge was one who could testify to that. She wouldn't be healing for quite some time from that broken arm I gave her when I pushed her down those steps. Serves her ass right. She should have stayed home and collected disability like she was supposed to.

Wil finally showed up at work about two hours later and went straight into his office. When he walked by my desk he didn't smile, smirk or anything like he usually did. It was obvious there was something wrong with him. I was sure it had something to do with his wife. That was okay, though. It was time to make him feel better, Mimi style. I grabbed a pad and pen for appearances and slipped into his office, locking the door behind me.

"Hey, handsome, I was expecting you to come back last night."

He had his back turned to me as he hung his coat in the small office closet behind his desk. "I never said I was coming back to your place last night."

"You said you'd think about it." I walked up behind him and rubbed his back tenderly. He didn't shrug me off or anything, but he didn't turn around and kiss me, either.

"Is everything all right?"

"Sure. If you call making a fool outta yourself all right, then I'm fine." When he turned around I became a stuttering fool, keeping him at arm's length. His shirt was spotted in dried blood.

"Wh-what happened?"

I swallowed hard, praying he hadn't killed or assaulted his wife. The last thing I wanted was for him to go to jail right when it looked like we might get together. If he really wanted her dead, I could have always arranged an accident.

"How'd that blood get on your shirt?"

He looked down, then shook his head as if he were angry at himself. "Shit, I forgot that was even there."

I stared at him in amazement. "Forgot it was there? Where'd it come from? Wil, please tell me you didn't do anything stupid."

"If you call beating up the mailman stupid. Then yeah, I did something stupid."

"Beat him up? Oh, God. Why?" I closed my eyes briefly.

"Why do you think, Mimi?" he spat, reaching into the closet and taking out a spare shirt. "Because I thought he was fucking my wife."

"Thought," I repeated. "You don't sound so convinced anymore."

"That's because I'm not. That man ain't fucking my wife."

"He isn't? But you said she admitted she was fooling around." This was not going according to plan and I was afraid the truth might come out.

"She did. But I can assure you she's not fucking the mailman."

"Then who? Who?" He stared at me and for a brief second I thought he knew the truth.

"I don't know, but I'm gonna find out." I took a step forward and placed my hands around his waist, no longer caring about the blood.

"Wil, why are you stirring things up? Sometimes it's better not to know." I gave him a concerned look. "I'm worried about you. Do you know you could go to jail for attacking that man?"

"Yeah, I know. And I know you're right. But I just can't shake the feeling that there's more to this story. There's gotta be." He frowned.

"Hey, cheer up. Why don't we go back to my place after work? We can figure this out together. Besides, you could use a home cooked meal. I make a mean teriyaki steak. And my sister just made me a pan of those brownies that you and Jeanie Brown like so much."

"Keisha made brownies, huh?" He smiled for the first time just as the phone rang. "Can you get that please? I wanna change my shirt."

I nodded my head, releasing his waist before I picked up the phone. "Sales department, Wil Duncan's line. How can I help you?"

I smiled as I watched him remove his shirt. Tonight he was gonna remove a hell of a lot more than that shirt.

"This is Mrs. Duncan. Is Wil in yet? It's an emergency." I was tempted to say no and hang up the phone. 'Cause I knew the only emergency she had was that she thought she was going to lose Wil to me. And she was right.

"Please hold." I hit the hold button. "It's your wife. She's been calling every half hour since nine. She says it's an emergency. You want me to tell her you're not here?"

"Nah, give me the phone." I handed it to him right after he slipped into his new shirt. He sighed like she was nothing more than an annoyance before he said, "What, Di?"

Whatever Diane said next must not have been good news because his grim face became grimmer. He shouted, "Is he okay?" Then he mumbled, "Thank God." He listened for a while longer, then said, "Tell him Daddy's gonna be right there. I'll meet you in the emergency room." He listened again. "I know. I know this is not your fault." He hesitated, taking a deep breath, then releasing it. "Yeah, I love you, too."

Hearing him say those words was like taking a punch in the stomach from Mike Tyson. How could he say that? She didn't love him and he didn't love her. We were the ones in love. God, I hated the way he patronized her. Why didn't he just tell her the truth, that he wanted to be with me.

"I gotta go," he said sadly after hanging up the phone.

"What happened?"

He got up from his chair. "My little boy Teddy fell off the swing set. He's hurt pretty badly. The paramedics said his leg might be broken and he may have a concussion."

"Oh, no, Wil. I'm so sorry. Is he all right? Is he gonna be okay?" I tried to sound as overly concerned as possible. Even though I wanted to wring that little brat's neck for ruining my plans for tonight.

"I don't know. It sounds pretty serious."

"Do you want me to go with you?"

"No," he said without hesitation. "His mother and I can handle this."

Wil grabbed his coat from the closet and disappeared out the door without another word. I sat down in his chair glaring at all his family photos that I should have been in. This hospital thing was not good. Things like this brought families together, and I could not afford to have Wil and Diane get back together. So I was gonna have to come up with something that would keep them apart. Something just short of an accident.

22

Trent

"Have a seat, Trent." Big Mike gestured, but his voice sounded more like a command than a suggestion. I felt like I'd been summoned by the Mafia the way Mike, Beverly and Jasper were staring at me when I walked into the office. Mike was chewing on the end of his cigar like it was a piece of gum instead of holding it gently on the side of his mouth, savoring it like he usually does.

"What's up? Why y'all looking at me like this?"

Big Mike glanced at Beverly and Jasper and both of them walked out of the office without saying a word. When they were gone Mike stood up, staring at me like I'd just committed murder.

"You know, Trent, today I got some of the best news of my life. A friend of mine over at Aggressive Records offered us a high six-figure deal for Indigo. We're supposed to bring her over there tomorrow to see him."

"What? That's great!" I pumped my hand in the air but Mike raised his hand, quickly ending my celebration. "Yeah, I thought so, too. But then I got some bad news." He cut his eyes at me. "Some news that fucked up my whole day."

Uh-oh. What did I do now? was the first thought I had before I said, "Like what?"

"I called Indigo to tell her the good news, only she answered the phone crying. You know why she'd been crying, Trent?" He pointed an accusatory finger at me. "Because your stupid ass broke off your engagement!" He slammed his hand down on the desk and I sat back in my chair abruptly. "She says she's too upset to go to the meeting. Too upset because of you, Trent!" He said my name like it left a bad taste in his mouth.

"I didn't exactly break it off, Mike. I just didn't give her a ring like I promised. I mean, I haven't had a chance to tell you, but . . ."

He raised his hand, again with a frown. "I know. You gave Indigo's ring to Michelle. You stupid ass."

I sat up in my chair, astonished. "How the fuck did you know that? I just asked her to marry me yesterday."

"Man, this is South Queens. Don't nothin' go down without me finding out about it. Besides, your boy Ray is so pissed off he's telling the world, hoping it will get back to Indigo and blow up your spot."

"Damn. That nigga is really out to get me."

"Why the fuck did you ask Michelle to marry you? I thought we agreed you were gonna marry Indigo," he shouted. "Do you realize you're fucking up millions of dollars for us all?"

I let out a long exhale. "I hate the thought of losing all that money, Mike, but I did it because I love Michelle. You were right. Marcus is my son. You were also right when you said I love Michelle. I can't live without her, Mike." I tried to sound convincing but he laughed at me.

"Oh, you can't, huh?" He laughed again. "Well let me ask you a few questions, Mr. I Can't. How you gonna live *with* her? You ain't got no job, Trent. What you gonna do to support her and the baby? Have you ever thought of that? How you gonna live with no money?"

He was right. I never thought about the fact that I would have to support Michelle. She'd never asked me for anything until the baby was born. She'd always supported herself, or at least her momma did. Maybe Mike was right.

"I can get a job," I replied with much less conviction than I would have liked.

Mike laughed. "Doing what? McDonald's, Burger King? Shit, I hear Sears is hiring."

"I know this chick whose husband runs the Honda dealership on Hillside. She can get me a job as a salesman anytime I want."

"But you gotta fuck her, don't you?" He gave me a sinister smile when I didn't answer. "And how long you gonna keep that job when her husband finds out you fucking her ass? 'Cause you know he's gonna find out. They always do. Face it, Trent. The only job you're good at is running women. You're a gigolo, kid. Not a family man. And you're about to fuck up millions trying to be something you're not."

"But I love her, Mike. And money can't buy you love."

Mike's sinister smile widened.

"Can't it? Show me a woman who doesn't want a rich man, and I'll show you a lying ass bitch." Mike stared at me long and hard. It felt like he was trying to analyze me before he continued. "Besides, you're already in love, Trent."

"I am? With who?"

"With your lifestyle. You love the life you live, the Mercedes, the house on the water, the different women fawning over you every night. You love that shit, don't you?"

I didn't answer and he prodded me more.

"Come on, Trent. You can lie to me but you can't lie to yourself. You love the life you live. Admit it."

"Yeah, I love it," I finally admitted. "But it's not real love. If you take it away, it doesn't hurt."

"Oh, yeah? Tell me it didn't hurt when you had your car repossessed. How did you feel when you didn't think you was gonna get it back?" I didn't reply, I just listened to what he had to say. "I bet it didn't hurt that much the night you left Michelle in the delivery room, did it? What'd you do when you left the hospital that night, Trent? Go out and get some ass?" I looked away from him and smirked because that's exactly what I did. "I bet when your car got repossessed that you didn't go look for another car, did you? You just wanted the old one back. That's 'cause you love your car. Are you sure you love Michelle?"

Ouch. Now that hurt. Because as much as I wanted to think I loved Michelle, I did love my car. And Mike's words made more sense than I wanted to admit.

"I never thought of it that way before."

"There's all kinds of love, Trent. You just have to decide which one is more important." He walked around his desk and patted my back before sitting on his desk. "Now you gotta make a decision. Either you're gonna marry Indigo and be rich, or you're gonna marry Michelle and pump gas at Exxon. What's it gonna be?"

A smile came across my face for the very first time since I walked in that office. "Why can't I have them both?"

"Because we have polygamy laws in this country." He laughed. "If you could have two wives, I woulda done it a long time ago."

"Yeah, but who says I have to be married to both of them at the same time?"

Mike stared at me as he puffed his cigar. He must have seen the light go off in my brain. "What are you getting at, Trent?"

"You still got that ring your ex-wife gave you back after the divorce?"

"Yeah." Mike nodded. "I still got it. Why?"

"Because I need it. It's worth a million dollars to us."

"It is?"

"It sure is. Right after I give it to Indigo."

"But I thought you said you're not gonna marry them both."

"I said I'm gonna marry them both. I am. I just never said anything about marrying them at the same time." A smile came across Mike's face as he started to understand where I was coming from. "You see, right now Michelle is content just to have a ring. I can probably string an engagement out two, maybe three years."

Mike's eyes lit up. "Right! I get it. You marry Indigo now, stay married to her at least a year or two. Then you're entitled to half of everything she's made, plus a share of her future earnings." Mike's smile widened. "Now you're acting like the Trent I know. Only one problem. How you gonna keep Michelle from finding out about Indigo and vice versa?"

"Simple. I'm gonna move Indigo to Atlanta. I'm gonna give her some bull about how all the top singers are moving there and how you can get a house cheap. Trust me, she won't be hard to convince."

"What about Michelle? Is she gonna give you a hard time about being in Atlanta?"

"Nah. Michelle's used to me being in and out. I'll just tell her I'm in Atlanta a lot on business. If I hit her off with some money each month and tell her it's to go toward a down payment on a house she'll be cool. Women always go for that security shit."

"I gotta tell you, Trent. I was worried about you there for a minute. I thought you were getting soft on me. But this plan, this plan is brilliant."

23

Wil

The second I pulled in the driveway Diane jumped out the car and ran in the house, leaving me to carry my son, Teddy, upstairs and put him to bed. We'd spent about five hours in the emergency room and barely said anything to each other that didn't pertain to Teddy. I guess Diane's conscience was still bothering her. And now after what happened at Mimi's last night, mine was bothering me, too. Although I must admit part of me just wanted to think up an excuse to get out the house so I could go see Mimi. The last thing I wanted to do was be in the same house alone with Diane.

I kissed my son good night, then said a quick prayer of thanks. Teddy had come out of this with just a nasty black eye and a fractured wrist. I was really scared there for a while. Originally the doctors were trying to get us to let him spend the night because they thought he had a concussion.

I left my son's room, then stepped into my daughter's room. She was already asleep so I assumed my sister, Melanie, must have put her to bed hours ago. Thank the Lord for Mel. It was times like this that you really needed family, and she always came through. She'd left work early and had gone to my neighbor's house to get Katie right after Diane called her and told her what happened.

I kissed my daughter, then went downstairs to offer my sister a lift so I could get out the house. Just as I walked past the bathroom, Diane came out. The two of us stared at each other without a word until she broke our silence.

"Is he 'sleep?" She walked over and, surprisingly, wrapping her arms around my waist, sighed deeply. It felt so good to be held by her. I wanted to hold her and stroke her hair but I couldn't.

She may have forgotten what happened last night but I sure as hell didn't.

"Yeah, he's 'sleep. So is Katie."

"Good," she whispered, then pressed her head against my chest as she held on to me tighter. This time I gave in and wrapped my arms around her.

"Wil," she whispered, "I'm not fooling around with the mailman."

"I know that, Di," I answered back.

She lifted her head and looked up at me with surprise. "You do?"

"Yeah, me and the mailman had a little talk this morning."

"You did?" Her eyes widened.

"Uh-huh. But what I wanna know is, if he didn't send those flowers, who did?"

She reached for my hand and gently caressed it as she stared in my eyes. "I honestly don't know."

I pulled away from her with a scowl on my face. "Come on, Diane. Do you really expect me to believe that? Now I wanna know who you're having an affair with. And I wanna know now."

"Wil, I'm telling you the truth. I'm not having an affair."

"Yeah, right. What you're telling me is a bunch of bull!" I rolled my eyes. "I thought you said you had a guilty conscience."

"I do have a guilty conscience," she said quietly. "I've had one for quite a while now. But it's not about cheating. It's about . . ." She stopped herself in mid sentence. "It's just hard. It's just hard to admit."

"Admit what, Di? That you're fooling around? I already know that, I just wanna know who it is."

She looked up at me with these sad eyes, filling up with tears just as my sister turned the corner.

"Hey, guys, do you need me to do anything for you before I go home?" Melanie stopped in her tracks when she saw the two of us standing there. She glanced back and forth between me and Di. "What's going on? Diane, why you crying? I thought the doctors said Teddy was going to be all right."

"This isn't about Teddy, Mel. This is something personal between me and my wife," I explained.

"Well," said Mel, "I know you two must be going through a rough time right now. Is there anything I can do to help? I can take the kids for a while so you all can spend some time alone. As long as you don't mind if Prince stops by."

"There's nothing you can do, Mel, unless you can tell me who my wife's been cheating with." I couldn't hide the disgust in my voice when I thought about my wife's betrayal.

"Cheating?" Melanie shouted at me. "Have you lost your mind?" Then she looked over at Diane who hadn't said a word since Melanie approached us.

"Oh, my God. You haven't told him yet, have you?" she asked Diane.

"No." Diane sounded so sad.

"Tell me what?" I demanded.

"Jesus, Diane!" Melanie said. "No wonder the man is acting all funny. Wil, your wife is sick."

I looked at Diane. "What is she talking about, Di? What's wrong with you?"

Diane's voice was so weak when she finally answered me. She couldn't even look me in the eye. "I've been to see the gynecologist a few times already." She started to cry. "Wil, I have to have a hysterectomy."

"Hysterectomy? Oh, my God. Baby, what's wrong?" I pulled Diane toward me and wrapped her in my arms. My anger was now concern.

Diane was so upset she couldn't even answer me, so Melanie told me, "She has severe fibroids."

"Fibroids? What does that mean?" I was confused and starting to get scared.

"Fibroids are tumors," Diane answered between tears. "I've got one the size of a grapefruit in my uterus. That's why I haven't been having sex with you, Wil. It's just too damn painful and I'm always bleeding."

I closed my eyes briefly. Silently scolding myself. It was all starting to make sense. My poor wife had been suffering this whole time and I'd only been making matters worse. "Is it cancerous?"

"No. It's benign."

"How long have you known?"

"I've known something's been wrong for about three months. I found out about the fibroids about a month ago."

"Why didn't you tell me, Di? You know I would have stuck by you."

"I tried, Wil. I must have tried a dozen times but each time I'd stop myself because I was afraid you'd look at me as less than a woman."

"Diane, I love you. I could never look at you as anything other than my woman." I held her tight. "Come on. I need you two to explain everything you know about these fibroids."

It was after three in the morning when I finally went to bed. I'd dropped my sister off at her new boyfriend's and came home. Diane was 'sleep so I got on the Internet and started to research fibroids. It was a real eye-opener because I had no idea so many black women were affected by them. Hell, I didn't even know what they were until tonight. I wanted, no I needed more information. I even ordered a book called *It's a Sistah Thing* by a woman named Monique R. Brown, to learn more about my wife's condition. I wasn't about to let Di have a hysterectomy if she didn't have to.

When I finished my search on the computer I went upstairs and got in bed.

"Wil," Diane whispered. I was surprised she was up.

"Yeah, Di?"

"Come here. I want you to hold me." She grabbed my hand and pulled me up close to her. I wrapped my arms around my wife and snuggled up close, stroking her hair. "Wil, I have no idea who sent those flowers."

"Neither do I, Di. But those flowers were no worse than the pictures so let's forget about them."

"I love you, Wil Duncan."

"I love you too, Di. And I'm gonna stick by you no matter what. We can do this, we've been through rougher times before. We just have to stick together."

"I know that now, Wil, and I'm sorry I didn't tell you all this before."

"You don't have to apologize anymore, Di. It's all right, but no more secrets. Okay? We're a team and there's no I in the word *team*."

"You're right," she replied as we snuggled up closer. "Wil?" she whispered.

"Yeah, babe?"

"Did you sleep with her?"

"Who?"

"Your secretary. Did you sleep with her last night? Or any other night? You can tell me. I'm not gonna get mad."

"No. I didn't sleep with her." I could feel her let out a long sigh of relief. "But . . . but I'm not gonna lie to you, Di. I did kiss her."

There was a silence between us. "Do you wanna be with her, Wil? If you do I'll let you go."

"No, Di. The only woman I wanna be with is you."

"Then you know she's gotta go. If we're gonna survive, she has got to go. You understand that, don't you?"

I kissed her neck. "Yeah, Di, I understand."

But the question is, will Mimi understand?

24

Melanie

"What's up, baby? You wanna dance?" I looked up at the tall, handsome brother who'd tapped me on the shoulder and smiled politely. He was probably the best-looking of the five men who'd asked me to dance. But I'd promised myself I wouldn't dance with anyone until I had a chance to dance with Prince first. Only problem was Desiree. She'd dragged Prince on the dance floor before we could even get our seats warmed up. I was starting to wish I'd never suggested we bring her with us. Desiree had been acting like a real ass almost the entire three weeks Prince and I had been going out. She always had a smart comment or sarcastic look whenever Prince did something romantic or sweet. She would even bang on the walls when we were having sex, telling us to keep it down. This was something I could have done to her a thousand times before, but instead I would always turn up my radio or TV to block out the noise. I knew it was just a jealous phase she was going through after what happened with her and Tim, but Prince was starting to get sick of it. And I didn't wanna lose him because of her. So I figured if we took her out with us instead of leaving her in the house to sulk, she wouldn't be so evil when we got home. The club we were at was always full of plenty of handsome men to shower her with attention. So why did it look like she was trying to spend all her time with my man?

"So what's up? You wanna dance or what?" Mr. Tall and Handsome asked again.

"No, thanks. Maybe later."

"What about a drink? Can I get you a drink?" He pulled out a chair like he was about to sit down. I lifted my recently refilled apple martini glass.

"I already have a drink, thanks. And if you don't mind, please don't sit there. I'm here with my boyfriend. I'm sure he wouldn't appreciate finding you in his chair when he gets back."

"Boyfriend?" He leaned over, getting up in my face with an attitude. "Where the fuck he go to? Siberia? Baby, I been watching. You been sitting here alone for almost forty-five minutes."

Forty-five minutes? Damn, had it been that long? I glanced on the dance floor where Prince was trying to dance conservatively. I say trying because Desiree looked like she was auditioning for the lead in *Dirty Dancing II.* She was all over him. If she had been anyone else I would have dragged his ass off the dance floor a long time ago.

"You know what? You bitches ain't shit. If you don't wanna dance, why the fuck you come to the club?" I was about give him a piece of my mind when someone else beat me to it.

"Yo, player, if I was you, I'd get the fuck outta her face unless you wanna be wearing this bottle." I looked up and there was Trent brandishing a Corona bottle like it was a deadly weapon.

"Aw'ight, man. I was just asking the sister to dance." He pushed in the chair and walked away with an attitude.

Trent pulled the chair out and plopped down next to me.

"I could have handled that, Trent."

"I hear you, Mel," he said sarcastically. "Where the hell is Prince anyway? I shouldn't have to do his job."

"He's over there dancing with Desiree." I pointed to the dance floor.

"Dancing? Don't look like they dancing to me. Looks like your girl's trying to fuck him." Trent shook his head. "I told you about that chick."

"Don't start, Trent. That's just Desiree," I told him, glancing toward the dance floor with a little more concern.

"Aw'ight, don't say I didn't warn you."

"So what's up with you?" I decided to change the subject. "You don't look like your regular self. Something bothering you?"

"No, nothin's bothering me." His nothing was definitely something. I could always tell when something was bothering either of my brothers.

"Don't lie, Trent."

"Look, Mel, it's nothing. I'm just mad at myself."

"Mad about what? What you got to be mad about?"

"I got engaged last week." He made it sound like it was the worst thing in the world. I wasn't sure if I should congratulate him or feel sorry for him. I did tell him not to ask that girl Indigo to marry him.

"So I guess you're having some reservations now, huh?"

"Nah, I really love Michelle and the baby . . ."

I cut him off. "You asked *Michelle* to marry you?" I couldn't believe it. He might not have been happy, but I was elated. Michelle was my girl, and I loved my nephew Marcus to death.

"Uh-huh. I asked her." He shook his head. "But—" I cut him off again.

"Then why you mad at yourself? Trent, that's great news. I love Michelle. And so do Momma and Wil." I wrapped my arms around his neck and hugged him tightly. "And I know she loves you."

"That's the problem. I love her, too. I mean I really love her, Mel." It was good to hear him say that because it meant he was finally growing up.

"Why's that a problem? Now you, her and the baby can be a family. Trent, I'm so proud of you." I hugged him again.

"Well, as Paul Harvey would say, save the accolades until you hear 'the rest of the story.' "

Uh-oh. I didn't like the expression on his face at all. "There's more?"

"Oh, yeah, there's more."

"Like what?"

"Remember when you was over my house a couple of weeks ago and I told you I was thinking about asking Indigo to marry me?"

"Yeah, I remember. Thank God you didn't do that." I smiled.

"I did do it, Melanie. I asked her to marry me and she said yes. We're supposed to be getting married next month."

It took me a few seconds to totally comprehend what he was saying but when I did my eyes became huge and my jaw felt like it had hit the ground.

"You gotta be kidding me. You're not saying what I think you're saying, are you?"

He lowered his head. "Yeah, I am. As of last night I became

engaged to two women. And I'm supposed marry one of them in less than six weeks."

"Oh my God! Are you fucking crazy? What is wrong with you?" I couldn't help myself. I hit him. Not hard, but enough to get his attention.

"Hey, why you hit me?" He leaned back as he rubbed his shoulder.

"Because you're stupid. Why would you ask Michelle to marry you if you were already engaged to Indigo?"

"I don't know. It just seemed like the right thing to do at the time." He gave me this stupid ass expression.

"The right thing to do at the time?" I raised my hand like I was gonna hit him again.

"Yeah, but now she's bugging me to set a date." He started to explain to me the confrontation between him, Ray and Michelle. I didn't agree with it, but I did understand his rationale, because I knew how Trent's mind operated, as sick as it was. He did love Michelle, that I was sure of, but he'd asked her to marry him more out of spite for Ray than love for Michelle.

"You can't do this, Trent. You have to make a choice. This is not right. Those women love you. This isn't some game."

"I know that, Mel. It's just hard."

"Well, you can't marry both of them. So which one do you want?"

He shrugged. "I don't know. I want them both."

"What do you mean you want them both? I thought you said you love Michelle."

"I do."

"So if you love Michelle so much, why don't you just break things off with Indigo?"

"I can't. I've got love for her, too."

I was surprised to hear that. "Do you have love for her or do you have love for her money?"

"As a wise friend of mine told me recently, 'who's to say that loving her money isn't loving her?' The way she treats me, I can't have one without the other. I've run game on a lot of women, Mel. But none of them treated me like Indigo has and that includes Michelle. She gives me anything I want and I don't have to ask. If things go right with her music I'll be set for life. Then I'll be able to take care of Marcus and Michelle properly."

"I can't believe you, Trent. She's not just doing those things out the kindness of her heart. She's doing those things because she loves you. And when she realizes you don't love her, you better watch out. That girl's a little more ghetto than you think."

"Don't worry. I've been doing this for a while. She's not gonna find out."

"You better hope she doesn't," I told him flatly, turning my attention to the dance floor where Desiree was grabbing Prince's hand, trying to get him to slow dance with her. I was about to get up outta my chair until I saw Prince refuse the dance and pull his hand free from Desiree's grasp. He walked toward me.

"I need a drink," Prince declared, placing his hand on my shoulder and standing behind me. If I didn't know better I would have sworn he was trying to put some distance between himself and Desiree. "Anyone else want one?"

I reached up and held his hand. "I've already got one, boo."

"Yo, player. Get me some cognac. Doesn't matter what brand, just make sure it's top shelf."

"I'll go with you. I don't know what I want." Desiree smiled, walking over and grabbing his arm. Evidently, she didn't see the look I gave her or she would have let go of him.

"Well, I gotta go to the bathroom first," Prince told her. It was obvious he'd seen the look I gave her and was making sure to avoid my wrath.

"Yeah, so do I," I cut in. "Why don't you go with me, Dez?"

Desiree must have sensed trouble because she said, "That's all right, I'll stay here with the fellas till you get back."

"No, I insist. I need to talk to you." I pulled her arm off Prince's and stood up.

"Oh, shit. Looks like it's on." Trent laughed.

"Shut up, Trent," I snapped before I tugged at her arm and pulled her toward the bathroom.

"What's got your panties in a bunch?" Desiree asked when we got in the bathroom.

"You! You're what's got them in bunch!" I placed one hand on my hip and pointed with the other.

"Me?" she asked innocently. "What did I do?"

I was all attitude now. "Don't play stupid with me, Desiree. You know what the fuck you did. Why were you all over my man?"

She rolled her eyes as if I'd offended her. "Is that what this is all about? You mad 'cause I danced with Prince? Melanie, he ain't all that. Besides, what're you worried about? You the one who's going home with him. Jesus, I don't believe this shit."

"Believe it, 'cause your ass was doing more than dancing. Everybody in the club could see you were trying to seduce him. Damn, why don't you get your own fucking man instead of trying to steal everybody else's." I regretted saying that right after it came out my mouth because her facial expression told me I'd hurt her more than I wanted.

"Fuck you, and fuck them, Melanie! I'm your fucking best friend. I don't want your man. I was just trying to have a good time. I always dance like that and so do you." She was so upset she looked like she was about to cry. I was starting to feel bad. Maybe it was just innocent after all, but friend or no friend, I had to get my point across.

"That's the only reason I'm talking to you instead of going upside your head."

"Goin' upside my head?" She took a step toward me like she was gonna do something. "You know what, Melanie? This conversation is over. Matter of fact, you don't have to worry about me dancing with Prince again 'cause I'm going home and I ain't ever going out with y'all again. I can be miserable all by myself." She turned toward the door and I watched her, unable to think of anything to say.

When she got to the door she spoke again, making me feel even worse. "You know what's really pissing me off, Melanie? I never thought a man could come between us."

She reached for the door and I called out her name, "Dez." "What?"

"Don't leave. I'm sorry." I gave her a weak smile. "I must be PMSing."

She let herself smile at me, just a little. "You must be, girl, 'cause you was trippin'. All I was doing was dancing. I know Prince is fine, but I would never do anything to hurt you, Melanie. I love you too much for that."

I walked over and wrapped my arms around my friend, feeling like a fool. "I love you too, Dez. I'm sorry. You can dance with Prince anytime you want. You're right. I know who he's coming home with."

When we got back to the table, Prince and Trent were in deep conversation. Probably about Trent's double engagement.

"Oh, my God. That's my song," I shouted when Fifty Cent's "In Da Club" came on.

"Mine, too," Desiree replied, swaying from side to side in her chair. "You wanna dance, Prince?"

There was a silence before he answered. He glanced at me as if he wanted me to answer for him. "Well, I haven't danced with Melanie yet."

"Oh, don't worry, you can dance with her later. She don't mind. Do you, Mel?"

All eyes were upon me now and I'm sure I surprised both Prince and Trent when I said, "No, I don't mind."

"You sure? I mean, I haven't danced with you yet."

"Yeah, I'm sure. Go 'head and danced with her." I gave him a little shove in her direction.

Prince stood up reluctantly. "Aw'ight. Come on, Desiree."

25

Mimi

I waited up for Wil half the night hoping he would come by but he didn't show, and I was more than a little disappointed. I must have called his cell phone a dozen times, but I got no answer. Yeah, I know his son went to the hospital but he could have at least called. We were trying to build a relationship, weren't we? When I got to work and his office door was open I think I might have been the happiest woman in New York. Taking out my perfume, I sprayed myself one good time, then unbuttoned the top two buttons on my blouse.

"Hey, Maxine." Wil smiled as I entered his office. But it wasn't the same God, I'm-glad-to-see-you smile he usually gave me in the morning. It was more like the "just trying to be friendly" smile he gave everyone else. I wondered why he was calling me Maxine instead of Mimi, too. I got my answer when the chair in front of his desk spun in my direction to reveal that smart-ass bitch, Jeanie Brown from upstairs. Her greedy ass was eating one of the brownies I'd left for Wil.

"Hello, Maxine. We were just talking about you." Oh, God, this bitch was about to fire me. I could feel it by the way she was staring at my blouse. Why the fuck did she always show up at the most inopportune times.

"Oh, really. What about?" I lifted my hand and tried to nonchalantly button my blouse as I waited for an answer.

"How'd you like to work for the company permanently, Maxine?" Wil asked. "Full benefits and salary."

"I'd . . . I'd love it. It's what I've wanted since I started temping here." I was grinning at them from ear to ear. I'd gone from wanting to smack this bitch Jeanie to wanting to kiss her. "Is this for real? You guys serious?"

"We sure are." Wil smiled.

"Then I accept." I wanted to close my eyes and jump up in the air and shout hallelujah. A full-time position working with Wil. God, this was like a dream come true. "Thank you so much. I can't tell you how happy I am."

"Good. You start in shipping the first of next month. Congratulations, Maxine." Jeanie stood up and offered me her hand.

"Shipping? But that's in the building next door." I glanced out the office window at the shipping and receiving building. It was only a hundred feet away, but the thought of being in a different building than Wil made it appear miles away.

"It sure is," Jeanie added with what looked like a smirk as she now adamantly offered me her hand. I took it, but I was no longer grinning.

"But what about this department? It's busy season. Who's gonna be the secretary in sales?"

"You will be till the end of the month," Wil explained.

"Don't worry about these guys. We're gonna get them another temp, and Marge will be back soon enough," Jeanie answered smugly. I wanted to smack her ass because this whole thing smelled like a setup.

I glanced at Wil who was coming around his desk. "They really need a go-getter like you over there in shipping, Maxine. That's why I called Jeanie this morning and recommended you for the job. Congratulations." He gave me a very professional hug that was all arms and no body.

"You recommended me?" I gave him a dumbfounded look as I watched him slide back behind his desk and sit down.

"Of course I did. After all the hard work you put in for me during this busy season, I didn't wanna see anyone else get that job. You deserve it, Maxine." If he called me Maxine one more time I was gonna wring his neck.

"Well, thanks a lot, Wil," I replied. It was meant to be sarcastic but I don't think he took it that way.

"You're welcome. Now if you don't mind, Jeanie and I have to go over a few of the temps' résumés. Can you close the door on your way out?"

Oh, my God, he just dismissed me. I went back to my desk

and sat there irate for almost forty minutes while I waited for Jeanie to leave. When she did, she stopped at my desk, munching on another one of those brownies I'd left in Wil's office.

"What if I don't wanna go to shipping?" I asked.

"Then you can stay home, Maxine. I don't know what's going on around here, but whatever it is, I'm gonna put a stop to it. Do I make myself clear?"

She didn't wait for a reply, she just walked away. I watched her disappear down the corridor, then headed straight into Wil's office, locking the door behind me

"Why the hell did you recommend me for a job in another building?" I shouted.

"What are you saying, Maxine? You don't want the job?"

"Will you stop calling me Maxine? And yes, I'm saying I don't want the job. I wanna stay in sales. I don't wanna go to another building. I wanna be with you, Wil. Don't you want me to be here?"

"Sit down, Mimi, and lower your voice," he said sternly.

I sat down and folded my arms with a pout. He got out his chair and walked around until he was standing in front of me. He leaned back against the desk before he spoke.

"The reason I recommended you is exactly what I said before. Because you deserve it. It's a permanent position, for twice as much money, and full benefits. You needed the benefits, Max . . . ah, I mean Mimi. For yourself and your son. Positions like this don't just pop up. I had to pull a lot of strings to get you this job. We're in the middle of a hiring freeze."

I let out a sigh of relief. I didn't like what he'd done, but at least he was thinking about me and my son. At least he was showing me he cared. "Okay, but I wanna know something. Are you trying to get rid of me? Because I'm getting the feeling you're trying to push me away."

He exhaled. "No, Maxine. I'm not trying to get rid of you, but I do think we should keep some distance between us. We've been spending too much time together. People are starting to talk."

"People like who, Jeanie Brown?" *That bitch was gonna have to have an accident.*

"Yeah, she's one of them. She and my wife—"

I cut him off before he could say another word. "Your wife? What does she have to do with this?"

"She doesn't feel comfortable with you in this department."

"Who cares what she thinks? She's having an affair herself. Aren't you leaving her?" Wil was starting to annoy me.

"No, Mimi, she's not. And I care what she thinks because I'm not leaving her."

What was he saying? This couldn't be happening. I wasn't gonna let him throw away what we had.

"But, but what about us?"

"Mimi, I'm sorry, but there is no us."

"What do you mean there is no us? How can you say that after the other night? You liked the way I kissed you, Wil, and don't you dare say you didn't."

He swallowed hard, staring at me. "I like you, Mimi. I like you a lot. You're the type of woman I would wanna be with *if* I wasn't married. Only I am married. I have children, and I don't wanna lose them or my wife. And if you stay in this office, Diane's gonna take them away from me. Please, you gotta understand."

I'd never seen him like this. She really had him scared. He looked like he was gonna cry.

"Okay, Wil, I'll go. But I want you to answer one question for me. Honestly."

"Sure, all right." He nodded.

"The other night, when you came over my apartment."

"What about it?"

"If your friend hadn't called, would you have slept with me?"

He took a breath and held it in a while as he mulled over my question.

"No, Mimi, I wouldn't have slept with you," he answered. But I knew he was lying. His entire face was flush, and for the first time during our conversation he wouldn't make eye contact with me. His words might not have been what I wanted to hear but his body language told me everything I needed to know. Wil wanted me just as much as I wanted him. It's just that his wife and Jeanie Brown were getting in the way.

I let out a deep breath of my own. "Okay, then. I guess we're only going to be working together another couple of weeks."

"Mimi, I hope you understand. I wish this could have turned out another way."

"Oh, I understand, Wil." *And this will turn out another way once I get rid of that wife of yours.* I turned around and walked back to my desk. By the time I sat down I'd formulated a plan. I wasn't sure how it would work, but I sure as hell was determined not to lose Wil.

26

Melanie

I walked into my bedroom, slipped outta my robe and hung it up on my closet door. I glanced at Prince who was snuggled under the covers, 'sleep. We sure put it on each other last night. I was tempted to wake him up for another round but he looked so peaceful sleeping and I really didn't have time. I'd have to get mine when I got back from my hair appointment. I slipped on some underwear and a bra, then into my jeans and a sweatshirt before looking in the mirror. I added some lip gloss, then pulled my hair back in a ponytail. God, how did I ever live before I had dreads? They just made life so much easier. Picking up my purse, I walked over and kissed my sleeping boyfriend on the cheek. I hoped Andrea finished my hair quick so I could get back, 'cause just kissing him on the cheek was getting me hot.

I'd never had a relationship with a man like Prince before. Not only was he great in bed, he was so attentive and unselfish in every aspect of our relationship. If we ate pizza and watched the game today, the next day he'd take me out to dinner or rent a romantic movie and make popcorn. I could never get any other guy to do something like that without him being all over me before the movie was even over. And we had such intelligent conversations. Yep, not only was my boo fine, but he had to be the most well-rounded man I'd ever met.

"Hey, where you going?" He opened his eyes, reaching for me as my lips left his cheek. I let him pull me down on the bed and we kissed.

"I'm going over to Nu-Tribe to get my hair twisted. I'll be back in a couple hours. Go back to sleep."

He sat up immediately. "No, I'll go with you." He smiled, then pulled back the sheets. I pulled the sheets back over him.

"Nah, baby, stay here and go back to sleep. I'm already

dressed and you'll just get bored." I sat up and kissed him again, smiling. "Besides, you're gonna need some rest for when I get back." I winked at him.

"I should go with you, Mel." He had this kind of pleading look on his face.

He reached for the sheets and I pushed him back gently with a sigh. "Prince, lay back down. It's eight o'clock. You know you don't get up before ten on Saturday. Plus, I know you're tired. Aren't you?"

"Yeah, a little, but . . ."

"No buts, boo. You've been working all week and hanging out with me all night. You need to get some rest." I stood up. "I'll be back soon. Keep the bed warm for me, okay?" I looked at him again as I reached for my purse.

"Where's your roommate? Is she going with you?"

"She went to the store to get some cigarettes."

"She coming back?"

"I think so. You want me to have her make you breakfast?"

This time he didn't say anything. He just pulled back the covers and sat on the edge of the bed.

"What are you doing?"

"I'm getting dressed so I can go with you," he said sternly as he took his pants off my dresser and stepped into them.

"Why? I told you I'd be right back."

"Look, Mel, either I'm going with you or I'm going home." He gave me this dead serious look before pulling his shirt over his head. I wasn't sure what was bothering him, but he sure had an attitude all of a sudden.

"Prince, this is ridiculous. Why are you so insistent on going to the beauty parlor? I told you I'd be back in a couple hours."

"Yeah, that's what you said last time." He had to be referring to when I went to Wil and Diane's and didn't get to his house until after midnight.

"What's that supposed to mean?"

"Nothing, all right? Just let me go to the bathroom. I don't want you to be late for your appointment." He walked out the room.

When he returned, I was not about to drop the subject. This wasn't like Prince. He never had a problem explaining himself.

"What's wrong with you? Why you playing me so close, like you don't trust me."

"I don't trust you?" He chuckled. "Look, baby, let's not get into it, okay?"

"No, Prince. Let's get into it. Don't you trust me?"

"Yeah, I trust you."

"Then why are you so insistent on going with me?"

He gave me an annoyed sigh. "Why you playing games, Melanie?"

"I'm not playing games, Prince," I snapped. "Now would you tell me what's going on?"

He took a deep breath. "Your roommate. She . . ." He hesitated, studying me with these distant eyes. He really did think I was playing some sort of stupid game. "Melanie, are you trying to test me or something?"

"Test you for what? Why would I test you? I thought you said this has to do with Desiree." I didn't know what the hell he was talking about. He had me totally confused.

"You know what this has to do with," he said in an accusatory tone.

"No, Prince, I don't. Why don't you tell me?"

He studied me some more, then came out and said exactly what was on his mind. "Are you trying to test my loyalty? Is that why you had Desiree come on to me?"

I wanted to ask him to repeat himself, but I couldn't speak because it was hard to breathe. I felt like I was going to faint. When I finally had enough air in my lungs I screamed, "No, you didn't! No, you didn't just say that you think I had Desiree coming on to you."

"Yeah, I did," he replied. "I thought you put her up to it."

"Put her up to it? I ain't put her up to shit," I spat. "And what you mean she came on to you?"

He stood there in silence.

"I asked you a question, Prince."

He exhaled. "Remember the other day when you left for work early?"

"The day I had to register for school."

"Yeah, Wednesday."

"What about it?"

"Well, when I woke up Desiree was in the bed with me and she was butt ass naked."

"What the fuck! You lying? Why didn't you tell me this before?" I wanted to choke him, and when he didn't answer fast enough for me I answered for him. "Because you fucked her, didn't you? You fucked my best friend."

"No, I didn't, Mel. I swear I didn't. She wanted to but I told her no."

"So why didn't you tell me this before?"

"Because she said she was just testing me. To make sure I wasn't trying to play you. Said that if I told you, she was gonna say I was lying. That you'd known her all your life and only knew me a month. That's why I asked you if you were testing me. When you said you were gonna leave me here I thought you were trying to see what I'd do."

He reached for me and I pulled away. I wanted to cry but I knew that wouldn't do any good until I got to the bottom of this. There were always two sides to every story. I was just afraid to hear what Desiree's was.

"I don't like this, Prince. You better not be lying to me."

"I have no reason to lie to you, baby." We both got quiet until he asked, "What're we gonna do?"

"I'm gonna get my hair done, then me and you and Desiree are gonna have a talk."

When Prince and I got home from the hairdresser Desiree wasn't there, so we sat and waited, silently watching TV for almost two hours. We'd barely said a word to each other and the tension in the apartment was thick enough to cut with a knife. Part of me just wanted to forget the whole thing. For me this was a no-win situation. I was either gonna lose my best friend or my man. There really wasn't any middle ground, and that gave me a migraine. But that was nothing compared to the nausea I felt when Desiree walked through the door smiling like she'd won the lottery.

"What's up, y'all?"

Neither of us answered and she didn't seem to notice until she placed a bag of groceries on the kitchen table.

"What's wrong with you two? Trouble in paradise already?" She laughed and my whole attitude changed.

"How could you, Desiree?" My eyes got real small and it was a good thing I was sitting on my hands or I mighta jumped up and smacked the shit outta her.

"How could I what?" She gave me this condescending look that sent me into a rage. I had told myself I was gonna act like a lady about this, hear her out, listen to what she had to say, but I'd seen her give that same patronizing look a thousand times. It usually meant she was gloating about something.

I jumped up off the couch and it was lucky for her that Prince grabbed one of my arms to hold me back. "You call yourself my friend, bitch?"

"I am your friend!" She stared at me like I'd lost my mind. "And who you callin' a bitch?"

"I'm calling you a bitch." I swung at her wildly with my free hand. "Lemme go, Prince!"

"What the fuck is wrong with her?" Desiree screamed as she jumped out the way of my fist, staring at Prince.

"Calm down, baby," Prince pleaded.

"I ain't gonna calm down. I'm gonna kill this bitch! Now lemme go!" I was twisting and turning all over the place trying to get to her ass. Somehow I finally connected with my free hand in a loud *slap!*

"Awww!" she screamed, grabbing her face. "What the fuck is wrong with you, Melanie?"

"You! You what's wrong with me, you stupid bitch! Lemme go, Prince." I struggled until I was close enough to get in another blow.

"You dirty ho!" she screamed.

"I got your ho, bitch! Lemme go, Prince!"

She touched her face again, then balled up her fist. She finally looked like she was ready to fight. "Yeah, Prince, let her go."

"You think you gonna play me? You think you can fuck with my man? In my bed? I'ma kill your ass."

Desiree's eyes went straight to Prince. "Is that what he told you? That I was trying to fuck him in your bed?" She shot Prince a look, then turned to me.

"You damn right! He ain't got no reason to lie."

"Why not? He's a man, isn't he? And you called me a stupid bitch."

That was it. I couldn't take it no more. I went absolutely berserk. I don't know if I pulled free of Prince or if he let me go, but within seconds Desiree and I were rolling around on the ground fighting like cats and dogs. I had a hand full of her weave and she'd ripped off half my blouse.

"Stop it! Y'all stop it!" Prince yelled, pulling us apart. I'm not gonna lie. I was glad he did because I was huffing and puffing so much I thought I was gonna pass out. Not to mention Desiree was starting to get the best of me toward the end.

"That nigga is trying to play you," Desiree huffed.

"The only one trying to play me is you. You call yourself my friend, then you try to fuck my man."

"I just told you I wasn't trying to fuck him. That nigga was trying to fuck me!" She backed away and grabbed her bag. I was afraid she was gonna pull out a knife. "Here!" She threw an envelope at me.

"What the fuck is this?"

"It's a letter I wrote you. I know how much you care about him, Melanie, but he ain't shit."

"See," Prince said, "I told you she was gonna try some shit like this, baby."

I ignored him and opened the letter.

Dear Melanie

It's about three o'clock in the morning and I haven't been able to sleep. Actually, I haven't been able to sleep in a couple days because there's something I need to tell you. Something I should have told you days ago, but I was afraid it might hurt you, and even worse, that you might not believe me. You see, the other day when you left the house early, Prince walked into my room half naked while I was getting dressed. He made a pass at me. Now I'm not gonna lie, I was tempted. He is one fine man and when he started talking about sucking my toes and shit like that, I almost melted. But then I remembered what was important—that you are the best friend I have in the world

*and I love you like a sister. I told Prince this and he
suddenly swore he was just joking. When I told him I was
gonna tell you what he did, he threatened to reverse things
on me, so I kept my mouth shut. But I can't keep it shut
anymore. Now I know this may end our friendship but
you need to drop this fool before he hurts you. To borrow
a phrase you always use, "If he'll do it once, he damn sure
is gonna do it again." Melanie, I hope you can forgive me
for not telling you this sooner.*

> *I love you and I'm sorry,*
> *Desiree*

When I finished reading the letter, I read it again. When I finished reading it the second time, I glanced at Prince, then over at Desiree, who was staring at me, all bruised up with a plug outta her hair. "I'm sorry, Dez," I whispered. Then I turned around and slapped the shit outta Prince.

"Get the fuck outta my house."

He took a step back, staring at me in astonishment. "Baby, don't do this. That bitch is lying. You playin' right into her hands."

"You the one lying," Desiree snapped. Prince took a step in her direction.

"I told you to get out my house, Prince," I screamed, pointing at the door. He approached me with open arms. "Now I know why you and Trent are so close. Your ass is just like him."

"Baby, that's not true. She's lying. I swear to God she's lying." He gave me a pleading look that I ignored

"Desiree, call the cops. This fool thinks I'm playin'." Desiree picked up the phone and started dialing. Prince shook his head and walked toward the door.

"I love you, Melanie. I hope you remember that when you find out the truth."

I watched Prince walk out the door, then turned to Desiree. "You got a cigarette?"

27

Trent

It was late, somewhere in the neighborhood of three or four o'clock in the morning, when I heard Indigo come in the house. She'd been working on her music with Big Mike most of the night, then said she was gonna head over to Manhattan Proper to check out karaoke night. I pulled the covers over my head when my bedroom door opened and pretended to be asleep. I was hoping she'd be tired and just lay down and go to sleep, 'cause if she wanted some, I was in trouble. I didn't think I had another round in me. I'd been over Michelle's house all afternoon, fucking my ass off. We'd dropped her mom and Marcus off at some church function that wasn't over until ten. Michelle hadn't even let me sniff her panties since our engagement because her mom always seemed to be around. When Rita wasn't around, Marcus's ass never seemed to wanna go to sleep. So after dropping off her mom and my son, Michelle and I took the opportunity to get to know each other intimately again, and again and again. By the time we were finished, I was shooting blanks.

"Trent, Trent. Wake up, Trent. Wake up!" Indigo crawled into bed and shook me, which meant I was in trouble. She wanted some, all right. Maybe, maybe if I was lucky I could get away with just giving her a little head, but I doubted it. She pulled the cover from over my head and I was surprised at how dark the room was. Usually she liked to light candles and incense to set the mood when she came in late and wanted some. "Wake up, Trent. I need to talk to you."

"What? What?" I grumbled, pretending to rub the sleep out my eyes. Not that she could see what I was doing anyway. The room was pitch black. I could barely make out her silhouette.

"Trent, do you love me?" She had a little uncertainty in her voice and I was wondering if Big Mike had mentioned my reservations about marrying her.

"Of course I love you. We're getting married next month, aren't we?"

"I don't know, you tell me. Ray Jenkins told me that you asked that girl Michelle, who keeps saying she had your baby, to marry you." Suddenly I was glad that it was too dark in the room for her to see my face. If she had, she would have known the truth. It looked like my old friend Ray was blowing me up again.

"Now, baby, I know you don't believe that, do you? Why would I marry her when I got you? I love you, Indigo." I reached up, taking hold of her waist.

"So you ain't asked her to marry you?" She sounded both skeptical and relieved at the same time.

"Hell, no! That nigga Ray is lying, baby. I bet he even tried to come on to you after he said it, didn't he? Didn't he?" She got quiet, which gave me a chance to go on the offensive. It was time to use a little reverse psychology to get my ass out of this. "You know I don't need this shit! How many times I gotta tell you I love you before you start to believe me? Damn! What you want me to do? Stand on the Empire State Building and scream out to the world, 'I LOVE INDIGO JONES!' 'Cause if that's what you want, I'll do it." I let out a pissed-off sounding sigh. "Shit, I've given you keys to my house, let you answer my phone, hell, I even quit my job to help you start your career. Why the fuck would I ask somebody else to marry me?"

"I don't know," she replied, still not sounding convinced. "Why would Ray just come out his face like that?"

"'Cause he's a hater, baby. But if you wanna believe some nigga off the street, who was trying to get some ass, then you need to bounce. Just get your shit and get the fuck out. I mean it! Get the fuck out my house." I rolled over and started to count to five backwards in my head.

Five, four, three, two, one, now.

"I'm sorry," she said sadly. "I know you don't love her. I know you love me." I smiled to myself thinking, *that reverse psychology shit works every time.*

"Well, I wish you would start acting like it." I turned over. "Don't you understand, Indigo? It's me and you against the world, baby. Everybody else has gotta step to the left. Now I want you to stay away from that nigga Ray. He's bad news, you hear me?"

"Yeah, I hear you but . . ."

"No buts," I snapped. "Just don't let it happen again."

"Okay, don't get mad. I love you, Trent."

"I love you, too, boo."

"I love you more," she told me playfully.

"As Fifty Cent would say, 'I love you like a fat kid loves cake.'"

We both laughed and she lowered her head and kissed me.

"Trent, I gotta tell you something. It's about that girl Michelle—"

I cut her off. "I know, I know. You wanna know if the baby's mine, right?"

"Well, yeah, but that's not it. She's—"

I cut her off again. "Well, I just want you to know . . ." I hesitated. I didn't wanna renounce my son. I loved the little guy. Hell, I loved his mother but I was too close to the prize to be worried about moral obligation. I had to convince this girl that it was all about her so I could get paid. "That baby's not mine, Indigo. I want you to know that."

"Oh, no, you didn't just deny my fucking baby!"

All of a sudden the ceiling light flashed on and my eyes were fighting to adjust to the lights. I couldn't see shit, but one thing was for certain. I'd been set the fuck up, 'cause that was Michelle's voice and it sounded like it was getting closer.

"I could take that other shit. I been taking that for years, but I can't take this! That's my fucking son! That's your fucking son, Trent! How could you deny him? You son of a bitch! I'm gonna kill you!"

Next thing I knew, I felt a hard slap across my face and Indigo was screaming, "Get the fuck off my man, bitch! I told you he ain't want you!" Then I heard a loud thump.

My eyes finally adjusted to the light and I could see Michelle and Indigo tousling on the floor like two WWE wrestling superstars. Indigo was on top and she was definitely getting the best of

Michelle. I jumped outta bed and separated them, trying my best to keep Indigo off Michelle.

"How could you, Trent? How could you do this to me and Marcus? I thought you loved us." Michelle wasn't trying to fight anymore; she was crying hysterically.

"Michelle, I'm sorry . . ." I didn't know what else to say. On top of that, I was still trying to keep Indigo at bay.

"Save it, Trent, all right? Just save it." She sniffled. "I don't need you and neither does Marcus. From this day forward the only family he's got is me and my momma. So keep yours away or they might get their feelings hurt."

"Michelle, don't . . ." I stopped myself in mid sentence. What do you say to a woman you're engaged to, who just heard you tell another woman you're engaged to, that you don't give a shit about her or her child? Well, I guess it really doesn't matter 'cause even if I had thought of something, Michelle didn't seem to wanna hear it. She turned around and walked out the door. I wanted to run after her, but like both Melanie and Big Mike had said, I had to make a decision. Was it going to be love or was it going to be money? I wanted it to be love, but what the hell was love without money? Besides, the chances of talking my way back into Michelle's heart after this one were almost none. So I retreated to the safety of money and placed my arm around Indigo.

"Fuck her, Trent. You shoulda let me whoop that bitch's ass," Indigo told me.

I should whoop your ass for bringing her here, I thought.

28

Mimi

The end of the month had come much quicker than I would have liked, and I was saddened because it was my last day as Wil's secretary. I was gonna try to spend as much time as I could with him tonight. The sales department was giving an end-of-the-busy-season party at Antun's, a little catering hall in Queens Village. I was hoping that afterward I'd be able to talk him into stopping by my apartment for a nightcap. We didn't spend as much time together as we used to, but we were still close, and he took me out to lunch at least once a week, which was nice. The only problem was, we always seemed to have a third wheel around like someone from the sales department or that pain in the ass, Jeanie Brown from upstairs. Don't get me wrong. I'm not complaining. I understood what was going on. Wil was trapped in a marriage he didn't wanna be in and it was my responsibility, not his, to free him if I wanted us to be together. The only problem was, it wasn't that easy coming up with an accident that everyone was going to believe. It took a lot of planning and a lot of thought.

Wil walked out of his office carrying his briefcase. He smiled. "You still here? I thought you left for the party an hour ago."

"I'm about to. I just have to take care of a few things with human resources before I leave on Monday."

"You want me to wait for you?" he tempted.

If you do, we might not make it to that party, I thought.

"No, I'll be along shortly. I wanna make a grand entrance. It is my last day in sales."

"Yeah, it is, isn't it." He sighed sadly. "Mimi, I hope you're not gonna be a stranger around here, 'cause I'm gonna miss you."

"I'm gonna miss you too, Wil. But I promise, in the long run you're gonna see a lot more of me than you'd ever expect."

"I hope so," he replied, giving me that smile that always made me feel like I was melting. "Well, don't take too long. I'm expecting a dance."

"Only if it's a slow one." I smiled, thinking of how nice it would be to wrap my arms around him and dance the night away. He was mine tonight. I dare a bitch to get on the dance floor with him.

"I'll see you at the party," he told me, walking away.

I watched him walk down the corridor, then stood up to retrieve my coat and bag from the closet behind my desk. I folded my coat over my arm, then opened my bottom desk drawer to remove the nine-inch box I'd hidden there this morning. I placed the box on my desk and opened it, staring at the contents with a satisfied grin. Covering up the box, I tucked it under my coat, then pushed in my chair and walked over to the window to see if the red convertible was still parked in the executive parking lot. It was, and I smiled as I walked to the elevator and pushed the "up" button.

"You going to the party, Mimi?" John, a nerdy sales intern, asked.

"Yep, I sure am."

"You wanna catch a cab?"

"No, I have to drop off some paperwork upstairs first. I'll meet you over there, okay?"

The elevator bell rang and the arrow indicated it was headed down. I watched John disappear into that elevator, then waited for an another one heading up. When it arrived, I stepped in and pushed four, for the executive floor. When the elevator door opened on the fourth floor, it was like a ghost town. All the secretaries and the receptionist had left for the weekend. I made my way down the hall unannounced until I was in front of Jeanie Brown's office. I tried to steady my racing heart, then knocked on the door.

"Come in."

I opened the door and walked in. Jeanie was sitting behind a glass desk, pecking away at a computer. "Maxine? What are you doing here? I thought sales was having a party tonight." I couldn't read her expression, but she definitely didn't seem overjoyed to see me. Not that it mattered to me. Her attitude toward me was not gonna be a problem much longer.

"They are, Ms. Brown, but I wanted to talk to you before I went over there."

"I'm kind of busy right now but have a seat."

I sat down in one of the two leather chairs in front of her desk.

"What's on your mind, Maxine?"

"Well, there are a few things. First, I wanna say thank you. I know I acted a little unappreciative about the promotion you gave me, so I wanted to give you this." I handed her the box I'd been hiding under my coat. She got a huge grin on her face when she opened it.

"Oh, Maxine, thank you. You really know how to get on a person's good side, don't you?" She was all smiles.

"You always seemed to be fond of my sister's brownies, so I had her whip up a batch just for you."

She reached in the box and pulled out a brownie square, closing her eyes as she bit into it. "Mmm, would you like one?" She offered the box to me.

I smiled. "You know, I don't mind if I do."

I took out a square and bit into it. Jeanie was already on her second square. She was grinning from ear to ear like she'd had the ultimate orgasm.

"Oh, my God, these are so good. Tell your sister I want the recipe."

"Oh, I can give you the recipe."

"You can?"

"Sure." I took a pen out my purse as I watched Jeanie pick up another brownie square and shove it in her mouth. "It's really pretty basic. You know, just a couple'a eggs, some flour, oil, baking soda and chocolate. She uses both cooking chocolate and those little Hershey Kisses. But this batch has a secret ingredient. I think you'll like it."

"Oh, yeah? What's that?" she asked in a suddenly raspy voice.

"You wouldn't believe me if I told you."

"Sure I would. What is it?" Her voice had gotten raspier and now she was holding her throat.

"Sesame seed oil." I smirked at her as I said, "I had her replace the cooking oil for sesame seed oil."

"Sesame seed oil? Oh, God! I'm allergic to sesame seeds." Jeanie's panic was written all over her face. She pushed the box of brownies across her desk like it was poisonous. Actually, I guess it was to her.

"Oh, damn. That's right. You did tell me you were allergic to sesame seeds, didn't you? I must have forgot. Are you okay?" I watched her face go pale and her eyes start to water as she struggled to get her desk drawer open. She pulled out something that looked like a white tube, the size of a pen. She tried to stick it in her arm but I snatched it out of her hand.

"Uh-uh-uhhh." I shook my head and waved my finger at her. "What's this, one of those EpiPens?"

"Give it to me." She coughed, lunging at me as she struggled for air.

"Oh, that's right. You need this to stop the swelling in your throat so you can breathe, don't you?" She nodded her head. "Well, why didn't you say so? Here." I extended my hand, dropping the pen on my side of her desk. "Ooooops." I laughed.

"Nooooooo," she struggled to get out. "What are you trying to do, kill me?"

I stood up straight and smirked. "You know, you're a lot smarter than you look. I didn't think you'd catch that for at least another couple of minutes."

"What are you, crazy? You're not gonna get away with this, Maxine." Her lips were turning blue and she was knocking shit all over her desk just trying to breathe.

"Really? Why not?" I hesitated as if I was waiting for her to give me an answer. "If the cops ask me if I gave you the brownies, I'm not gonna deny it. Everyone in the building knows you love my sister's brownies. And how could I know you're allergic to sesame seeds? Besides, why would I hurt you? You just gave me a promotion. The cops are gonna look at this like it was just one unfortunate accident."

"You are crazy," she managed to murmur.

"That's what the doctors say but I am not crazy! But one thing's for sure, Jeanie. Your ass is dead." She fell on the floor, kicking, then suddenly stopped. I bent down and picked up her EpiPen, wiping it clean of my fingerprints before tossing it near her body. "It was nice knowing you, Jeanie. I'll send a wedding invitation with your friend Diane. She'll be coming to see you real soon."

29

Melanie

Oh, no. This can't be right, I told myself as I stared down at the small white object in my hand. *This can't be happening to me.* I walked out of the bathroom and into my bedroom. The phone started to ring but I ignored it as I sat down on my bed and stared blankly at the object I was still holding. I knew who was calling on the first ring. It was Prince. Since we'd broken up, he'd made a habit of calling at least five times a day, starting about seven o'clock in the morning. Now it was only a few minutes past seven, so I was pretty confident it was him. I contemplated answering the phone, then decided against it. Most of the time I wouldn't even think about picking up the phone. I'd just listen to him plead on the answering machine. When I did pick up, I usually ended up hanging up on him or cursing him out because he'd start calling Desiree a liar.

Ring, ring, ring, ring, beeeep!

"Hey, Mel, it's Prince." He chuckled. "Like you don't know my voice by now, right? Look, I don't know if you left for work already or if you're just screening your calls, but I just wanted to tell you that I love you." There was a sigh and a pause before he said, "I miss you, Mel. I don't know how things got to this point or why that bitch Desiree is lying on me. But what I do know is that I can't sleep, I don't eat, and without you, baby, I'm not complete. I love you, boo. Please give me a call."

Damn, why couldn't he just get it through his thick-ass skull? It wasn't gonna happen. He'd fucked up and we were over. Even if I did miss him, too.

Knock, knock.

Desiree stuck her head in my door before I could reply.

"Was that him?" She walked in wearing her waitress uniform and carrying her journal.

"Yeah, that was him. I just let the answering machine get it."

"Did he leave a message?" she asked. I don't know why but it seemed like Desiree was more concerned about what Prince was doing than I was.

"Uh-huh."

"What'd he say?"

"The usual." I said it like I was bored by Prince's constant attempts to win me back. "He wanted me to know how much he loved me and that he missed me. Oh, and how much of a liar *you* are."

"Fuck that nigga," Desiree snapped.

I wish I could, I thought.

"Well, I'm outta here. I'll see you tonight. You still down to go to The Shadow?"

"I guess. It depends on how I feel." Desiree had been trying to get me to go out and meet someone else ever since Prince and I broke up. I hadn't gone to the clubs with her yet, because no matter how mad I was at Prince, I still missed him, and I wasn't interested in getting with anyone else. I'd been making up excuses why I couldn't go out with her, but as I rubbed my stomach and told her I wasn't sure about tonight, I wasn't lying.

"You still got that stomach virus? I heard you throwing up in there this morning."

"Worse." I handed her what I'd been holding.

"Oh, shit! Is this what I think it is?" She glanced at me, then down at the white plastic stick she was holding. "Is this a . . . Oh, my God, it's got a plus sign. You're not? You're not pregnant, are you?" She gave me a bug-eyed stare.

"According to that EPT you're holding, I am. Not to mention the fact that I'm about three weeks late."

"Damn. What you gonna do? You're not gonna keep it, are you?" Desiree looked more scared than I was.

"I don't know. I just found out. I haven't given it much thought," I lied. Of course I'd been thinking about it. That's why I went out and bought the EPT in the first place. I also knew what I was gonna do. I just wasn't sure if I could go through with it again.

She sat on the bed next to me. "Is it Prince's?"

"Ain't no one else's it could be."

"You gonna tell him?"

"I guess I have to at some point."

She turned to me. "No you don't. Melanie, you don't need no baby and you don't need no man pressuring you into keeping it. If I were you, I wouldn't tell him shit. I'd just go down to the clinic and take care of my business."

"That's not right, Dez."

"Neither is Prince for grabbing my ass every chance he had. But that didn't stop him."

"This is not a conversation I wanna have right now. The last thing I wanna hear about is what Prince was trying to do to you," I stated.

"I'm sorry." She gave me a quick hug. "You want me to stay home? We can do the girlfriend thing. Just sit around, eat chocolate and watch soaps."

"Thanks, Dez, but I've got a lot of thinking to do. I'd prefer to do it alone, if you don't mind."

"Okay, but we're gonna talk about this tonight when I get home." She hugged me again, then got up and walked to the door. "Hit me on the cell if you need me, all right?"

I nodded and she walked out. I opened my nightstand and pulled out a yellow piece of paper, dialing the number on it.

"Choices Women's Clinic. Nadine speaking."

"Hi, my name is Melanie Duncan. I have an appointment tomorrow morning at nine o'clock. I just wanted to confirm."

"Yes, Melanie, we have you for nine o'clock. Please don't eat anything after midnight and you have to be accompanied by another adult or the doctor won't perform the procedure."

I hung up the phone, then picked it up again, dialing Trent's number.

"Yeah, hello," he grumbled. It sounded like he'd just woken up.

I started to get emotional the second I heard my brother's voice. There was something about talking to him or Wil when I was in trouble that just made me feel like I was a little girl again. I guess it had something to do with the fact that my father died when I was young and they were the only two male role models I'd ever had.

"Trent." I sniffled.

"Melanie? What's d'matter? Are you all right?" Before I could answer he blurted out, "What happened? Did Michelle call you?" He sounded like he had his own problems. I was tempted to hang up.

"No," I whined like a little girl as I burst into tears. "I'm pregnant."

"Pregnant? Oh, shit." I could hear him struggling to sit up in the bed. "Did you tell Prince yet?"

"No." I shook my head like he could see me.

"Well, you need to talk to him. I know you're supposed to be mad at him, but if you're gonna have a baby, you and him need to talk."

"I'm not having the baby, Trent. I made an appointment at Choices. I just need you to go with me." There was a long silence on the line. The only thing I could hear was his breathing. "Trent? Trent, you there?"

"You sure about this, Mel? We went down this road before, and you didn't like it."

I didn't reply right away because he was right. When I was seventeen, I became pregnant by this guy named Rodney. To this day, I haven't even told my mom about that. The only person I told was Trent, and he took me down to Choices to have an abortion. Believe it or not, he didn't try to force me to have an abortion. He let me make my own decision. A decision I've regretted ever since and he knows it.

"I know I didn't like it, Trent, but I can't have a baby. Not without a father," I told him adamantly.

"Wait a minute. Isn't Prince the father?"

"Yeah, and? What's that mean? That don't mean he's gonna be a daddy to his baby. Look at you."

He got quiet again. I didn't mean for it to come out that way but Trent knew I was pissed off at him because of what he did to Michelle. She was so upset she wouldn't let any of us see Marcus now.

"He's not like me, Mel. He's gonna be there for his kid. Prince is a good man. He wants to marry you."

"Well, I don't wanna marry him." I ran my hand through my

locks. "Look, Trent, this is hard enough as it is. Please don't give me a hard time, okay? Now are you gonna take me or not?"

"Yeah, I'll take you," he answered unhappily. "What time?"

"I gotta be there at nine tomorrow morning. Why don't you pick me up around eight?"

30

Wil

Halfway to the party I got a message from Diane asking me to come home right away. She didn't give me any details but the urgency in her voice had me running stop signs and dodging pedestrians until I pulled in the driveway. I jumped out the truck and ran up the walkway as fast as I could. All the lights were out and that wasn't a good sign. When I opened the door I prepared myself for the worst. Was something wrong with the kids? Was it her illness? I'd just read a story on the Internet about a woman bleeding to death due to fibroids.

"Di! Diane!" I hollered but didn't get a response, so I hollered again. "Diane!"

"I'm upstairs, Wil. Stay right there. I'll be right down."

I walked over to the stairs and looked up. I didn't give a damn what she said. I wasn't about to stay downstairs after running five stop signs and nearly running over two joggers. I wanted to know what the hell was going on. But before I could climb the first step, she was gazing down at me from above.

"Hi," she whispered in this sexy voice I hadn't heard in quite some time.

"Hi, yourself," I replied, swallowing hard as I watched her seemingly glide down the stairs. She was wearing a red-and-black lace bustier with red panties, a black garter and black stockings. Oh, and let's not forget the five-inch black heels. Those heels just completed the package. Yeah, my wife was a big woman, but as far as I was concerned, her luscious curves should have been on the cover of *Playboy* magazine.

When she reached the bottom of the stairs she gently touched my face and walked around me three times, strutting like a supermodel.

"Have you been working out?" She grabbed a handful of my ass, startling me. I must've jumped about a foot in the air.

"What's got into you?" I glanced around for the kids. "And where are the kids?"

"The kids are at your sister's. Now stop talking and kiss me." She pulled me in close and we kissed like I can't remember us kissing in years. My hands instinctively began to roam her body, which was as soft and warm as I could ever remember. My manhood sprang to attention and I'm sure she could feel it rubbing up against her.

"I got some good news and some bad news today. Which do you wanna hear first?"

I hadn't stopped rubbing my stuff against her. "Tell me the bad news first, then the good news. Maybe the good news will cheer me up."

"Linda and Ralph are getting divorced." Linda was Diane's older sister by seven years. She and her husband, Ralph, had been married for way over twenty years, but I can't say that the divorce surprised me. Ralph had been complaining about their sex life the entire ten years Diane and I had been married. I always thought that his complaining was just his way of trying to make Linda step up in the bedroom. I guess he finally decided it was time for him to step out.

"Oh, damn. I'm sorry to hear that."

"So am I. He moved in with some twenty-five-year-old bitch. Can you believe that? They were married before that home wrecker was even born." She kissed me again, this time lightly. "I don't want us to be like them, Wil."

"Neither do I, Di." I kissed her back and then remembered she had more news. "So what's the good news?"

"Well, there's a little bit more bad news." She frowned.

"Oh, God, more? What is it?"

She looked up at me. "I know you've been patient but I'm still in too much pain to have sex."

I tried not to look disappointed, but I was upset that she teased me with her outfit. You couldn't have paid me to think I wasn't getting some a few minutes ago. Oh, well, that's what I get for assuming things. Another day, another cold shower.

I exhaled. "What's the good news?"

"I spoke to the specialist we went to see last week."

"Yeah, what'd he say?"

"He said the tumor isn't quite as big as he originally thought and that I'd be a perfect candidate for fibroid embolization. Wil, he's gonna shrink the tumor. I'm not gonna have to have a hysterectomy."

I closed my eyes and thanked God. Now that was good news. "When's he gonna do it?"

"Next week at L.I.J. Hospital. He said it'd be a little painful but I could come home the same day."

"Now that's what I call good news." I squeezed her tight.

"And I've got some more good news."

"You do?"

"Yeah, I do." Her voice got sexy again. "I meant what I said about not ending up like my sister. She forgot what got her Ralph in the first place."

"What do you mean?"

"She forgot about meeting her husband's needs." She started to kiss my neck while her hand fiddled with my zipper. "I might not be able to have sex, but I can still . . ."

"Ohhhhh, shittttt," I moaned. Her warm hands had taken hold of me and she could have led me to hell and back with the way she was making me feel.

"Like I was saying, I can still take care of my baby."

She slid to her knees and I gently cradled her head as she went to work using her tongue and mouth, making me moan and groan loud enough for the entire neighborhood to hear. When she finished, she stood up and smiled. "Happy now?"

I couldn't talk. All I could do was nod my head and smile at the woman I loved. I felt like I was a virgin and I'd just been deflowered by an expert.

She winked. "Good. Now whenever you want some more, just ask. There's plenty more where that came from." Again I didn't speak. I just nodded. "Now don't we have a party to go to?"

"We?"

"Yeah, I wanna go. I haven't missed an end-of-the-season party since we started dating." She walked over to the foyer closet and took out a red dress that had obviously been put there earlier for this exact moment. She took the dress off the hanger and slid into it. "I'm gonna change my shoes, but I want you to remember what's underneath this dress for when we get home."

"I don't think that's something I'll forget."

"I hope not." She turned around so that her back was to me. "Will you zip me up, please?"

"You sure you wanna go to this party?" I asked as I zipped her dress. "You know Maxine is gonna be there?"

"So." She walked over to the foyer mirror to fix her hair. "I don't have anything to worry about, do I? There's nothing going on between you two that I don't know, is there?"

"No. Not a damn thing."

"All right, then. I'm just going to have a good time with my friends and *my husband*." She turned around, smiling wickedly. "How do I look?"

I took one look at my wife in that dress and said, "Good enough to eat."

"The way I'm feeling right now, I might take you up on that later."

"Please do." I smiled. She took my arm and we headed out the door.

When Di and I arrived, I was not only surprised at the number of people who showed up at the party but at how many of them were actually dancing. Here I was thinking that I was working with a bunch of nerds the past few months, but these white folks were partying their asses off. I don't think I saw one person without a drink in his or her hand. So when a few of Diane's former coworkers accosted her at the door, I decided to head to the bar and grab a drink myself.

"Let me have a rum and Coke," I told the bartender.

"Hey, handsome. Buy a girl a drink?" Mimi slid onto the bar stool next to me just as the bartender brought me my drink. I glanced in Diane's direction. She was still gossiping with her friends, but if she headed in our direction I was planning on making a hasty retreat.

"Sure."

"I'll have an apricot sour," she told the bartender.

"So did you get everything straight with human resources?"

"Yeah I'd say everything I was concerned about is pretty much a dead issue up there." She took her drink from the bartender. "All I have is one more thorn in my side to take care of."

"Well, I hope you take care of it soon, because there's no one I can think of who deserves to be happy more than you."

"Thanks, Wil. That's sweet. I feel the same way about you."

I glanced over at Diane again. Her old boss, Juan Sanchez, had just dragged her on the dance floor. That was good, because I needed to tell Mimi that Di was here and that the slow dance she asked for was not gonna happen.

"You keep looking over there on the dance floor. Would you like to dance?"

"Nah, maybe later."

"Come on, Wil. You promised me a dance."

"I know, but . . ."

"But what? You don't know how to dance or something? Come on. I love Fabolous."

"Mimi, I have to tell you something."

"Tell me after we dance. Come on." She tugged at my sleeve.

Ah, what the hell, I thought. *Just one dance can't hurt. Besides, it will give me the excuse not to slow dance with her later.*

I let out a sigh. "All right. Come on."

We headed out to the dance floor.

Mimi and I were dancing for about five minutes and everything was cool except that I felt paranoid about Diane watching us. My fear was pretty much unwarranted, though, because Diane was on the other side of the dance floor minding her business, dancing with Juan. She didn't even seem to miss me at all. So I started to calm down and let my guard down. Big mistake. Diane wasn't the problem. The problem was dancing in front of me, as I discovered as soon as the DJ put on a Busta Rhymes record. That's when Mimi turned around and started to back that ass on up. The more she backed it up, the more I backed away. I backed away so much I backed my ass right into someone who grabbed my waist so I couldn't back up anymore. That someone was Diane, and believe it or not, she was starting to dance just as freaky as Mimi was. Those two had me in the middle of a size sixteen sandwich, with both Diane and Mimi trying to outdo each other on the dance floor. I had Diane grinding everything she had up against me from the back and Mimi bouncing her phat ass all over me in the front. And the funny thing is, they both seemed to be having a good time. They were both laughing and smiling, like we were all old friends. And that in itself scared the hell outta me. To make matters worse we'd attracted a crowd around us that was spurring Diane and Mimi's competition even more by chanting, "Go Wil! Go Wil! Go Wil!" At least they were until that stupid ass DJ put on a slow song and snapped the three of us back into reality.

That's when the axe came down on my head because Mimi grabbed one hand and Diane grabbed the other then they both said, "Let's dance, Wil," in unison.

"Who the fuck are you?" Mimi asked, taking a step toward Diane so that they were eye to eye.

"That's none of your business. Who the fuck are you?" Diane replied with attitude, shoving Mimi out of her face.

"Diane," I scolded, stepping in between them. I was facing Mimi, hoping I could stop her from retaliating. "Mimi, this is my wife, Diane. Diane, this is Mimi." Neither of them said a word; they just glared at each other.

"Wil, are you gonna dance with me or not?" Diane demanded.

"Yeah, Di, I'm gonna dance with you. I'll see you later, all right, Mimi?" Mimi didn't budge and it was pretty obvious she was about to explode at any second, so I thanked God when Henry Wickens, the vice president of sales, interrupted the song. Well at least until I heard what he had to say.

"Excuse me, ladies and gentlemen. I'm sorry to interrupt the party but I have a little bad news. Jeanie Brown, the assistant director of human resources, was found dead in her office. They haven't confirmed it but the police told us it looks like she had some type of allergic reaction."

31

Melanie

I was pretty much an emotional wreck the entire ride over to the clinic the next morning. I barely slept at all the night before and the little bit I did was filled with nightmares. Plus, I had Trent pulling over every ten minutes because I felt like was gonna puke my guts out, even though nothing came out. And if that wasn't enough, I was having a damn nicotine fit like you'd never believe. Trent offered me a cigarette but I declined. I was about to have an abortion, yet the mothering instinct in me wouldn't allow me to smoke while the baby was inside me. Like I said, I was a wreck.

Trent circled the block, then pulled the car up in front of Choices and turned to me. "Why don't you get out here while I park the car? It doesn't look like I'm gonna find a spot on this block."

"All right, I'll wait out here for you." I stepped out the car.

"Hey, Mel?" Trent called as he rolled down the window.

"Yeah?" I stuck my head in the car.

"You sure about this? 'Cause me, Momma and Wil, we can help you with the baby if you want."

"I know that, Trent, but I can't see myself having a baby right now."

"Aw'ight. I just wanted to make sure."

I watched him pull away, feeling a little woozy but happy to know my brother cared. Two minutes later I heard a familiar male voice call my name. A very familiar voice that made me feel even woozier.

"What are you doing here, Prince?" I hadn't even turned around when I started my question, but when I did my eyes were given a treat. Lord, he was the last person I wanted to see, but that man was fine.

"Your brother told me you were coming here."

"Damn it, why the hell couldn't he just keep his mouth shut?"

"He was trying to help," Prince said as he approached.

"Help how? By telling you I'm pregnant, so you can harass me. What do you want, Prince?" I used a nasty tone to mask the fact that I was actually a little happy to see him.

"I came to ask you not to kill my baby." He looked so sad I could barely take it.

"Who said it was your baby?" I glanced down the block to see where Trent was, then tried to step around Prince and walk into the clinic. I didn't think I was ready to handle this conversation right now. Prince didn't touch me, but he blocked my path with his body.

"Come on, Melanie. Let's stop playing games." His sad face became stern.

"This is not a game, Prince. This is my life. I can't have a baby now. I'm not married. I haven't even finished school. I can barely take care of myself. How the hell am I gonna take care of a child?" I was starting to get emotional. "So no, this is not a game."

"I understand that, and if you really wanna have an abortion there's nothing I can do about it. Sure, I could try to stop you today by acting the fool but if you're serious you're just gonna be right back here tomorrow. All I'm asking is that you hear me out. Let me tell you how I feel. And what I'm willing to do to help you if you keep the baby."

"And what's that?" I placed my hand on my hip. I had to keep reminding myself that I was really mad at this man for what he did to Desiree. He was not the kind of person I wanted to be connected with by a child for the next eighteen years. I was not about to change my mind, but he was right. The least I could do was listen to what he had to say.

"Well, first of all, I love you, Melanie and . . ." He reached out and put a hand gently on my shoulder. I shook him off with a look.

"Don't, Prince," I snapped. "It's not helping your cause. One bit."

He backed off. "Look, I know it's hard being a single mother. And I don't want you to be a single mother. I want us to be a team and raise this baby whether we're together or not. I'm willing to take responsibility."

"Responsibility, huh? How the hell do you expect me to believe that, Prince? I've heard so many guys tell girls that same bull when they was pregnant. But when the baby came? Sure, they stuck around for a while, but when they realized they wasn't getting no ass, *poof,* they were gone with the wind. No phone calls, no child support, not even a damn Christmas card."

"Look, Melanie, I'm not gonna pretend I don't want you. I do. But I want this baby just as much. I'm twenty-eight and I ain't got no kids and my moms ain't got no grandkids. I ain't gonna run out on my kid and neither is my mom. And I'm willing to give you this to prove it." He reached into his coat and handed me a thick brown envelope.

"What's this for?" I looked down at his hand but didn't take the envelope from him.

"That's my guarantee that I'm willing to be a good father if you have this baby." He put it into my hand and his eyes pleaded with me to open it. "That's a copy of my birth certificate, my driver's license, my social security card, my pension plan, my last three W-2's and a $100,000 life insurance policy I took out on myself with you as the beneficiary. Everything you need to collect seventeen percent of what I make for the next twenty-one years of my life or a little more if I die. You tell me what man who's not willing to be a father would give you that?"

"Prince . . ." I didn't know what to say as I thumbed through the contents of the envelope. As emotional as I already was this morning, I wasn't prepared for this. It was so hard for me to comprehend that the same man who could try to get with my best friend was now making such a heartfelt plea to do the right thing by me and my baby. He was starting to melt some of my defenses.

"Melanie, please don't kill our baby." His voice was so gentle and so sad. "I'll stay out your way. I promise."

"I can't have a baby, Prince." I fought to hold back my tears. I was crying for the decision I had to make, I was crying for this unborn baby, and I was crying for the relationship Prince and I had lost.

"Yeah, you can. You already have one inside you." His eyes

went to my still flat stomach, and he looked like he wanted to reach out and stroke it to be close to our child. "You're not concerned about having a baby, Melanie. You're concerned about raising it."

"I don't know if I'm ready to give up my life yet, Prince."

"Then just give up nine months. Me and my moms will raise the baby. You can come get the baby on the weekends if you want."

That snapped me out of the fog I felt like I was in. Did he really believe I would have a baby and just hand it over to him? At the time, my pride made that seem worse than an abortion. How would I look, not able to mother my own child, giving it to the man who tried to get with my best friend? Oh, no. Oh, hell no, that was not gonna happen.

"Look, Prince. I'm getting rid of it." My voice was flat as I got my emotions under control.

"Hey, Prince. Funny seeing you here," Trent announced as he came around the corner. He'd probably been lurking around there, waiting for us to finish.

"Cut the shit, Trent," I told him angrily. "I already know you told him I was coming."

"All righty, then. Y'all getting anything straight?" Trent asked.

"Yeah, we got things straight. She's gonna kill my baby." Prince turned around and started walking, but then he stopped. He turned to look at me, and the sadness was gone from his eyes. Now he looked as angry as I was. "Melanie, you don't have to worry about me calling anymore."

I didn't answer him. What else was there to say?

"Well, you gonna do this or what?" Trent asked as he opened the door to the clinic.

"Yeah, I'm gonna do it," I told him as I watched Prince disappear around a corner.

Twenty minutes later I was in an examination room thumbing through the contents of the envelope Prince had given me. Before I started to look through the envelope I'd been daydreaming about what our child would look like. I know Prince told me once that he wanted a little girl. But me, I'd always wanted a boy. The door opened and a petite Asian woman in a nurse's uniform came in, interrupting my thoughts.

"Hi, Ms. Duncan." She smiled. "My name's Donna Lee and I'm the clinic's social worker. I hope you don't mind but before you have this procedure I have to ask you a few questions."

"Ask away," I told her.

"Okay." She gave me a comforting smile. "I know you've probably been asked this quite a few times already but are you sure you want this procedure?"

I shifted the envelope Prince had given me from hand to hand, then glanced at her with a weak frown. "Miss Lee, I'm not sure of anything right now."

"Have you thought about some of the other options? There is always adoption or you could keep the baby."

"Yeah, I guess I could, couldn't I?" I replied more serious than I wanted to admit.

"We can help you put together a support system if you'd like." I thought about Trent who was sitting in the lobby waiting for me and then my mom and Wil and Diane. Then I glanced down at the envelope again.

"No, I have a mother and some great brothers. Not to mention a baby's father who's willing to do the right thing. No, I think I have a support system."

The woman smiled. "So does that mean you changed your mind?"

"No, it just means I need to give this whole thing some more thought. Can you hand me my clothes?"

She smiled at me. "I sure can."

32

Wil

"Wil," my new secretary Linda called.

It had been almost three weeks since Jeanie Brown's death and things had finally started to calm down around the building, although they were nowhere near back to normal in the sales department. Mimi was now in another building working in shipping and receiving while Linda was trying to fill her absence the best she could. To be honest, she wasn't a very good secretary, and even less attractive to the eye, which was part of the reason I hired her but it made me miss Mimi all the more. It didn't help that Mimi stopped by almost every day during lunch to say hi, wearing those low cut blouses and tight skirts of hers. To make things even worse she'd always end up sticking around her entire lunch break doing some of incompetent Linda's work.

"Yes, Linda," I replied, looking up from my paperwork.

"There's a Keisha Smith waiting out here to see you. She says it's important."

"Keisha Smith?" I scratched my head. "I don't think I know a Keisha Smith. Does she have an appointment? What company is she from?"

"She's not with a company. She said to tell you she's Maxine Graves's sister."

"Oh, Mimi's sister Keisha. Yeah, send her in." I stood, smiling as Keisha walked into my office. God, she really was just a darker version of her sister. Fine as hell with an outrageous body. "Hey, Keisha, how you doing?"

Keisha skipped the pleasantries and got right the point. "Where's my sister?"

I shrugged my shoulders. "I don't know. I spoke to her yesterday but I haven't seen her today. Have you checked shipping? She usually doesn't stop by here until around lunchtime."

"What do you mean stop by? I thought she was your secretary." She looked confused and was obviously out of the loop when it came to her sister's business.

"No, Maxine hasn't been my secretary in almost a month," I explained. "She's working in shipping."

"What? But, but I thought." She hesitated. "Oh, dear God. Where's shipping?"

"It's in the building next door. Hey, is something wrong?"

She sighed, "I sure as hell hope not. Can you call shipping and find out if my sister's over there?"

"Sure." I reached down and dialed Maxine's desk, letting it ring on speakerphone.

"Shipping and receiving, this is Joyce. How can I help you?"

"Hi, Joyce, this is Wil Duncan in sales. Is Maxine Graves around today?"

"No, Maxine won't be in until around one o'clock today, Mr. Duncan."

"Okay, thanks." I hung up the phone and looked up at Keisha. If I didn't know something was wrong before, I knew it now. I could see it all over Keisha's face. "What's wrong?"

"Look, I don't mean to be personal, but are you really divorcing your wife?"

"Divorcing my wife? No! I'm happily married. Who told you that?" I gave her a strange look, then realized I probably knew the answer to my own question. "Mimi told you that, didn't she?"

"Yeah, she told me. But what I wanna know is why the hell are you fooling around with my sister if you're so happily married?"

"I'm not fooling around with your sister." I gave her an insulted look. I was gonna have to have a talk with Mimi. She'd taken that one kiss way out of context.

"Yeah, right. You weren't over her house last night watching the game when I called?"

"No. I talked to her on the phone but that's about it. I was at the hospital with my wife yesterday. We didn't get home until close to midnight. Do you wanna call her?" I picked up the phone. This whole conversation was taking a terrible turn and I was starting to become annoyed.

"So you and my sister aren't having an affair?" Keisha asked. This sounded like it was news to her.

"Look, Keisha, I know your sister likes me and I think the world of her, but I'm a married man. I've explained that to her. That's why she was transferred to shipping."

"Well, then we've got a problem." Her brow was furrowed. She looked truly worried.

"What do you mean *we've* got a problem? How do I have a problem?"

"Does Maxine know where you live?"

"Yeah, why? What's that have to do with our problem?'"

"I think you better sit down, 'cause I have a few things to tell you about my sister that I doubt she put on her résumé."

I did as she asked and sat down. She sat down in the chair in front of me looking real serious. From that point on I started to get a real bad feeling about this.

"Look, you've gotta promise me that this stays between you and me. If I'm wrong and Maxine's just at the dentist or something, I don't want her to lose her job by telling her personal business."

"You don't have to worry about that. She's not in my department anymore. Besides, I like Maxine. I would never do anything to hurt her."

"I sure hope you feel that way after I tell you this," she said, leaning forward. "Wil, my sister is manic depressive. She's been seeing psychiatrists ever since she was a teenager—"

I cut her off. "What are you trying to say, that Mimi's crazy?"

"Delusional is more like it."

"Delusional? She seems fine to me." I gave her a look of disbelief. I was starting to think Keisha was the crazy one.

"And around you, I would expect her to appear fine."

"Well, what's she delusional about?"

"You." She pointed at me.

"Me?" I sat back in my chair, making a face as I pointed to myself. "Why is she delusional about me? I've always been nice to her."

"Exactly," Keisha began to explain. "That's her delusion. She takes your kindness for love. She thinks you're in love with her,

Wil. That you're having a relationship. She told me y'all were getting married."

"Married! But I'm already married and I'm not leaving my wife. She knows that."

"That's the problem. That's always the problem with Maxine, Wil. She has these amazing fantasies about nice men like you sweeping her off her feet. I'm no doctor but I think married men are even attractive to her because you're more of a challenge. Then when you stupid asses end up sleeping with her, you just make things worse."

"I didn't sleep with her," I reiterated.

Keisha gave me a skeptical glance. "Well, you'll be the first."

I didn't bother to respond to her, although I did want to know more about Maxine. "So, is she dangerous?"

Keisha was silent for a while before she spoke. "Let's put it this way. The last guy she thought she was in love with was this guy named Philip. His wife fell off the platform of the Long Island Railroad into an oncoming train." I closed my eyes at the image. Then a thought flashed in my head. Marge had fallen and reinjured her arm right when she was supposed to come back and replace Mimi. Did Mimi have something to do with it?

"Did Mimi do that? Did she hurt that man's wife?"

"Nobody seems to know for sure. The district attorney deemed it an accident because there were no witnesses. But Maxine was there, and what she was doing in Hempstead at that time of morning when she lived in Queens is beyond me."

"Look, Keisha, what about my wife? Is she in danger?"

"I hope not but that's why I'm here."

"What do you mean you hope not? What's that supposed to mean?"

"I'm not sure but I think Mimi took a gun I keep for protection out of my beauty shop this morning."

I picked up the phone immediately and dialed my house. The phone kept ringing until I got my answering machine. "Diane, as soon as you get this message, call me right away. It's important. Call me right away. And don't open the door for anyone." I hung up the phone and dialed her cell phone. Again I got no answer, so I left the same message.

"Wil, I think you need to call the police."

I dialed 911.

"Nine-one-one emergency. Please state the emergency."

"Can you send a car to 176 234th Street?"

"We'd be glad to, sir. What's the emergency?"

"I think someone is going to my house to hurt my wife."

"Are they there already?"

"I'm not sure. My wife's not answering the phone."

"Sir, we can send a car over to your address but the officers will not enter the house unless they find a disturbance."

"Fine, just send a car." I hung up the phone, staring at Keisha. "I'm going home, you wanna come?" She nodded and the two of us ran out of my office.

33

Mimi

I drove past Wil's house and circled the block for the fifth time, admiring the flowers and shrubs along his well-manicured lawn. It's amazing the things you miss at night that seem almost impossible to miss during the day. I must have driven past Wil's house a thousand times before, wishing it were me in there with him instead of Diane, but not once did I ever notice how beautiful his landscaping was. It was something I was gonna have to keep up after Diane was gone and I moved in.

I parked my car on a side street about two blocks away, then started walking toward the house. I was carrying a box of my sister's brownies with me. When I got to the front door I opened my pocketbook and slipped on a pair of black gloves to match my black and white outfit before ringing the bell. Diane answered the door a few seconds later wearing a pair of jeans and a sweatshirt.

"Yes?" She stuck her head out the screen door, staring at me as if she wasn't quite sure if she knew me or not. I was so dressed up she probably thought I was a Jehovah's Witness.

"Hi, Diane. Remember me? I'm Maxine, from Wil's office." She stared a little a harder and her eyes shifted evilly. I'm sure she must have thought I was over there to finish what we'd started at the party.

"Wil's not here. He's at work," she told me in a curt tone, turning toward her house.

"I know. I didn't come here to see Wil. I came here to talk to you, woman to woman, about him."

"Look, I don't have time for this. My phone is ringing." She pulled the door closed.

"Let it ring. I think we need to get everything out in the open about your husband and me! That is, if you can handle it."

I think my suggestive words threw her for a loop because her reply, although positive, was less than confident. "I can handle it." She sighed, opening the door.

"Good, can I come in? I promise it'll be brief and you'll never see me again."

She pushed the door open and I stepped into the house just as the phone stopped ringing.

"This is a lovely place you have here. I plan on having a place just like it, real soon."

Just as soon as your ass is buried and gone, I thought to my-self as I followed her down the hallway.

She walked into the kitchen and sat down at the table, gesturing to a chair across from her. I ignored her and set the box of brownies on the table. She glanced at it, but it didn't seem to interest her.

"What do you have to say about Wil?" she questioned.

I walked around the table slowly, admiring the kitchen before taking the seat directly in front of her. "This is a beautiful kitchen. I always wanted a large eat-in kitchen. Although I'd probably change the color of the curtains." I smirked.

"Look, are you here to write an article for *Good Housekeeping* or are you here to talk about my husband? 'Cause I have to pick up my kids from day care—" I cut her off with a smirk.

"Please, you don't have to pick up them kids until two o'clock," I quickly retorted.

Diane's expression was priceless. She looked like someone had smacked the shit out of her. "How did you know what time I pick up my kids?"

"Wil told me." I chuckled. "He tells me everything, you know. Including the fact that your ass is frigid and you're not giving him any."

She was so shocked by my comment her mouth was wide enough to catch flies. When she gained her composure she pointed at the door. "I think you should leave."

I smiled. "I thought we were gonna talk."

"This conversation is over." She started to stand.

"It's not over until I say it's over. Now sit down, Diane," I demanded.

"Who the fuck you think you talking to? This is my house."
She balled up her fist, glaring at me.

"Not for long," I snapped.

She looked like she was about to jump across the table and
beat my ass but she stopped abruptly when I pulled a handgun
out of my bag and pointed it at her chest.

"Now I think I told you to sit down, didn't I? That is, unless
you want me to blow your ass away. Then who's gonna pick up
those kids at two?" I shook my head. "Not me. I'm supposed to
be at work at one."

"Don't you hurt my babies." She slowly sat down, keeping
her eyes on the gun.

"Hurt them? You disappoint me, Diane. I would never hurt
them. Matter of fact, I brought these brownies for them." I
opened the box of brownies with my free hand, taking one out
and biting into it. "Have one?" I smirked as I told her, "You
know, your girl Jeanie loved these brownies. I guess you could
even say they were the death of her."

"You're one crazy bitch," Diane said, trying to sound brave
even though fear was all over her face.

I laughed and pointed the gun at her head. "Crazy? You
know, that's the same thing Jeanie said right before she took her
last breath."

"Jeanie? Jeanie's death was accidental." She sounded like she
was still hoping that was true.

I laughed again. "Accidentally on purpose." She didn't reply
so I continued. "Did you know Jeanie was allergic to sesame
seeds? I did. That's why I had my sister use sesame seed oil instead of vegetable oil in her brownies. You should have seen
Jeanie's face when I told her." I took another bite of my brownie.
"You have any allergies, Diane?" She didn't answer so I waved
the gun at her. "I asked you a question."

"No. I don't have allergies."

"Neither do I." I finished off the brownie. "You sure you
don't want one?"

"Why are you doing this? Jeanie didn't do anything to you.
Neither did I."

"You mean you haven't figured it out yet?" I was enjoying the look on Diane's face as she sat there trembling. "I'm doing it because I'm in love with Wil and he's not gonna be mine until you're gone. What do you think, I just go around killing people?"

There was a knock on the door and she moved like she wanted to answer it.

"You expecting company?" I lifted the gun to her head.

"No."

"Good. It's probably just some Jehovah's Witnesses."

When the knocking stopped I waited a few minutes, then gestured for Diane to get up.

"Where are we going?"

"Upstairs."

She gave me a puzzled look. "Why?"

"You'll see." When we got to the top of the stairs I ushered her into the master bedroom. I'd never been in her house, but I knew where it was from sitting across the street staring at their window late at night, hoping to get a glimpse of Wil. Their bedroom was pretty. A combination of pastel paints and flowered wallpaper. I was impressed by the way the curtains and bedspreads matched the wallpaper. But the most impressive thing of all was the king-size bed. God, the things Wil and me were going to do on that bed. Just the thought of it made me wanna smack Diane for having the opportunity to do it first. But I regained my composure, remembering that she was about to get hers in just a few minutes.

"In the bathroom," I ordered, directing her with the gun. She did as she was told and I relished in the power I held over her. "Did you take a bath today?" I lifted the gun.

"No. I—" I stopped her in mid sentence.

"Don't make no excuses. I thought I smelled something funky. You know you nasty. Run some bath water."

"Are you serious?" She snapped, obviously forgetting who was in charge.

"Did I stutter?" I lifted the gun again.

She bent down and turned the water on, then looked up at me.

"What's wrong? You don't put bubbles in your bath?" She

shook her head, but reached for the bubble bath on the tub's rim and poured it in. When the tub was filled I leaned against the sink and told her, "Get your clothes off."

"For what?" she asked defiantly. "What are you gonna do, drown me in the tub?"

"I'm gonna blow your ass away right now if you don't get them fucking clothes off."

"You're never gonna get away with this," she told me as she slowly unbuckled her jeans. "You realize that, don't you? Do you really think Wil's gonna wanna be with a woman who killed his wife?"

"Why not? All I gotta do is make it look like an accident. Like I did Philip's wife and your girl Jeanie. Now stop stalling and get your fucking clothes off."

I watched her painstakingly take off her clothes until she was completely naked. "Now get in the tub," I ordered. She gave me this look that made me think she was going to do something stupid. I raised the gun to her head and smirked. "I guess you don't want an open casket." She didn't reply. She just stepped in the tub. "Now sit down."

This time she did as she was told and I sat on the toilet seat to give Diane her last rites.

"You know, I mentioned to Wil one time that I love to sit in a warm bubble bath and listen to R. Kelly." I smiled at the thought. "You know what he said to me? He said, 'Diane loves to listen to music in the tub, too.'" I nodded my head before I continued. "Yep, he said you have a clock radio that you keep right on a shelf above the toilet." I stood up for a second and took the radio off the shelf. I held it in one hand. The gun, pointed at Diane, was in my other hand. "Is this it?"

"Yeah."

"You already have it tuned into KISS." I flipped it on and Luther Vandross's "There's Nothing Better Than Love" came out of the small speaker. "Oh, I love this song." I started to sway back and forth, then dropped the radio on the bathroom rug.

"Oops!" I picked up the radio, making a face. "My God, I almost dropped this in the tub. You know, you should really buy a new clock radio, preferably a battery-operated one. This plug-in one is real dangerous, especially near a bathtub. You could have one hell of an accident in here if this thing falls in the tub with you."

Fear sparked in Diane's eyes as I dangled the radio over her bath water.

"Any last words? Maybe something I can tell your kids?"

"Yeah," she answered, then stopped when we both heard a sound downstairs. I thought I heard Wil's voice calling for her, but I didn't know how that could be possible. He was supposed to be at work now. This plan was supposed to be foolproof.

Diane looked toward the door and my eyes followed her gaze. Within seconds I heard water splashing. I turned back to Diane but before I could react, she was halfway out the tub and on top of me, trying to wrestle the gun from my hand.

"Oh, my God, Wil. Wil! Help me! Please, help me!" She was screaming for her husband.

"Get off me, you bitch!" I screamed as we wrestled to the bathroom floor. The radio fell out of my hands, but I managed to keep hold of the gun. I had no idea where the radio went, but I couldn't worry about that now. We tousled back and forth and I had to give her credit. She was a lot stronger than I thought. But not quite strong enough. Somehow I pulled the gun free and pointed it at her. "Back up, bitch!" She did and we both stood up just as Wil entered the bathroom doorway.

34

Wil

We rushed into the house and I called out Diane's name as I quickly searched the first floor. I was positive she was home because her car was in the driveway and her keys and purse were both on the living room sofa. I was just praying that she was in the backyard working on her flowers, or upstairs taking a nap.

"Wil," Keisha called from the kitchen. When I entered she was holding a box of brownies. "Maxine was here. I gave her this box of brownies this morning."

"Shit," I cursed. I was truly afraid for my wife's life for the first time. "Where could they be? I didn't see Maxine's car outside."

"Did you check upstairs?"

"Diane," I yelled even louder than before in frustration.

"Wil! Help me! Please, help me!" I heard my panicked wife scream from upstairs.

"They're up there." I tossed my cell phone to Keisha and said, "Call the cops." Then I ran to the stairs and up them as fast as I could.

When I reached the top of the stairs, my heart was almost beating out of my chest. *Okay, Wil, what are you gonna do when you find them? Keisha said Maxine has a gun.* I heard the commotion in my bedroom and rushed in without hesitation. I found them both in the bathroom and I couldn't believe my eyes. Maxine was dressed like she was going to church, or maybe a funeral. She had a gun in her hand and it was pointed at Diane, who was naked as the day she was born and obviously scared. And she wasn't the only one.

"Wil," Diane called out in fear.

"It's all right, Di." I tried to give her a reassuring look. "Maxine? What are you doing? Put that gun down."

"Wil?" She actually smiled at me. "What are you doing here? You're supposed to be at work."

"I came to stop you from doing something stupid. Now, please, put down that gun before you hurt someone," I told her calmly, extending my hand.

"I can't."

"Yes, you can. Now give me the gun," I said sternly.

"No, I can't!" she snapped, lifting the gun to Diane's head until I pulled back my arm. "Don't you understand, Wil? I'm doing this for you. For us. With her out the way, me, you, and the kids can be happy. Now I want you to leave. This has to look like an accident." Damn, she really was delusional. *God dammit, Keisha, where the hell are the cops?* I wondered as I tried to keep myself from panicking.

"I'm not leaving, Maxine. I can't let you do this. This is not Diane's fault."

"Yes, it is!" she screamed.

"No, it isn't. It's my fault. Diane doesn't have anything to do with this."

"No, Wil. It's not your fault. It's her fault! It's all her fault! You'd be with me if it wasn't for her." Her face was screwed up with anger, but tears were welling in her eyes.

"No, I wouldn't, Maxine."

"Yes, you would! And stop calling me Maxine!" She turned the gun toward me and I froze. "Now I don't wanna hear anything else negative about our relationship, Wil. Do you understand me?" I hesitated and she lifted the gun.

"Do what she says, Wil. She's already killed Jeanie."

"Shut up, Diane." She turned the gun back on my wife.

"Oh, my God. You killed Jeanie?" I couldn't imagine what she'd done to Jeanie, but right now my only concern was for my wife.

"Yeah, she was getting in the way. She didn't want us to be together," Mimi said in a flat, cold voice.

"So you killed her? That woman gave you a job, Mimi. We wouldn't have even met if it wasn't for her."

I don't think she'd ever thought of it that way, because her expression momentarily changed to one of confusion. "Don't be mad with me, Wil." She almost sounded like a child. "It was an accident."

"No, it wasn't." I lost my cool. "You killed her. Keisha's right. You're fucking crazy. You should be in a mental institution."

"No, I shouldn't!" she exploded. "I'm not fucking crazy! Do you hear me, Wil? I'm not crazy! Now take that back! Take it back, now, or so help me God I will shoot you right where you stand." She pointed the gun at me and pulled back the hammer. Once I heard the click, I froze up, closing my eyes as I waited for the impact of the bullet. But the bullet never came.

"Leave him alone you crazy bitch!" Diane screamed.

I opened my eyes just in time to see Diane grab Mimi by the hair and pull her backwards into the tub. The gun went off, but the bullet missed me completely. I tried to grab Diane and pull her away from Mimi and that gun, but there was no need. Mimi was in the tub shaking uncontrollably. Then I heard a loud pop and all the lights went out. Only the sunlight illuminated the room. In the tub I could see Mimi's body, limp and still. I took a cautious step toward her and realized what had happened. Diane's clock radio was in the tub along with Mimi. She'd been killed pretty quickly.

"Is she? Is she dead?" Diane whimpered.

"Yeah, I think so," I replied, pulling my wife into my arms.

"That's what she wanted to do to me," she cried. I held her tighter and felt her shuddering with fear.

"I know, baby, but she can't hurt anyone anymore."

35

Melanie

It was Saturday afternoon. I was drinking a cup of tea as I watched my niece, Katie, playing with her dolls on my living room floor. Her brother, Teddy, was having a ball, pushing his trucks and cars as fast as he could up and down the tile floor of my hallway, then in and out of the bedrooms. After everything that had happened with Wil and Diane I'd offered to watch the kids for them so that they could get away for the weekend. I couldn't even imagine what they'd gone through last week with that crazy-ass secretary of his, but I had to give them credit, they seemed to be taking it all in stride.

I'd always loved watching Teddy and Katie, but especially now, because they made me realize just how precious the child growing inside me was. I still hadn't told Prince that I was keeping the baby, and it had been a struggle to get Trent to keep his mouth shut the past few weeks. I was going to have to tell him soon, though, because Trent had given me an ultimatum. He said if I didn't tell Prince I was keeping the baby before his wedding in two weeks, he'd make it his business to tell Prince during the reception. I'd picked up the phone to call Prince on more than one occasion, but each time I'd think about him trying to get with Desiree and hang up. I knew I was gonna have to get past that shit and at least be friends with him for the baby's sake, but I'd never had a man hurt me like that before. I guess part of me was waiting for him to call me, but true to his word he hadn't called once since leaving Trent and me in front of the clinic that day. I guess he was just as angry at me as I was at him. We had a true love-hate relationship.

"Auntie Mel, can you read this book to me?" Teddy came running down the hall carrying one of Desiree's journals.

"Teddy, gimme that. Where'd you get that from?"

"From Auntie Dez-ray's room." He handed it to me and it fell on the floor with its pages open. Desiree was always writing in these journals, and I'd never disrespected her privacy by trying to read them. They stayed in her room, and I'd never once gone to peek while Desiree was out. Hadn't even really been interested in what she was writing as long as she wasn't writing about me. Besides, Desiree was my girl, and she pretty much told me everything, anyway. But now that Teddy had brought one to me, I couldn't resist a glance at the open pages that were on the floor before me. And when I happened to see my name on the page, you know I had to pick up that book and see what she had to say.

> *Melanie and I went to the Shark Bar in Manhattan tonight. I don't know where she got the dress she wore, but that shit was hideous. It looked like she bought it out the thrift store. I was embarrassed to say she was with me.*

I sat back in my chair. Embarrassed? If I remembered correctly, she got mad because all the cute guys were buying me drinks and she was stuck with some over-the-hill, foreign taxi driver with a receding hairline. Damn, why she gotta hate? Now I had to know more, so I flipped through a few more pages, stopping when I saw Prince's name in bold print.

> *PRINCE ratings: 10 in the face, 10 in the body, I don't know what he's like in the bedroom, but I'd love to find out.*
> *Melanie and I went to Manhattan Proper tonight. I finally got a chance to meet this mystery man Prince she's been so head over heels about and I must say, he's even finer than she described. She's trying to act like she doesn't care about him because he didn't call, but I know she does. If she drops the ball with this one, I might have to pick it up and run with it. He's got to be one of the finest men I've ever seen. . . .*

Damn, girlfriend, it's like that, huh? Why didn't she tell me this shit to my face? What else did my so-called best friend have to say about me and my man in her book? A few pages later, I found another entry about Prince.

I have to admit I was a little jealous when I came home and found out Prince and Melanie had gotten together. Especially after what happened with me and Tim. But his stopping by with presents and flowers and shit is starting to get on my nerves. What the fuck makes her so special?

I knew she was jealous of what Prince and I had, but I had no idea how deep her feelings ran. I didn't know whether to feel sorry for her that she was so lonely or sorry for myself. I know it hurt reading that shit, but I had to read on.

Damn, don't these two ever stop? It's three o'clock in the morning and they're going at it again. They're making me so horny I think I'm going to masturbate as I listen. . . .

"Ahhh, now that's disgusting," I said out loud.
"What's disgusting?" Teddy asked.
"Nothing, sweetie." I smiled at my nephew. "Why don't you go back in the hall and play with your cars? When I'm finished reading I'm gonna take you guys to McDonald's."
"All right," Teddy shouted as he walked back toward the hall. I flipped through a few more pages.

Prince and I had a long conversation today before Melanie got home. I knew he was good-looking, but I never imagined that he could be so fun to talk with. I was actually pissed off when Melanie came home and we had to end our conversation. . . .

She was pissed off that I came home to *my* man? This was even more serious than I'd thought. I felt a little knot forming in my stomach, because the next entry was no better.

Melanie, Prince and I went out to a place called The Spot in Hempstead. I had a great time and I danced with

Prince most of the night. Things were pretty cool, although I did have to put Melanie in her place when she dragged me in the bathroom with some petty shit about the way I was dancing with Prince. Shit, I couldn't help it if her man wanted me. If he didn't, why was his dick hard when I rubbed my ass up against it?

If she was my friend she wouldn't have been rubbing her ass against my man in the first place! And she had the nerve to tell me that night that if I was taking him home I didn't have anything to worry about. What I failed to realize was that she was going home with us too. And from what I was reading, I don't think Desiree would have minded one bit if somehow I ended up out of the picture that night. I was just about ready to throw this damn book against a wall.

It's getting hard listening to Prince and Melanie having sex every night. I'm starting to wish it was me in there instead of her. I wonder if I would have a chance with him? I just might have to put his loyalty to the test.

That fucking bitch! Now I was seeing red as I flipped to the next page.

I've been doing everything I can to get Prince's attention, but he's either blind or stupid because he keeps ignoring my advances. I've done everything but give him an invitation to the pussy. I even went so far as to grab his ass a few times when Melanie wasn't looking, but he still ain't paid me no mind. But I haven't given up yet. I got something for him when Melanie goes to register for school in the morning. Something he's never gonna forget.

The more I read, the madder I got, and the clearer the picture was becoming. I was starting to get a sick feeling that Prince had been telling the truth all along. Maybe he wasn't the one who'd made a pass after all. But I was still so damn confused. Maybe he did finally give in to her advances. Shit, you almost couldn't blame the man with the way Desiree was throwing her ass at him. But one thing didn't make sense. If he had given in and made a pass, it was clear now that Desiree would not have turned him down like she claimed she had. That bitch wanted my man bad. I had to read further, because I had to know whose version of the story was true. I was becoming convinced that I'd made a very big mistake believing Desiree.

I'm in trouble and I don't know how to get out of it. This morning after Melanie left to register for school, I slipped into her bed with no clothes on. I figured Prince was just like every other man and wouldn't resist the opportunity to get some new pussy. Especially if I made the first move. But I was wrong and that bastard rejected me like I was a used condom. He threatened to tell Melanie what I'd done. I had to blackmail him into keeping his mouth shut. Only I don't think he's going to keep his mouth shut for long. He's one of those guys with a conscience.

By now I felt like I was about to hyperventilate. How the fuck did I let her get away with this? I flipped to the next page to find out what else she had been up to.

Prince has started to act real funny whenever I'm around. I know it's just a matter of time before he tells Melanie everything. But I'm not worried. I've devised a plan that will turn back any attempt he makes toward exposing me. And all it entails is a letter. A letter I'll carry around with me for the next six months if need be.

That was it. I couldn't read one more word. If I had, I would probably be going to jail for murder, and I had a baby to think about now. Desiree had cost me not only the best man I had ever been with, but the father of my child. Now I wasn't about to fight that bitch in my condition, but she was getting the fuck out my house. I picked up the phone and dialed Trent's number.
"Hello."

"Trent, I need you to come over and pick up Teddy and Katie for a few hours. I got something important I have to take care of."

"Like what? Everything all right?"

"No, but I'll explain it to you when you get here."

"Aw'ight. I'm on my way."

A couple hours later, I was sitting on the couch with Prince, feeling emotionally drained. Trent had come by like I'd asked. I gave him the short version of everything I'd learned in Desiree's journal, then he went out to the hardware store and bought a new lock for my door. After he changed the lock for me, he took the kids and wished me luck. As soon as Trent was gone I'd called Prince and told him we really needed to talk. At first he was a little hesitant. I wasn't sure he would even agree to see me after how I'd pushed him away in front of the clinic. But when I told him that I hadn't gone through with the abortion, his attitude seemed to relax. I think he might have even been smiling on the other end of the phone, but he was doing his best to mask any feelings. I didn't blame him, though. We'd both been really hurt by this whole mess. That was why I wanted him to come over to see if we could mend any of the damage that had been done. If there was any hope, I wanted us to be together not just for the sake of the child I was carrying but because of the love I have for him.

We'd talked through the whole thing about Desiree. Prince was relieved that I'd found the journal and I knew the truth, but he was still really hurt that I had believed Desiree in the first place. He understood the whole thing about her being my girl, but that wasn't good enough. If there was any hope that Prince and I could get back together now, we had some serious trust issues to work out. I needed to believe that he was going to be faithful to me. But then again, now that the truth was out, he'd never really given me a reason to believe otherwise. So it was more important at this point that Prince could trust me. He needed to trust that I would have his back if an issue like this ever came up again. And the first step in proving that to him was to end my friendship with Desiree. That was gonna be no problem after what she'd done. In fact, I was looking forward to it. We waited for quite a while in silence until I heard her fumbling with the lock. When she couldn't get in, she finally knocked.

I took my time getting up from the sofa to answer the door. "Who?"

"What you mean, who? It's me. Let me in. Something's wrong with the lock. My key won't work."

I opened the door and gave her a cross-eyed smirk as she entered.

"What's wrong with the lock? And why are all those garbage bags out in the hallway?"

"Ain't nothing wrong with the lock," I snarled at her. "I just felt like changing it."

She looked at me like I'd lost my mind. "For what?"

"To keep out unwanted visitors."

"What? Prince still harassing you?" she asked nonchalantly.

It took everything I had not to smack her ass as she walked into the kitchen. She was lucky I was pregnant and had to worry about my child or I would have whooped her ass.

"No, Prince is right there in the living room." I pointed at the sofa and Desiree's jaw almost hit the ground as she did a triple take.

"What's he doing here?" she asked defensively. She was too worried about herself to notice my attitude.

"He's my baby's father. He's welcome here anytime he wants. Too bad I can't say the same thing for you."

Desiree took a step back. If she didn't sense there was a problem before, she sure sensed it now. "What's that supposed to mean?"

I shook my head from side to side. I might not be able to fight right now, but I sure could get ghetto when I wanted to. "It means get the fuck out my apartment. That's what it means."

"Your apartment?" She sucked her teeth. "Please. I pay rent here, too."

"Well you should have put your name on the lease when I asked you to, because now you don't live here no more. Oh, and that pile of garbage bags you asked about? That's your shit. Every last funky bit of it."

She was speechless for a few seconds as she looked with wet eyes from me to Prince and back to me. "What I do? Why you doing me like this for some nigga?"

"Why you calling him a nigga if you wanted him so bad?"

A look of fear flashed across her face for a second, but she recovered pretty quickly with her attitude. "Him? I don't want him." She gave Prince a look like something in the room smelled bad.

"Please, Desiree. I read your journal. And I know what you did."

"You read my journal?" She looked pissed off, then realized she was the one in the wrong. "I was just—"

I cut her off. "Don't lie, bitch, 'cause it ain't working, okay?"

"I can't fuckin' believe you read my journal! That's my private shit, Melanie!" She looked like she was about to step to me, but Prince got off the couch and headed toward us. Desiree stopped herself and offered one more threat.

"This shit ain't over, Melanie."

"Maybe not, but our friendship is."

36

Trent

I walked out the Queens courthouse doors in need of a cigarette and some fresh air. I was greeted by my brother, Wil; my sister Melanie; and Prince, who'd been back in my sister's life ever since she kicked Desiree out. I was glad they were gonna try to make it work for the sake of their child.

No one spoke as I approached, but their faces told me everything I needed to know. They'd been talking about me. They'd been talking about this whole damn fiasco. I musta looked like a real loser right about then. And the last thing I wanted to do was look like a loser in front of Wil. Not after everything he'd gone through and still come out smelling like roses. I still don't believe he wasn't fucking that chick Mimi.

"Momma okay?" Wil asked.

"Yeah, she fine. She's in there talking to Diane. She just wants to know what's going on."

"She ain't the only one," Melanie replied, rolling her eyes.

"Y'all seen her?" I asked, although I knew the answer. I took out my pack of cigarettes and nervously lit the last one.

"Nope. I don't think she's coming, Trent," Prince replied honestly.

"Ain't no think, Prince. She ain't coming," Melanie stated, checking her cell phone for the time. "It's quarter to five. Now I know a bride's supposed to be fashionably late but damn, this shit is ridiculous. She should have been here two hours ago."

"She's coming, Mel," I snapped, looking her in the eyes. "Indigo loves me. She wouldn't stand me up." I'm not sure if I was trying to convince them or myself. Not that it mattered. I don't think any of us was convinced.

"Have you tried to call her?" Wil encouraged.

"Yeah, three times. Maybe she was in the shower or something." I pulled out my cell and dialed the house again. No answer.

"It's time to face facts, Trent. I know it's hard to believe, but you've been stood up." Wil placed a big hand on my back and rubbed my shoulder. He was trying to be nice, but to me it was like torture.

I took a drag of my cigarette, then dropped it to the ground and stomped it out. I didn't wanna believe it, but the truth was the truth. Indigo had made a fool out of me. I'd invited a small group of friends and family, including my mom, to see us get married at the courthouse. Only I'd been left looking like a fool at the altar. I couldn't believe this was happening. Women didn't do things like this to me. Not to me. I'm Trent Duncan.

"Aw'ight," I told them. "Let's go inside so I can tell Momma."

I walked with my head down back into the courthouse to room 203 where they performed all the weddings. Wil, Melanie and Prince followed me. When I stepped in the room all eyes were upon me, and I had a hard time looking anyone in the face. I walked over to my mother and sat down next to her and placed my arm around her.

"What's going on, son? Isn't she coming?"

"Well, Mom." I took one look in my mother's face and I just couldn't tell her the truth. I could not tell her that her son had been left at the altar. "Hold on, Momma, my phone is vibrating. Maybe it's her." I slid my phone off its belt holster and flicked it open as I stood up.

"Hello," I said into the phone, then made a nasty face as I pretended to listen to someone. "Where have you been? Do you realize my entire family is here waiting for you?" I faked a look of concern as I pretended to listen. "Oh, is he all right?" I pretended to listen some more. "Okay, I'll be right there. I love you too, baby." I closed the phone slowly and looked sadly at my mother. She reached out and grabbed my hand.

"Is everything all right, son?"

"No, Momma, it's not." I furrowed my brow to show her how grim the fake situation was. "Everybody, can I have your attention?" All eyes were upon me. "I wanna thank you all for coming, but unfortunately we have to postpone the wedding."

"Why, what happened?" my mother's brother, Uncle Roy, asked.

"Indigo's father had a car accident on his way up here from Maryland. He's in critical condition." From the expression on everyone's faces, my performance must have been stellar. "Now there's food and drink, which my brother, Wil, was so kind to provide, over at Momma's house, so I hope you'll stop by."

My mother stood and kissed my cheek. "I'm sorry to hear about that girl's father, son. But God works in mysterious ways. Maybe this was His way of telling you that next time you should get married in a church." I never did tell Momma that I was the one who insisted on getting married in the courthouse. Indigo really wanted a big church wedding. I just figured that if we didn't make a big production out of our wedding, maybe I could keep it a secret from Michelle and still get with her once she cooled down a bit.

"Come on, Momma. Let's get you home." Wil offered her a hand.

"Just a minute, Wil." She turned toward me. "Trent, I know you say you love this girl, but maybe this is your chance to get back with Michelle so I can see my grandbaby."

I didn't reply. I just nodded. It wasn't that Momma disliked Indigo so much. She just really missed being able to spend time with my son. Michelle had been true to her word since our fight. She'd kept Marcus not only from me, but my family, too. I hated to see how much it hurt my mother.

Ten minutes later, everyone had left except for Big Mike, who hadn't said a word to me since he and Beverly arrived over three hours ago. He looked a little pissed off himself. Not that I could blame him. After the reception we were all supposed to go back to his place and meet with the people from Aggressive Records so Indigo could sign her contract and get her signing bonus. Mike's cut was fifteen percent, plus whatever he was gonna make as producer.

"I gotta give it to you," Mike told me, clapping his hands. "You really made the best outta a bad situation."

"What are you talking about, Mike?"

"You know what I'm talking about. I've been working pretty

close to Indigo these last few weeks. She told me her father died last year in a car accident."

"Yeah, I know, but I didn't know what else to say."

"She skipped out on you, didn't she?"

"I don't know what happened, Mike. I left her at my house at 1:30 and she was fine. She was taking a shower and getting ready to put on her dress. She couldn't wait to get down here. I don't know what the hell happened."

"Well you better find out and get her over to my house, 'cause those brothers over at Aggressive are bringing a check for seven hundred and fifty grand tonight."

"Seven hundred grand!" I could hear the cash registers going off in my head. "Don't worry, Mike. I'll find her." Any embarrassment I felt over being stood up vanished as I remembered my ultimate goal, the almighty dollar.

After two hours of driving around searching for Indigo, I finally just said, "fuck it," and brought my ass on home. I must have sat in front of my apartment in my car for about twenty minutes, feeling sorry for myself. It's not every day you get left at the altar and humiliated in front of your family, and then lose three quarters of a million dollars all in a five-hour period. So to say I was mad was an understatement. I was pissed the fuck off. And not only about the money. Hell, I could always get more money. What hurt the most was that I was such a bad judge of character. I really thought Indigo cared about me. The funny thing was, now that she seemed to be gone, I had to admit I kinda cared about her, too.

I got out the car and walked over to my door. When I stepped into my apartment and turned on the light I couldn't believe my eyes. It looked like a war zone. Everything I owned from my big screen TV to my brand new leather sofa had been either broken to bits or shredded to pieces.

"Indigo!" I roared, but got no response. I was so pissed off that tears were coming out my eyes.

I walked down the hallway where I saw the light shining from my office. It was just as bad in there as in the living room. Maybe a little worse. She had smashed everything in the room, including the gold records that had been hanging on the walls.

Then I saw the worst part of all. On top of my desk was a six-inch-high pile of ripped up business cards, which meant she had found my stash. I opened the closet door nervously, knowing what I would probably find. I was right, too. Every single fake plaque and degree I had was missing. If I hadn't been sure before, now I was positive that I'd lost the money I was looking to get out of Indigo's record deal. Even if I could find her, there wasn't much chance I'd be able to convince her I really was a record exec. But damn, I still wanted my plaques and degrees back. I glanced at my ruined things. If she was out of the picture, I was gonna have to go on the hunt for a new sugar momma.

Damn, what the fuck did she do with those things? I was determined to find my shit, but I didn't even know where to start. I walked back out my office and across the hall to my bedroom. The door was locked, which meant Indigo was probably in there.

"Indigo!" I banged on the door. "Indigo! Open this god-damned door!" I started pounding on the door even harder. "Open this fucking door!" I was so aggravated that I went back into my office, got a head of steam and ran into the bedroom door. The lock snapped with a loud crack and I fell to the floor onto a pile of shredded up clothes. I was ready to kill when I saw that the lapel to my favorite Armani suit had been cut off. Now she had gone too damn far.

"Indigo, you bitch, where the fuck are you?" I pushed myself to a standing position as fast as I could. But what my eyes saw next humbled me beyond belief. Indigo was lying on my bed, dressed in the gown she was supposed to be wearing to our wedding. She looked lifeless, lying there surrounded by my plaques and degrees. On the night table were five pill bottles, all of them empty.

"Oh, my God, Indigo. No!" I cried as I ran over to the bed. I touched her and she was cold. "God, please, please don't let her be dead." I shook her. "Come on, Indigo, get up. Get up, baby," I pleaded. All my anger had disappeared. I wiped the tears from my eyes and rested my head on her chest, praying I might hear a heartbeat. I did, however faint it was. I let out a sigh of relief as I reached for my cell phone and dialed 911.

As soon as the 911 operator said the paramedics were on

their way I hung up my phone and cradled her in my arms.
"Hang in there, baby," I kept repeating as I rocked her. "Hang in
there. They're on the way." As I rocked her, I glanced toward my
dresser and noticed some lavender stationery on top. I reached
for it and unfolded it. The paper shook in my hands as I read
what she'd written.

Trent,
I guess you know by now that I discovered your little
secret. You're not a vice president of Def Jam and never
were. You know the funny thing? When I first saw you in
that bar I didn't give a damn what you did for a living. I
just thought you were cute and wanted to get to know
you. So imagine how lucky I felt when I found out that not
only were you cute, you were the man who could help me
achieve my dream of becoming a singer. The only thing I
ever wanted in life. I thought I had it all when I was with
you. A man who could promote my career and who loved
me. Like you said, it was you and me against the world.
We were going to take the music industry by storm and be
together forever.
That's why it was so painful when I stumbled upon your
little stash of business cards and fake degrees while I was
trying to find a hiding place for your wedding present.
That's when I realized you never loved me at all, did you?
That I was nothing more than a meal ticket you could dis-
card at any time. All you loved was the money and presents
I gave you, and I hate you for that. You're nothing but a
con man and I was your score. Well, that's over now. You
can forget about that. You'll see I've destroyed everything I
ever bought for you and a little more—the leather couch,
the big-screen TV, the clothes and the cologne. Everything's
destroyed, just like you've destroyed my life. Now, with
these pills I'm going to take away the most important thing
to you, the thing that could have made you millions—my
voice. You won't be able to use me anymore, Trent, because
by the time you find this I'll be dead.
As for you, just remember I didn't do this because I

hated myself. I did this because I hated you and what you did to me. Every time you walk in this house I want you to remember that my death is on your hands and that I died in your bed. I hope my death stays with you the rest of your life. I hope you learn your lesson and stop trying to play women. But I don't think there's much chance of that. So maybe I'll just hope that someday you'll know how bad it feels to be played. Maybe someday you'll run into the ultimate player hater.

Indigo

"No! You're not gonna die. You're not gonna pin this on me!" I yelled at her lifeless body. I laid her flat on her back so I could listen to her heartbeat again. "I am not gonna have your death on my hands. Do you hear me, Indigo? I'm not gonna have it! So get up, baby, please get up. I never meant to hurt you. I never meant for this to happen. Now wake up!"

The warm sun peeked over the ocean, shining into my living room through the holes of my shredded curtains and onto my depressed face. I'd been sitting on what was left of my leather couch reading Indigo's letter repeatedly since the paramedics had carried her outta my house last night. I know I should have gone to the hospital with her but I just couldn't after I overheard the paramedics tell a cop that she was probably not gonna make it. I'd done a lot of shitty things to a lot of people in my life, but being responsible for Indigo's suicide had to be the worst. I still couldn't believe she actually went through with it.

A knock at the door startled me from the daze I was in, and before I could react the knocking had become a loud banging. "Trent! You in there?"

"Come in! The door's open!" I yelled at whoever was at the door. When I looked up, Wil and Melanie were coming in. As they surveyed the damage Indigo had done to my place, their expressions changed from mild concern about their brother who got stood up at the altar, to confusion, then to shock.

"Oh, my God!" Melanie gasped as she looked around.

"Jesus! What the hell happened in here?" Wil demanded. "This place looks like a cyclone hit it."

"Yeah, a cyclone named Indigo," I replied sadly.

"Indigo did this?" Wil looked surprised.

"Yeah, and a whole lot worse." I handed him the letter.

I know I was supposed to be a man but I couldn't help it. Having my sister and brother around brought down emotional barriers that I couldn't control. I broke down and started to cry for the first time in ten years.

"What is it, Trent? What's the matter?" Melanie came over and wrapped her arms around me, which only made things even worse. The tears flowed even stronger. I felt like a little kid in my sister's arms.

"I didn't mean it, Mel. I swear I didn't mean it. I was just trying to get paid. I didn't want her to die." I continued to sob.

"What are you talking about, Trent?"

"She tried to kill herself, Mel. She tried to kill herself because of me." I sniffed.

"Who? Who tried to kill herself? What are you talking about?"

"Indigo," Wil answered for me. His voice was stern, almost a little accusatory. "She found out Trent was a phony and took some pills. Here, read this." He shoved the letter toward Melanie. I buried my head into my sister's shoulder in shame.

The phone rang and Wil walked over to answer it. When he hung up I could tell it wasn't good news.

"That was the hospital. Indigo's in bad shape, but it looks like she's gonna live."

I sat up and wiped my tears away. "Thank you, God."

"Don't be thanking Him unless you gonna change," Wil said angrily. "Just because she's not dead doesn't mean you didn't almost push her there. You're my brother, Trent, but you're not a very nice person. You don't even take care of your own damn kid the way you're supposed to. I'm glad Daddy's not here to see this."

"Wil, maybe this isn't the time," Melanie started to say.

"No, Mel." I cut her off. "He's right. I'm not a very nice person and Dad's probably rolling over in his grave right about now. I do have to change."

"So what you gonna do? How you gonna change?" Wil challenged me.

"First thing I gotta do is get a job. Then I gotta go talk Michelle into letting me spend some time with my son. She might not want me, but that little boy needs me and right now I need him."

Wil thought about what I'd said for a minute, then said, "It goes against my better judgment, but I can help you with the job. We've got an opening in sales. It's entry level, but with all the game you got, you'll probably make a million dollars in commission." His voice softened a bit and he almost smiled at me.

"Thanks, Wil," I told him sincerely. "I won't let you down."

"You damn right you won't. I'm not gonna give you that chance. Now go take a shower and get your ass over to the hospital and see that girl."

I'd gone by the hospital to see Indigo, but her people wouldn't let me near her. It seems she called her mom and told her about me before she commenced to tearing my apartment to shreds. I stopped one of the doctors on the way into her room, and he told me it looked like she would probably make it, so at least I could leave with that much peace. I left and drove to Michelle's. Only I didn't have the courage to knock on the door when I saw her mother's car in the driveway. I'd had a pretty bad day as it was. I didn't need a frying pan upside my head to make it worse. Luckily, a cab pulled up a few minutes later and Michelle got out of it.

"Michelle," I called. She turned in my direction.

"Trent? What the fuck are you doing parked outside my house? I told you to leave me alone. Don't make me get an order of protection."

"Look, I didn't come here to fight. I came to apologize. I just wanna talk to you. I wanna see my son."

"Son? You don't have any kids, do you?" She scratched her head. "Isn't that what you told your fiancée?"

"Stop playing, Michelle. I'm trying to apologize. I'm sorry."

"You're right. You are sorry. A sorry excuse for a man." She turned and started walking toward the house.

"Michelle! I just wanna know what it's gonna take for me to see my son again."

She turned back around.

"You wanna know what it'll take? I'll tell you what it'll take. But I'm sure you'll never agree to it . . ." She came across the street and got in my car.

37

Wil

"Hurry up, Wil," Diane yelled excitedly as I walked into the room. She was sprawled out in the heart-shaped Jacuzzi, surrounded by bubbles, waiting for our favorite show to come on the television. I'd just gotten back from taking a dip in the pool and had lost track of time. I hurried to get my trunks off, then slid into the water next to my wife. I kissed her and my hands roamed her body as we made out like teenagers. It was our tenth wedding anniversary and we were spending it in the beautiful Pocono Mountains at the Caesars Pocono Resort. After a rather painful few weeks after the fibroid embolization, Diane was back to her old horny self and I couldn't have been happier. With everything that happened with Mimi, Diane and I had been working on our marriage even harder than before. We'd both promised that nothing would ever come between us again.

"Relax, baby." She pushed me away gently. "The show's coming on. I'm not going anywhere. I'm gonna take care of you right after I see your brother make a fool outta himself on national TV." She laughed as we both turned toward the TV. I picked up the remote and turned the station to BET.

"You sure you got the right station? You know the channels are different up here in Pennsylvania," she snapped playfully, leaning her head on my shoulder.

"I know how to get BET," I told her with mock insult.

"So what do you think? Do you think he's gonna go through with it?"

"If he wants to see Marcus he will. Michelle seemed kinda adamant about that. The question is, is he gonna be the player or be played?"

"I'm betting on played. Your brother's not too bright. And

you know that Sylvester Harrington, he always got some twist on his show."

"Trent's smarter than you think, Di. And he really wants this thing with Michelle to work. That's all he's been talking about at work."

"Yeah, but has he really changed? This could all be a front to get Michelle back in his life."

"It could be, but I don't think so. I think he's going on this show to make a point."

"What kind of point?"

"Shhhh, it's coming on. We'll talk about it after the show," I said as the camera focused in on Sylvester Harrington, the host of *Two Sides To A Story*.

"Welcome, ladies and gentlemen. My name's Sylvester Harrington and this is *Two Sides To A Story*. Our first guest tonight is Michelle. Michelle's been dating Trent off and on for almost ten years. Matter of fact, last year she was pregnant, and Trent walked out of the delivery room on her because he said the baby was too dark to be his." The studio audience let out a collective sigh as the host turned toward Michelle.

"Welcome to the show, Michelle."

"Thanks for having me, Sylvester." Michelle smiled.

"Michelle, this Trent sounds like a *real* piece of work." The camera panned in on a picture of Trent sitting in the green room, then back to Michelle.

"You don't know the half of it, Sylvester. Trent is a cheating, lying dog. Not only did he walk out the delivery room, but about two months ago he came crawling back to me with a wedding ring."

"Oh, really?" Sylvester smiled for the crowd. "So did you accept his proposal?"

"Yeah." Michelle nodded, her face revealing her embarrassment. "I accepted it until I found out he was engaged to another woman."

Now the audience was really enraged. There were people booing and hollering about what a dog Trent was. A few of them were yelling at Michelle for being so stupid.

"What about your son? Trent's saying that you're not letting him or his family see the baby. Is that true?"

"You damn right it's true. You not gonna treat my baby like a yo-yo."

"What do you mean by that?"

"He told his other fiancée right in front of my face that my son was not his child. And I told him if he's not your child then tell your family not to come see him. And I meant that." A few people in the audience shouted their approval.

"So let me get this straight. You're mad because Trent keeps denying your son?"

"Yeah. He denies Marcus whenever it's convenient for him."

"Well I hear you, sister, 'cause I was out back and I saw your son. He does look just like Trent."

Pictures of both Marcus and Trent came on the screen, and you could tell by the audience's reaction that they felt the same way as the host.

"Well, Michelle, as you know, the name of our show is *Two Sides To A Story,* so we're gonna have to bring out Trent and hear what he has to say. Ladies and gentlemen, welcome Trent to the show." Before Trent even walked out on the stage the crowd was on their feet, booing loudly.

"Trent, welcome to the show."

"Thanks," Trent said timidly. Clearly the audience's reaction had him shook. He wasn't used to this kind of treatment from people.

"I've been hearing some bad things about you, Trent." Sylvester smiled as he leaned in closer to Trent.

"Well, don't believe everything you hear," Trent snapped back sarcastically. "By the way, sending that beautiful woman to my room last night was a great touch. I hope your producers weren't too disappointed when I sent her home."

Sylvester did his best to hide his embarrassment as his eyes quickly shot toward the producer. The audience laughed.

"Well, enough about the producers. Michelle here tells me that you like to envision yourself as a player."

"I think reformed player is probably the best way to describe it. I'm trying to be a family man now. That is, if I can get Michelle to let me see my son."

"So you wanna see your son? I was under the impression that you don't think he's yours. Michelle claims that you walked out of the delivery room because he was too dark."

"I did. And it was probably the most ignorant thing I've ever done in my life." My brother actually sounded sincere. Then again, he'd sounded just as sincere whenever he was handing out his phony business cards.

"Well, if you know it was ignorant, why are you here?"

"Because Michelle doesn't believe me. She still thinks I'm the ignorant person I was. But I've changed. I got a new job. I wanna be in my son's life and I don't want there to be any question about that."

"So you're willing to pay child support and everything?"

"No doubt. I wanna be a father to my child. I love Marcus. He's the only thing I got left."

"What do you have to say about that, Michelle?"

"Talk is cheap. He could say that today and tomorrow he'll get mad at me and take it out on my baby, start telling people he don't even know my son. I want him to take a paternity test. I want him to have undeniable proof that this is his son and then I want him to take responsibility for his son."

"Well, as you know, Trent didn't have a problem with that, Michelle. The only thing he asked is that you give him a chance to be a father. Are you willing to do that?"

"Yeah."

"Well, I have the paternity results right here. Anything either of you wanna say before I reveal them?"

"Yeah, I got something I wanna say," Trent cut in as he turned to Michelle. "First off, I wanna say, Michelle, I love you, and I wanna apologize for all the BS I've put you through over the years. You're a good woman and I'm sorry you had to go through this. I also wanna thank you for having my son and being such a good mother. He doesn't even have to open that envelope. I know Marcus is my son and I love you for that." Trent had done it again. He'd charmed the audience over to his side, and now they were applauding his words. Even the host looked like he was rooting for Trent now. Michelle was smiling at Trent.

"Well, from the looks of it, y'all are gonna live happily ever after," Sylvester said. "I guess you don't need me to read the results, do you?" His words were a tease for the audience, who started shouting, "Read the results! Read the results!" just like you would expect a talk show audience to do. After all, those people didn't really care about my brother and Michelle. They were just looking to be entertained.

"No, Sylvester, things might look good right now, but I know Trent," Michelle said. "I still need those results in case the 'new Trent' decides to go back to his old ways when the camera is off."

She looked at Trent, who looked a little disappointed that his speech hadn't been enough to win her over completely. "Trent, I do love you, but I still gotta do this. It's like insurance for Marcus, you know?"

Trent looked away from her, but kept his cool. His face didn't reveal any emotions. "That's cool, Michelle. I'm gonna do whatever it takes."

"Okay," said Sylvester as the audience cheered and chanted. "It's time to read the results." He pulled a paper out of the envelope he'd been holding. Trent looked at Michelle and reached for her hand. She held his hand and they both actually looked pretty happy.

"Trent, you are one hundred percent *not* the father of Michelle's baby," Sylvester announced. There was a collective gasp from the audience. The camera zoomed in on Trent who was grimacing like *he* was about to give birth.

"What?" Trent yelled.

He snatched the results out of Sylvester's hand. By the time he read them and turned to Michelle, she was halfway to backstage.

"Did you see his face, Wil?" Diane asked with a laugh.

"Yep, I sure did," I replied. "I'd say that's the face of a player reborn."

PLAYER HATERS

CARL WEBER

ABOUT THIS GUIDE

The suggested questions are intended to enhance
your group's reading of Carl Weber's
PLAYER HATERS.

DISCUSSION QUESTIONS

1. Do you know or have you ever run into a man like Trent?

2. Be honest. If someone gave you a business card would you question whether he or she was a doctor or lawyer?

3. Have you ever paid the bills for someone you were dating?

4. Things worked out for the best but should Melanie have slept with Prince that first night?

5. What kind of brother do you think Trent was to Melanie?

6. What did you think about Prince? Is he the type of man you'd like to meet? How many men would give a woman all his personal information like Prince did?

7. Do you think Prince and Melanie will stay together?

8. Did Desiree get hers or should Melanie have whipped that butt?

9. Was Diane wrong for not telling Wil about her fibroids?

10. What would you have done if you were Diane and Mimi had called your house at five in the morning?

11. Did you think Wil slept with Mimi? Should he have slept with Mimi if he wasn't getting any at home?

12. When did you realize that Mimi wasn't just a home wrecker but crazy?

13. Were you surprised by Jeanie Brown's death? Did you think Diane was next?

14. Did you realize that Mimi's sister, Keisha, was the same Keisha from my previous book *Lookin' for Luv?*

15. What did you think about Trent's double engagement?

16. Did you think Michelle's baby was Trent's?

17. Have you ever thought about killing yourself over a man or a woman?

18. What did you think of the ending?

19. Did you expect more characters from *Married Men?*

The following is a sample chapter from
Carl Weber's eagerly anticipated upcoming novel
THE PREACHER'S SON.

This book will be available in February 2005
wherever hardcover books are sold.

ENJOY!

Prologue

Blue Johnson's metallic blue Jeep Cherokee rolled south down Merrick Boulevard. The windows were down and the radio was blasting 50 Cent's "*21 Questions*." The bass was so loud that not only could nearby pedestrians hear the music, they could feel it, too. It was the first eighty-plus day of the year and Blue and his best friend, Dante Wilson, rocked their heads to the music as they flirted with one pretty woman after another. When the car stopped at a traffic light, Dante winked at the beautiful twenty-something-year-old woman who'd pulled up next to them in a red Honda Civic. She winked back with a smile and Dante nodded, his face now flush with color as he turned toward Blue. He was the shyer of the two, but not by much.

"Yo, check out baby over here in the Civic," he yelled as he turned back in her direction, smiling like he was in a toothpaste commercial. He'd decided to impress Blue with his pick-up skills. "What's up, baby girl? Can a brotha get them digi . . ." He stopped himself abruptly and Blue fell out laughing. Dante hadn't seen quite what he was expecting. Oh, there was a woman there all right, but it wasn't the fine sister he'd been flirting with. She had made a right on red and was halfway around the corner. In the place of her car was a black Lincoln Continental. The driver was a dark-skinned, heavyset woman in her late fifties, wearing an expensive but ugly blond wig. Dante knew her quite well, and by the scowl on her face it was clear she didn't appreciate his comment, their music or Blue's laughter in the background. Her name was Deaconess Lillian Wright, better known to Dante as The Bitch. She was one of his mother's closest friends along with being one of his father's church's biggest supporters.

"How you doing, Deaconess?" Dante raised his hand as he

smiled meekly. He turned back toward Blue, who'd stopped laughing and was back to rocking his head to the music.

"Blue, turn the radio down," Dante said through gritted teeth.

"What?" Blue shouted, wondering why Dante was whispering.

"I said turn the motherfuckin' radio down!" Dante yelled this time. He reached for the volume knob, doing it himself. He turned back to Deaconess Wright, who was already punching buttons on her cell phone. Dante knew that could only mean trouble. Especially when he heard her speaking into the phone about something that sounded suspiciously like, "Oh yes, he's drunk. I'm sure of it."

The light turned green but before Blue could hit the accelerator, Deaconess Wright swerved out of the right turn lane and into his, speeding down Merrick Boulevard.

"Aw, shit." Dante slammed his hand on the dashboard. "Man, I bet that bitch is headed straight to the church to see my momma."

"So what?" Blue shrugged.

"So what? Do you realize how much trouble I'm gonna get into?" Dante's face showed his concern.

"Trouble for what?" Blue sighed, rolling his eyes at his friend. "How old are you, Dante?"

"Man, you know how old I am." Dante snapped with attitude. "Twenty-one. Same age as you."

"Okay, so you're old enough to drink in this state and buy cigarettes, right?" Blue asked sarcastically.

"Yeah, what's the point, Blue?"

"The point is . . ." Blue took his eyes off the road and glared at Dante. "Why the fuck are you so worried about some old church biddy with droopy titties calling your mother? You a grown man. What your moms gonna do, give you a beatin'?"

"Look, Blue, I been trying to explain this to you for years. Everything that my sister and I do is a reflection on my parents, and a reflection on the church. My pops is Bishop T.K. Wilson, for crying out loud. He's one of the most powerful pastors in the city, possibly even the state."

"And? What's that supposed to mean? You know I like the

Bishop, Dante, but he ain't God. He's just a man. He likes pussy just like the rest of us heathens, otherwise you wouldn't be here."

Dante couldn't help it. He let out a frustrated laugh. Blue had a way with words that was always colorful if not true.

"You don't understand how hard it is being the Bishop's son, Blue. That old bitch, Deaconess Wright, has had it in for me ever since her homely ass daughter Mary married Reverend Reynolds. She seems to think I'm the only thing standing in the way of her son-in-law becoming the next pastor when the Bishop retires."

"Yeah, and she's right. You are the only one in his way."

"But I don't wanna be—"

Blue cut him off. "Don't even start that shit, Dante. Not unless you're willing to tell your peoples the truth."

"I can't tell them the truth. Not yet anyway. My momma wants me to be the pastor one day, and so does the Bishop. I can't let them down."

"Let them down! What about letting yourself down, Dante? You got a chance to intern at Aggressive Records under Black Barron himself." Blue's face looked pained at the thought of Dante passing up that opportunity. "Man, you need to stand up to your parents. Shit, man, you don't even wanna be a minister. How you gonna be a pastor?"

Dante shrugged his shoulders but remained silent. They'd had this conversation a hundred times before, and the result was always the same. Dante agreed with Blue, but he never actually had the nerve to confront his parents about his true aspirations. Blue turned his attention back to the road, but not before he turned up the volume again.

A few minutes later Blue pulled his truck in front of the church and smiled at Dante as he stuck out his fist. Dante tapped Blue's fist, stepped out of the truck and stretched. At an even six-feet, three-inches tall, Dante was a well-built man with a basketball player's body and smooth, handsome, almond-colored features. His friend Blue, not an inch over five-eight, was also well built, and considerably darker. His real name was Neal, but Dante couldn't remember anyone other than a few teachers calling him anything but Blue since they'd met. He and Dante had been best friends since the sixth grade, and against Dante's mother's better wishes, they had just gone apartment hunting together.

"I'll check you later. You gonna be up there by Manhattan Proper tonight?"

"Probably. Yo, you sure you don't wanna come in? The women's choir rehearsal's about to get out and you know they gonna have some food and some good-looking honeys downstairs."

Blue glanced over at Deaconess Wright's Lincoln Continental and Dante's mother's champagne Mercedes-Benz parked in the church's parking lot. Dante's offer was tempting. Not only was Blue hungry, he loved messing with them church girls. Still, he really wasn't up for any drama. And with First Lady Wilson around and Deaconess Wright there, there was sure to be some drama. If things went as they usually did, Blue would be the one who ended up getting blamed for it, too.

Blue pointed at the two cars. "I think I'll pass, bro. It looks like you about to have some drama with your momma. Ain't no need for me to stick around. I'll just make things worse for you."

"Chicken. What, are you scared of my mother?" Dante teased.

"Pretty much," Blue replied.

"I thought you said I should stand up to her."

"I said *you* should stand up to her. You're her son. Me, I'm gonna carry my ass on home where it's safe. Only time your moms wants to see me is on Sunday and that's only if I'm putting something into the collection plate."

Dante chuckled. "You know she loves you, Blue."

"Yeah, like a snake likes a rat. Did you forget what she did last Saturday? She got on the mike at the church bazaar and told everyone who'd listen to hold on to their daughters 'cause Satan just walked in. Them people started staring at me like I had horns and shit. Now I've been called a lot of things Dante, but to have the first lady of the church call you the Devil has got to be the worst."

Dante lowered his head. He had to laugh at his mother's antics. Despite her actions, she really didn't dislike his friend. She just loved her son and didn't wanna admit that he was human and could make mistakes. It was easier for her to make Blue the

scapegoat for any of Dante's missteps. "She didn't mean anything by it, Blue."

Blue rolled his eyes. "Dante, face it, man. Your mom doesn't
like me. She never has. She thinks I'm a bad influence on you."

"Yeah. Little does she know I'm probably a worse influence
on you than you are on me." They both laughed as Dante closed
the Jeep's door and headed for the side entrance to the church.
When he entered the building he was greeted by the loud cack-
ling of women gossiping, then a sudden silence. Dante smiled as
he approached the thirty or so women of the First Jamaica
Baptist's award-winning women's choir standing in the church
recreation area.

"Hi, Dante." One woman smiled.

"What's up, Latrice?" he replied with a nod. That started a
chain reaction of his, hellos, shy waves and blushing if he happened to make eye contact. The women seemed to part like the
Red Sea to allow Dante to pass through and enter the hallway to
his office. He could feel their eyes still on him as he passed. He
thought he even heard a few sighs.

Dante had been given this type of attention from the young
women of the church for years, and it seemed like most of their
mothers encouraged it. As the son of the Bishop, he was treated
like royalty, the crown prince of the church. Like all princes,
every young woman in the village wanted to be his princess. For
years Dante had taken advantage of that, fooling around with
half of the women in the congregation who were younger than
twenty-five.

Dante walked into his office and closed the door. He sat behind his desk and listened to the women of the choir leaving. He
checked over the schedule for the youth basketball league, which
he ran as director of the church's children's activities. Not long
after he sat down, there was a knock on the door. A knock he'd
been expecting ever since he and Blue pulled in front of the
building. He got up and walked toward the door, but there was
no need. The door opened before he could get there.

Dante stopped dead in his tracks when he realized it was not
his mother, as he had expected. It was the vibrant and sexy Anita
Bell, the only woman he'd ever loved, or at least thought he
loved.

"Anita," he gasped as his eyes quickly roamed her body. Anita was dressed in a very conservative white church dress with white heels, but her voluptuous body made anything she wore look provocative. One of the things Dante had loved about her was that she knew how to use that body like no one he'd ever met.

"Dante," she said, smiling. "I guess some things never change."

"What's that supposed to mean?" Dante was truly confused until Anita pointed at his crotch. Dante looked down and blushed. When it came to Anita, it was obvious which one of his heads was in control. Dante took the folder he was holding and tried to hide his swollen manhood.

"Don't hide it now. I've already seen it." She smirked, reaching behind her and locking the door then stepping closer to him. She kissed his full lips. "I missed you, Dante," she whispered.

She kissed him again before he could respond. This time she wrapped her arms around him and he did the same. Their kiss was so passionate it took his breath away. When it was finally over, they stayed wrapped in each other's arms and stared lustfully into each other's eyes.

"God, I missed you, Dante," she whispered as her right hand moved from his backside to his crotch.

"I missed you, too," he said as he gently pushed her away. "Just not enough to commit adultery. Where's your husband?"

Anita took a step forward and looked up at him with a frown. "Why'd you have to mention him?"

"I don't know," he said sarcastically. "It seemed kind of important when I realized you were unzipping my fly." Anita sighed. "So where is he, Anita? Where's your husband?"

"He's at our new house in Hollis, unpacking our things. But you don't have to worry about that. Only thing you need to be worried about is what's in front of you. I want you, Dante. And I've missed you. I've been thinking about you every day since I left."

He glanced at her and his mind went down memory lane. He and Anita had been going together since he was nineteen, although very few people other than Blue and his sister knew about it. They'd kept things on the low because Anita was his father's secretary and ten years his senior. The age difference didn't bother Dante, though. As far as he was concerned, he was going to marry Anita. But she knew better. She knew that his mother and father were never gonna go for that. That's why she started secretly dating Deacon Robert Emerson. Deacon Emerson was an arm amputee in his early forties. He was well known around the church and had considerable assets. He'd been trying to get Anita to date him since she'd started working at the church. For almost four years she'd told him no, but one day she smiled and agreed to go out with him. Three months later, much to Dante's chagrin, they were married and moved to Florida at Anita's request. She knew she needed to get as far away from the temptation of Dante as possible. She may have denied it, but she was in love with him. Now after eight months Anita and the Deacon were back, and since she had mentioned a new house, it appeared they were back to stay.

"I'm back, Dante. And once I ask your father to give me my old job back we can get right back to doing everything the way we did before. And I mean everything." She posed flirtatiously and gave him this sexy look that made his rock hard penis even harder.

"What about your husband?"

"What about him? We kept your parents in the dark for almost three years. What makes you think we can't keep him in the dark too?" She stepped closer to him, rubbing his chest the way she knew he liked it. "I need you, Dante. He can't satisfy me. I haven't had an orgasm since I was with you." She frowned pitifully, like a child who was being punished.

Dante thought about how easy it was for him to make her climax. He knew her body better than he knew his own. He ran his finger down her spine, and she shuddered with excitement. He lowered his head and blew in her ear. Anita moaned out loud. *How could the Deacon not be able to do that?* he wondered, then smiled at his own ego. Anita was his pussy. She had always been his pussy. He looked at her. He looked at her in the manner a man reserves only for his woman. Oh, those feelings were starting to come back. But instead of making him want her, they made him angry. He pushed her away.

"Well, I don't want you. Not if you're married. Not if you're his wife instead of mine. What are you doing back here anyway, Anita?"

"I hated Florida. I hate him. I needed to get back to you. I love you, Dante. Please, baby, let me show you how much I love you," she pleaded.

Dante didn't say a word. He just silently watched Anita unbutton her dress until she was no longer wearing a conservative church dress. But she was still wearing all white—a white push-up bra, white panties, white garter belt with white stockings and of course, those sexy white stiletto heels. The contrast against her mahogany skin was stunning.

"Please, baby. Let me show you how much I love you." Anita rubbed her hands on his chest again then kissed him gently before she started to slowly kneel. Dante knew what she was about to do and was virtually powerless to stop her. Oral sex was his weakness and Anita was an expert.

"I can't do this, Anita," he whispered repeatedly, but that didn't stop her. Finally he just decided to give in. When it came to Anita, Dante's big head went on auto pilot and his little head took over. He placed his hand gently on her hair and stared blankly at the wall as he waited eagerly for the pleasure she would soon give him. Anita licked her lips as she stared at his pulsating manhood and prepared to swallow it whole. Unfortunately, that would not happen today because Dante spotted the picture of Jesus hanging on the wall. Anita may have been the master of his penis, but she was not the master of his conscience or faith, neither of which would allow him to commit adultery.

"Oh, dear Lord, forgive me," he said, his eyes focused. He jerked her head up. "I can't do this. This is wrong. You're married."

Before she could reply, there was a knock on the door and a jiggling of the doorknob.

"Dante, are you in here, son?" his mother called through the door.

Dante instinctively answered, "Yes," as both he and Anita stared at each other with panicked looks on their faces. They knew if they didn't open that door quickly his mother, a suspicious woman by nature, would put two and two together the second she saw Anita in his office. And Lord help them both if his mother had Deaconess Wright with her as he suspected. Anita reached down and picked up her dress then turned back to Dante, hoping to get some direction.

"Hide?" Dante was as panic stricken as Anita.

Anita glared at him. "Where?"

Dante's eyes searched the room for a hiding place. He jumped when his mother knocked on the door again. He pointed toward his desk.

"Dante, open this door," his mother said sternly.

"Under my desk," he whispered to Anita. She scrambled over there as he approached the door. He waited till she was out of sight then opened the door. His mother and his father, Bishop T.K. Wilson, greeted him.

"Have you been drinking?"

"No, Ma," he replied, opening his arms to give his mother a hug. In his mind, he was cursing the woman in the black Continental. *Damn, that bitch Deaconess Wright lied on me again.*

His mother sniffed him as she kissed his cheek then smiled with satisfaction. If he knew his mother, she'd been defending him tooth and nail and now felt vindicated in her actions. "Why was this door locked?"

"Huh? Oh, uh," Dante searched his mind for an excuse as his mother stared into his eyes. "Because I was changing my clothes and I didn't want any of the women's choir walking in and seeing my private parts. I just came from the gym and wanted to get out of those sweaty clothes." He casually turned his back and zipped up his pants as his mother walked by. She was surveying his office, as if she knew he was lying.

"Hey, Bishop." Dante offered his father his hand, still keeping his eyes on his mother and his desk. "So what brings you two down here?" His mother's suspicious look instantly became a jubilated smile, and she spoke before her husband had a chance to get out a word.

"Oh, Dante. We have the best news. Come sit down so we can tell you." Dante moved over to his desk quickly and sat down. His father had a habit of sitting at his desk and that wasn't something he could risk right now. As his parents sat down on the other side, Dante glanced under his desk. Anita, still half-naked, smiled at him. Dante pushed his chair back about a foot when she stroked the inside of his leg. He knew Anita too well. She was a freak and he wouldn't put it past her to try something crazy like pulling out his manhood to finish what she'd tried to start earlier.

"So, what's this great news?" Dante asked, slapping Anita's hand as she tried to unzip his pants.

"Well, Dante." His mother turned to his father with a huge smile. She looked like she was gonna bust a gasket she was so excited. "I'm gonna let the Bishop tell you."

Dante turned his attention to his father, who leaned forward with a paternal smile. "Well, son. Your mother and I just found out you've been accepted into Howard University's seminary school."

"I have?" Dante looked from one parent to the other then back again.

"Dante, I'm so proud of you." His mother had tears in her eyes.

"But, but I never applied to Howard's seminary school," Dante stuttered.

"I know. I applied for you," his smiling mother replied. "I bet you didn't even think you'd get in." She was so clearly pleased with herself and expected the same from him.

"Congratulations, son." His father nodded as he stood up. "Howard seminary is a fine school."

"Thanks, Bishop," Dante replied without thinking.

"Come on, Lydia. We're supposed to be over at the borough president's office in twenty minutes."

Dante's mother stood up and leaned over his desk. She kissed him. "Dante, I'm so proud of you. I can't wait till your first sermon."

"Neither can I, Mom," he answered weakly.

Dante watched the Bishop and his mother walk toward the door and suddenly he had unresolved courage. He had to tell them. He had to tell them he didn't want to go to Howard's seminary. He didn't wanna go to anyone's seminary. And he had to tell them before they started to blab their news to everyone in the church, because then he would be painted into a corner.

"Ma," he called, standing up quickly. Just as the words left his mouth he realized he had to sit down because his fly was unzipped and there was a hand attached to his private parts.

"Yes," his mother replied as she turned around. He sat down just in the nick of time.

"Nothin'. Just wanted to say thanks."